Bridle Path
Press

# DEATH
## — IN THE —
# ORCHARD

*A Trudy Genova Manhattan Mystery*

# M.K. GRAFF

Bridle Path Press, LLC
8419 Stevenson Road
Baltimore, MD 21208

www.bridlepathpress.com

Direct orders to the above address.

Printed in the United States of America.
First Edition.
ISBN: 978-1-7321630-8-9

Library of Congress Control Number: 2024932716

Book Design by Elizabeth Ryan Cole
Cover photo created using Adobe Firefly

Bridle Path
Press

For
**Anne Louise Reed Jacobs**
&
**The Sisters of No Mercy:**
**Laura Lea Borsman Hamilton**
**Judith Ann Altschuler-Lourine**
**Lee Pirnat Hershberger**

"I wouldn't trade it for anything, never, no. Never.
Your friendship is the best present ever."

Tigger, *Winnie-the-Pooh* by A. A. Milne

# DEATH in the ORCHARD CAST OF CHARACTERS

*In Order of Appearance:*

TRUDY GENOVA, RN, Medical consultant for NY studios

MARIO GENOVA, Trudy's deceased father

MEG PITMAN, Production Assistant for Passion Broadcasting Junction; Trudy's best friend

TROOPER WES BRADY, New York State trooper

SERVING SINCE BREAKFAST, Brady's rookie trooper

BOBBY COSTELLO, drug runner

DETECTIVE NED O'MALLEY, NYPD 20th Precinct, Trudy's boyfriend

HILDY GENOVA, Trudy's mother

BOB RILEY, Hildy's beau, Trudy's former high school English teacher

GREG DIETZ, Genova Orchards' newest staff member on prison re-entry program

LT. PAUL HOFFMANN, Schoharie PD

RICK GENOVA, Trudy's brother

AIDAN MCCARTHY, Rick's husband

BEN GENOVA, Trudy's oldest brother

GAIL GENOVA, Ben's wife, Trudy's high school friend

HARRY HOLLAND, boarder at Greg Dietz's halfway house

RON HANSON, Schoharie PD, Ben's high school friend

GEORGE ZIMMER, coroner

TONY BORELLI, NYPD detective, Ned's partner

DOUG DIETZ, Greg's brother

RUSTY, Doug's Springer Spaniel

GERALD DIETZ, Greg's father

CINDY DIETZ, Greg's mother

LARRY LONG, retired detective

WAYNE BAAR, Long's partner, proprietor of Veronica's Vintage shop

DR. FRANK BOZZELLI, retired medical examiner

WYNN GRAHAM, Bank manager, Mario Genova's friend

JAKE GRAHAM, Wynn's deceased elder son

JOHN MAYDAN, Trudy's high school crush

JIMMY CHANG, owner of Party Hearty

OSKAR JABLONSKI, proprietor of Jablonski's Olde Worlde Deli, Mario's friend

STEVE NORTHRUP, Warden, Troy Correctional

BRUCE AMES, owner of Ames Hardware Emporium, Mario's friend

VINCE RUSSO, Orchard staff, boards at Greg's Dietz's halfway house

MARY GRAHAM, Wynn's ex-wife

*In every man, of course, a demon lies hidden . . .*

Fyodor Dostoevsky, The Brothers Karamazov

# Death
## in the
# Orchard

# CHAPTER ONE

The hospital room held a bed with its head jacked up high, a night table with a stack of books, and an overbed table pushed to one side with a plastic pitcher and water glass. A beautiful young woman sat on the side of the bed with her blonde hair pulled back in a ponytail. She wore a blue T-shirt the color of her eyes; her slender legs dangled from a pair of gym shorts. A male therapist finished tying the laces on her sneakers and stood, his white jacket embroidered with *PT*. Close-up, his handsome face showed his struggle to hold back the strong emotions this woman stirred in him. He moved aside and placed a walking frame in front of her.

"Small steps, Grace, that's all I'm asking. Just a dozen steps to start, and in a few weeks, you'll walk right out the door and head home."

The agony the loss of seeing this young woman on a daily basis would cause was writ large upon his face. Grace let her feet slide to the floor. The therapist held her under her upper arms as he helped her stand and then hold onto the frame. "Get your balance first." He leaned in and half-closed his eyes as if inhaling the scent of her shampoo. Pure bliss lit his face.

"And . . . CUT!" The director's voice boomed above us. "That's a wrap, people. Thanks for coming in on a Saturday to get this in the can."

The actors quickly left the soundstage, ignoring each other, while the hot Klieg lights were turned off with a loud *thunk*, and I was free to leave for my vacation.

My name is Trudy Genova, RN, and I work as a medical consultant for a New York studio. Some days I'm sent to cover medical scenes for soap operas or television movies. On others I do what is known as "baby wrangling," which means taking child actors under sixteen to wardrobe, running their lines, and taking them up on set, where no parents are allowed, for rehearsals and taping. This was the last scene requiring my attention on a TV movie, and I could leave to head to my upstate family home on vacation with a clear conscience.

My best friend, Meg Pitman, appeared at my elbow. "Thank goodness we're done. You'd never know in real life those two loathe each other." She walked out of the soundstage with me, both of us stepping over the thick cables that ran along the floor. "I'll help you with your bags. Ned will be here any minute."

Meg was a production assistant at the studio. I'd left my suitcase, backpack, and computer bag behind her desk. "Thanks again for taking Wilkie Collins." My cat adored Meg and she was happy to watch him while I was gone. We reached Meg's office, where she handed me my computer bag, which I slung over my shoulder, then balanced my backpack on top of a larger rolling suitcase.

"Besides, it's only for a week," Meg continued, grabbing the backpack off the suitcase. "Then you'll owe me big time." She followed me to the studio door.

"I shudder to think what that will entail. Sounds like you have something in mind."

Meg tossed her streaked pale hair over her shoulder and widened her honey-colored doe eyes. "No biggie. Dinner with you and O'Malley with my parents when you get back. Maybe Tony won't feel he's under fire if there are friendly faces to provide a good distraction for their first meeting." Tony Borelli and my boyfriend, Ned O'Malley, were NYPD detectives.

"No distraction known will keep your parents from grilling Tony. But I'm game to watch him suffer." Ned's partner was from a large Brooklyn Italian family, light years away from Meg's wealthy upbringing as an only child. His nerves about their first meeting had taken on epic proportions.

I bounced the suitcase down the three steps to the studio door, and Meg followed with my backpack. It was a breezy autumn day that was unseasonably warm. Up the block where Columbus Avenue and Broadway crossed in front of Lincoln Center, traffic flowed with taxi horns blaring, and in the distance, I heard an ambulance siren. A mom walked past, holding her little boy by the hand. He clutched a sheaf of green, yellow, and orange paper leaves he'd colored.

"You've already met Ned's parents and made a grand impression by stopping a murderer in his tracks right in front of them." Meg sighed. "Tony needs all the help he can get."

I buffed my nails on my denim jacket. "I have my skills," I admitted, "and a nicely placed kick to the groin is one of them."

"It certainly did the job when it was needed. But you must remember you were worried about meeting them— you should appreciate how Tony feels."

"Don't worry. We'll be there, but I don't expect anything will make him comfortable."

"I'll work on my mother before then, extolling his virtues and his love of family."

"Keep at it." I looked down the road for Ned, who was borrowing his parents' car for our trip. As I had no idea what said car looked like, its color or make, I scrutinized each vehicle as it turned from Central Park West onto West 66th Street and drove past the studio, alternating feelings of excitement with nervous concerns about this trip.

I had asked Ned to accompany me home to attend my sister-in-law's baby shower in Schoharie in the Catskills, where he would meet my family. This was the first grandchild, my older brother Ben's child. His wife Gail was a close friend of mine from school, so this was a big deal in several areas.

Only Meg and Tony knew the real reason I was bringing Ned home this particular week. I'd asked him to help me investigate a cold case from eleven years ago.

I was convinced my father had been murdered.

# CHAPTER TWO

*ELEVEN YEARS EARLIER*

New York State Trooper Wes Brady sat in his patrol car near noon, his new rookie in the passenger seat. He'd parked right after exit 24 of the New York State Thruway, a major exchange where travelers had the choice of heading via I-90 east toward Buffalo, while choosing I-87, the Adirondack Northway, would bring them to Canada. "One more thing. Tomorrow, less aftershave. I like a neat patrol car. I don't need it to smell like a whorehouse."

The young man nodded. "Yes, sir. Sorry." He blushed, red creeping up his face.

"You get your off-duty squared?"

"Yes, sir." He recited as if from a manual. "'All serving officers after appropriate training will be issued carry concealed permits and expected to have either their service weapon or a personal off-duty weapon with them at all times.' That's pretty close, right?"

"Close enough. Get a good holster for it."

"Will do." The rookie looked out his window at the traffic. "Do you get many speeders on the Thruway, sir?"

Brady gave the kid a withering look. "What the hell kind of question is that, Serving Since Breakfast? Why would you think we wouldn't get speeders on the main road from the city line to Albany where creeps take the Northway to Canada? Can you read a map?" He shook his head. "Forget speeders. This route is a drug runner's paradise."

"Yes, sir." The rookie scrambled to present a better showing. "I meant, at this particular section, I'd think drivers would slow down."

"Some do." A flashy purple car caught Brady's eye as the driver sped up and cut off another driver. "And then there are others like this idiot." Lights flashing and siren screeching, Brady took off after a late model Chevy Nova. Someone had put money into restoring it, judging from the ugly grape-colored paint to the weird airbrushed design across the trunk. "Call in the plate."

"Yessir."

Brady could see the driver pound the steering wheel in frustration before putting on his blinkers to cautiously cross several lanes of traffic as if he were Driver of the Year. He pulled over to the right shoulder, and Brady watched him open both front windows.

"Plate registered to one Robert Costello at an Albany address, sir."

"Run his name and check for outstanding warrants. We'll let Mr. Costello sweat a minute." Brady saw Costello flip open his glove box. He had a feeling today would be a good learning experience for his rookie.

"Two previous speeding tickets; no warrants."

"You see all those air fresheners hanging from his rearview mirror?"

The rookie nodded. "I do. A whole bunch of them."

Brady shot the kid a glance to see if he was taking the piss. Nope. This one was as green as he'd thought. "That, my young rookie, is what is known as a Felony Forest. Those little pine trees are Costello's way of covering up the smell of the weed he smokes when he's in the car. Dollars to proverbial cop donuts he'll light a cigarette to cover the smell." They watched Costello shake out a cigarette and light up, blowing smoke into the interior of the car instead of out the window. "Bingo."

Brady got out of the car and adjusted his belt and hat; the rookie parroted his movements. "Check for a passenger and be aware of any weapons. I'll take the driver. Use your nose and keep your eyes peeled for probable cause."

The two troopers walked toward the Nova, the rookie

mirroring the older trooper's swagger. Brady put his hand on the trunk to leave his prints in case Costello sped away and explained his actions to the rookie. "Leaving my prints proves I've stopped this car if the driver takes off, or worse, if he pulls a gun and there's a shooting, my prints are proof that car has been at that site." The trunk's airbrushed design showed the head and shoulders of a smiling Mickey Mantle, with "The Mick" written in an arch over his head. Brady walked to the open driver's window and inhaled the unmistakable skunky scent of marijuana. The interior was surprisingly clean. "License and registration."

On the passenger side, the rookie took a deep breath and nodded to Brady.

"Yeah, sure." Costello handed over both, along with his insurance card, all in the name of Robert Costello. He looked straight ahead while he smoked his cigarette down to the nub. Then Costello's muscle memory had him doing what he always did after smoking a cigarette: he pulled open the ashtray to mash out his stub.

Trooper Brady saw the weed roach that sat amongst the ashes. "Hands on the steering wheel, Mr. Costello, and I'll take your keys. That roach gives us cause to search your vehicle."

"Shit." Costello complied. "I guess since we're gonna be friends, you can call me Bobby. No chance you fellas might look the other way just this once? It's a tiny roach. I could make it very worth your while."

"Now you wouldn't be trying to bribe me, would you, old pal?"

Two minutes later the rookie had handcuffed and secured Bobby Costello in the back of the patrol car after patting him down under Brady's watchful eye.

"You know how to search this car, rookie?"

"Yessir. Start at the driver's side and go around it." The rookie used his flashlight to check under the driver's seat and ran his hands up under the dashboard. He flipped the car mat and checked the visor, then moved to the center console, where he found a dented Altoids mints tin holding two fat rolled joints and several large roaches. Leaving the tin on the console, he walked around and searched the passenger side, then did the entire back seat without finding anything more. On surer footing now, the rookie told Brady, "The contents of the tin give us probable cause to open the trunk."

"You would be correct." Brady followed the rookie to the trunk. He glanced at the patrol car, where Bobby Costello appeared to look out the window as if he hadn't a care in the world.

The rookie used the key to open the trunk and remove a blanket he shook and draped over the trunk lid. He took out a baseball bat and tire iron and laid those on the ground. The blanket had covered the spare tire, laying there unattached, and he lifted it out and leaned it against the bumper while he searched the inside of the trunk. Next, he pulled up the interior carpet and lifted the compartment lid. Inside lay a dusty jack and a second rustier tire iron he checked and left in place, then patted the rug back down. He used his flashlight to check the underside of the trunk lid, running his hands along the seams. "Should I pop the hubcaps next?"

Brady looked at Bobby Costello and back at the spare tire the rookie was attempting to lift back into the trunk. "Just a sec." He hoisted the tire and turned back to see Bobby Costello throw himself back against the seat. "Guess you didn't realize this tire is a whole lot heavier than it should be."

# CHAPTER THREE

"What kind of car are we looking for?" Meg asked.

I admitted I had no idea. "Paddy loaned us his jalopy, as he calls it, for the trip. He said they wouldn't be leaving the city until after we came back." I had my head in my backpack, checking that I'd packed my cell phone charger.

"Really? Some jalopy."

A quick horn beep made me raise my head to see Ned glide to the curb in a baby blue vintage Mercedes Benz. I didn't know much about cars, but its rounded bumpers made me think this one was from the 50s or 60s. My shoulders slumped in dismay. This was not the way to fit in with the Genova clan, who drive SUVs and pickup trucks.

Ned jumped out of the car while I tamped down my misgivings and turned to hug Meg.

"Stay safe and keep me posted," she whispered and

then turned to Ned. "And you, keep an eye on her, please. Trudy has a habit of getting herself into trouble."

"Hey, I'm standing right here," I protested.

"I'm on it," Ned promised Meg and wheeled my suitcase to the roomy trunk of the Benz. I placed my computer bag on the back seat, then slid into the passenger seat next to Ned and shoved my backpack into the roomy footwell. The car's tan leather interior remained supple with a whiff of preservative. A modern radio and GPS had been added to the dash.

"This car must be your father's pride and joy." I clicked my seat belt. "I'm surprised he parted with it." I kept my tone light as we set off toward the Henry Hudson Parkway North.

"He was happy for us to give her a workout. My parents use it to ride out to the Hamptons or Montauk on occasion, but they haven't done that lately." Ned's father had cardiac stents placed recently and he was in the midst of a rehab program overseen by his formidable wife, Ned's mother Ruth. "I hoped this might be a conversation starter with your brothers. You know how guys and cars can be."

"Sure." Noncommittal; we would see. "You remember the route I mentioned, or do you want me to set the GPS?"

"Route 17 to 87 North to Exit 21."

"Good memory. I'll explain the local roads from there."

"Sit back and enjoy the ride then." Ned turned on the radio to the rock station he favored in his downtime. "U2 retrospective today, okay with you?"

"Sure. Driver's choice." I had to admit the car's suspension gave us a comfortable ride as we cruised along. This early on a Saturday we'd missed weekly traffic. Soon we were sailing north, and I tried to relax as the familiar songs played. Ned was a competent driver.

We had never been alone for an extended period. The week stretched ahead of us, and I fully intended to cash in on that end of the situation, too, as we navigated the early days of cementing our relationship. We'd been dating occasionally since meeting last spring at the studio when an actor had died suspiciously and upped our relationship more recently as it became clear we were good together.

This was an important trip home for me. I was excited to see Gail pregnant since she hadn't been when I'd been home last Christmas. I'd kept track by texts and the photos she shared on social media, following her monthly belly growth. She was due in six weeks, a Christmas baby, and when I'd asked her why she'd waited this long to have a shower, she confided it had taken her and my brother a long time to get pregnant, and she hadn't wanted to jinx things by having an early shower. Her choice.

Gail was a year older and had been a sister figure to me

during high school when I had two older brothers. We were the petite gals on the volleyball team, and despite endless teasing about players needing to be tall, Gail and I made up for our lack of height in high leaps and exuberant spikes. Her baby shower was the prompt for the visit; introducing Ned to my family was part of it, too, as only my mom had met him the previous spring when I'd been injured during that case at the studio. Part of me felt excited to show Ned where I'd grown up, even if I was edgy about how my brothers would get along with this New York detective who worked in a totally different world.

Those were great reasons for a visit, but not the ones that worried me. After I'd made a habit of involving myself in Ned's last two cases, I needed him to help me solve mine.

I watched Ned change lanes as he hummed to "Beautiful Day." When he caught my eye, he winked. I smiled back, feeling a zing of attraction in the pit of my stomach. I took a deep breath and tried to relax.

"Anxious about going home?" he asked.

I gathered my thoughts. "It's always bittersweet for me. When I'm away in the Big Apple, I miss my family, but being home . . ."

"Brings back the pain of your father's death," he finished.

*DEATH in the ORCHARD*

"Even more than that, Ned. Everyone else seems to have accepted that day as a tragic accident, but to me, the circumstances stink to high heaven." I was convinced there was far more to be unearthed. I'd decided not to tell my mother or brothers I had enlisted Ned to figure out what had happened until we'd found something worth telling.

But that decision meant part of me was terrified. I was opening a can of worms I wouldn't be able to close if the outcome of our investigation proved less than favorable toward the father I'd admired. He wasn't perfect, but he'd been a great dad to us. I couldn't understand why his body had been found at our town's railroad depot; nor why he'd closed out my parents' retirement and savings accounts, with the money never found. It had certainly not made sense to me then and still didn't now.

"Which is why I agreed to help you with this, Trudy. But are you certain about not telling anyone in your family about our plans?"

I knew I was taking a big risk, but this had gnawed away at me for the past eleven years, and I needed to find the truth, no matter where it took me. I would need to walk a fine line with my family while keeping what we were doing under wraps at first.

"I think my mom would understand, but I'm not certain how either of my brothers would react. Let's stick to our original plan." Back then, Ben readily accepted Dad's death as an accident as he took over running the apple orchard business my parents built, focusing on orders and finances. Rick generally kept his feelings more to himself as he finished school, and now managed the orchard and its workers. I'd decided there was no point in bringing up that sad time if we could avoid it for the moment, especially with the baby shower tomorrow.

After the shower, I'd start working to find the resolution to the questions that had plagued me for the past years.

And then all bets were off.

Ned signaled to take the Catskill exit. He glanced at Trudy, who seemed lost in her thoughts. Sun coming in the window picked out blonde highlights in her honey-colored hair, which she laughingly referred to as "dishwater blonde." He had readily agreed to come home with her, but it was the investigative side of their trip that had him more nervous than meeting her family.

There was the chance they'd uncover something unpalatable about her father, and he'd bear the blame for helping her find it. He'd learned that Trudy was stubborn and would have done this without his cooperation. By participating, he hoped to keep her safe. His main goal was to protect Trudy.

The road curved sharply and Trudy leaned closer to him. The citrusy scent of her shampoo reached him, and he felt his body react. He wondered where he and Trudy would be sleeping. When he'd met Trudy's mother last spring, she'd introduced herself as "Hilda," but Trudy said Bob had been calling her by the nickname used by family and friends that she preferred, and he should, too. Hildy it would be. She'd seemed like a modern mom, but who knew how she would feel when it came to her daughter and said daughter's boyfriend sleeping together under her roof? For that matter, how did *he* feel about sleeping together at her childhood home?

He'd deal with whatever Hildy wanted, but decided he wouldn't creep around at night to avoid squeaky floorboards in what Trudy had described as an old Edwardian house. It occurred to Ned that perhaps they shouldn't sleep together at all. Plus, there would be reactions from the two brothers he'd never met, one brother-in-law, one pregnant sister-in-law, and Hildy's beau. "You said everyone in the family lives at the orchard?"

Trudy nodded. "Ben and Gail live in a modern ranch

house between the cider barn and Mom's house. Rick is the middle kid. He and his husband, Aidan, live in a cabin at the back of the orchard property." He felt her eyes appraising him. "You're not nervous about meeting them, are you?"

"Not nervous, although older brothers tend to be protective of younger sisters. Must have been nice to have siblings."

"Mostly, but being the youngest meant they terrorized me with pranks, poked their noses in my business, and generally made pests of themselves. Routinely invaded my privacy, too."

Ned laughed. "All right then, maybe not all roses." Being an only child had bothered him from time to time growing up. He'd enjoyed school and stayed in touch with a few of his friends from there. His parents had exposed him to all that New York offered, from art and theatre to museums and more. But none of that provided someone who knew the inside jokes, to wrestle with, or play tricks against their parents. There was no sibling who had shared his childhood, as wonderful as it had been. He wondered how that had affected his decision to join the police. There was a camaraderie in his precinct that felt like extended family. Before he left on this vacation, he and his fellow detectives had each donated days of paid vacation time to a colleague in his precinct to allow the man to be at home to care for his wife after surgery. He liked that they'd step up for each other.

Ned shrugged off the dim shadow of loneliness and followed Trudy's directions along narrow country roads as the mountains loomed in the distance. Autumn in the surrounding woods was showy, the yellow, red, and orange leaves a colorful display along the twisty roads they traveled. It felt good to leave work behind for this break; he hadn't taken a vacation in a while. Helping Trudy was quickly feeling secondary to being with her. At this point in their relationship, everything was new and exciting. *She* was exciting.

"They're a good bunch," Trudy admitted. "Made it easier to move to the city and leave my mom after nursing school, knowing the boys and then Gail and Aidan were around. Gail had a lot to do with insisting I should leave. Now if I can only get used to the idea of Mom dating my high school English teacher . . ."

That had been the shocker last spring when Hildy had come down to care for Trudy. Ned had seen how Trudy grappled with this news. "The infamous Bob Riley. Guess I'll meet him, too. Didn't your mom say he was excited to hear about your classes and the mystery you've started?"

She nodded. Trudy's NYU classes were helping her advance the manuscript she'd started, set in England with an American protagonist. After a few stops and starts, she seemed to have hit on a storyline she liked, but more importantly, one of her profs thought it had promise. "Mr. Riley was my favorite teacher and always encouraged my writing efforts. Guess I'll have to start calling him Bob." She sighed. "It's thinking of him with my mom that puts a different spin on things."

Ned arched an eyebrow. "You mean sleeping with your mom?"

"Let's not go there, please. Mom was only fifty when my dad died and I'm sure she's missed . . . companionship. I try not to think beyond that. No, it's more that it feels awkward with the change in our roles, I guess. I mean I'm happy he wants to read my manuscript, but is he going to grade it? It's weird..."

He shot her a quick grin. "A change of subject, then. What do you have on our schedule once we arrive?"

"Lunch with Mom and Bob. Everyone else will be at work and we'll see them at dinner. Mom's eager to show off her new kitchen reno. I told her I'd give you a tour of downtown Schoharie this afternoon."

"Perfect. I've arranged for us to see your father's file."

Trudy sat up straighter. "You did? You're amazing."

"Glad you've noticed." He slowed as two deer crossed the road and disappeared into the trees with a flick of white tails. "It's routine courtesy to let local cop shops know when you're on their patch, especially as we're going to be asking questions When I told the local lieutenant, Paul Hoffmann, you asked to look at the case file, he had it brought from the archives, and said he'd be in this afternoon working on staff evaluations."

"Just like that he agreed?"

"After I let him know I'd be in Schoharie and did a bit of finessing. I explained you were sixteen when your father died and weren't told a lot of details. Now you're older, and dating a detective, you have a desire to know more about what happened."

"All true."

"He agreed we could see the file, but we can't copy anything. He did say it's slim."

She nodded. "I can work with that."

"Trudy," he warned, "no funny business."

"I have no idea what you mean." She touched his arm. "Thanks for setting this up, Ned. It means a lot to me."

"I know it does, Trudy, which is why I'm doing it. But you must be prepared for what you might learn. You may be convinced your father was murdered, but it might turn out to be an accident after all." He decided to tell her the truth. "I also don't want to be responsible for finding out negative information about your dad. Your family will hate me."

"I'll keep an open mind, I promise." She brushed her

hair back from her face. For a few moments they rode along in silence past older homes, farmhouses and Colonials in various states of repair, some set high on foothills with steep driveways.

Ned glanced at the dashboard clock and knew they'd be there shortly. Trudy had her head turned to look at the landscape.

Then she turned back to him. "It would be much easier if my father's death was truly an accident. Then we wouldn't have to hunt for his murderer."

# CHAPTER FOUR

Three hours after we left Manhattan, we turned onto Rickard Hill Road. I was hungry after my early start, the quick banana I'd gobbled from the craft table at the studio long gone.

Since I'd been home last Christmas, the sign proclaiming **Genova Orchards** at the head of the drive had been freshly painted, its dark green lettering standing out against a crisp white background with a garland of rosy apples surrounding the name. Underneath in smaller letters it read *All organic apples, cider, and herbs.* Beneath the main sign, three drop-down boards noted: *Gifts, crafts, antiques. Café open 9 AM to 3 PM. Dog-friendly on leashes.*

Ned paused with his blinker on to allow a minivan at the head of a line of cars to exit. Its rear section was laden with baskets brimming with shiny apples, while its middle row held two sleepy toddlers in their car seats. "Someone's going to be busy making applesauce. Who are the animals?" He pointed to a sign on a post inside the open gate. "SLOW: Animals, human and otherwise, on grounds." The string of cars leaving took advantage of him stopping. It was a busy day at the orchard.

"Rick and Aidan have a couple of barn cats to keep mice down, and Ben and Gail are holding off on a puppy until after the baby arrives. The sign is more for customers. Many bring dogs, especially during picking season."

"Does your mom have a dog?"

"Her sweet cocker spaniel died last year. I have it on good authority from Gail that Bob plans to surprise her at Christmas with a cockapoo that won't shed."

The car line ended and Ned turned into the drive. This early in the day there were still many cars, SUVs, and pickups in the lot, and I could see people moving among the apples. More would be in the shop. I felt a surge of satisfaction looking at the compound my father and mother had built, with buildings on either side of the drive and neat rows of apple trees stretching up a mildly sloped hill, acres and acres of them. I felt a shiver of anticipation—or was that trepidation for the days to come?

I directed Ned past the white cottage shop to our left. "That glassed addition off to the right looks out onto the herb and flower garden and has tables and chairs for the café. You can get take-out sandwiches, as well as Mom's baked goods, or choose to eat in. Gail dries and sells the herbs and some of the flowers but uses a lot of them in the wreaths she makes for the shop. The main room is full of handcrafted gifts like hers from local artisans mixed with vintage finds. Gail loves to poke around antique shops and estate sales."

"Smart, a nice income stream."

"Ben started the sandwich counter, which stays open all year with the bakery. That helps pay the bills in the winter when the apples are gone. Keep going." I pointed to the huge red barn on our right with a pumpkin patch beyond it. Pumpkins of different sizes and shapes stood on planking shelves, with clutches of Indian corn and bound cornstalks for sale. "The barn is where the apples are sorted for selling and carting out, and the cider is made, the guts of the place. It has fridges for the cider, and we sell local cheeses, too." Things hummed along nicely now in the large enterprise, but I remembered the days when money was tight after my father died, with Mom and Ben struggling to learn the business and Aidan rushing to finish school to help out.

My reasons for being here danced at the edge of my thoughts. A baby shower followed by my father's murder investigation presented a terrific contrast. Would this work out? Was I being unfair to my family?

Ned pulled over after the pumpkin patch, letting the

car idle as he looked at our operation.

Before he could speak, I said, "All right, I'm questioning my decision not to tell my family we're looking into my father's death."

"You have to decide, Trudy." Ned put his hand on top of mine and gave it a squeeze. "I'll go with whatever you choose."

I looked out the side mirror as doors slammed and several cars left, while more arrived behind us on this busy Saturday. "With Gail pregnant and the orchard at its busiest time, I think I shouldn't distract them without concrete news."

Ned peered through the windshield. "How big is this place?" Row upon row of trees, some boughs still hanging heavy with fruit, spread up the hill into the distance.

I looked at the orchard with new eyes, seeing it from the perspective of someone who hadn't grown up with these trees for their yard. "About thirty acres, minus the land the houses and buildings stand on. There were plans to extend west to the neighboring farm but those had to be canceled after my dad died."

Ned whistled. "That's still some enterprise."

"One of my dad's favorite sayings was, 'Go big or go home.'" What about Mario Genova? What would my dad say about the course of action I'd planned? Would he tell me to leave the past where it was, or be proud I wanted to push to find the truth?

Ned put the car in gear and slowly continued along the road. Off to the left we passed clusters of pick-your-own apple gatherers, where we could see people with baskets collecting their own fruit in the rows cordoned off from the commercial area. "Picking season is coming to an end, but the cider production will keep going for a while." I pointed to a cedar shake ranch house on the right, after the pumpkin patch, decorated for Hallowe'en. "Ben and Gail's house. She's a big decorator." My stomach growled, yet I kept stalling our arrival. Coming home also meant facing Bob Riley, who was not a monster, I reminded myself. Get a grip, Trudy.

"And here's Mom's."

Ned pulled up in front of our family home, a Tiffany blue Edwardian in the Queen Anne style. The window sashes were picked out in bright white, like icing on a huge cake, while gingerbread trim and fish-scale shingles were painted a pale lavender, ending with a shiny front door the color of an eggplant. "That was my bedroom." I pointed to the round turret room.

I knew my mom kept her SUV in one of the three garages; the older Ford pickup parked in front of one of the other doors must belong to Bob, as he and my mother weren't living together—yet. While it was taking me time to get used to the idea of my mom being with someone, at least Bob wasn't unknown to us. I knew him well enough to know he wouldn't take advantage of my mother, and that should be enough.

"Park in front of one of the other garages. The boys can pull in anywhere later when they come for dinner."

"Great. That way I can show them the car."

*Great.* "Let's leave the suitcases for now and head inside to say hello."

Mom must have been listening for the car. By the time we walked up the front steps, she'd thrown the door open and stood waiting to hug us both. "Trudy! Ned, come in. I'm so happy you're home."

Ned waited while I gave my mom a good long hug and inhaled her familiar light scent, overlaid with a hint of cinnamon. "Someone's been baking." Her stylish bob was streaked with gray strands. She wore faded jeans and a much-washed Genova Orchards tee under a plaid shirt and could pass for fifty instead of someone in her early sixties.

"Tonight's dessert and Gail's cake for the shower. Come say hello to Bob."

I smiled at Mom as she gave Ned a hug and led us from the entry into the hall past the dining room. 'I thought we'd eat on the back porch as it's only the four of us and sunny out there this time of day. You must be hungry after such a long drive."

*DEATH in the ORCHARD*

"Smells great in here." Ned admired the ornate woodwork and embossed anaglypta wallpaper that ran down the hall, typical of this style house. My artistic mom had stenciled period designs under the thick crown molding. The Edwardian look was completely different from the Biedermeier style of his parents' Upper East Side apartment.

"This is some woodwork, Hildy. Beautifully preserved," Ned said.

"I've tried to keep the period details without going overboard. This house was built in 1909 and the Edwardians liked things dark and ornate. I prefer a lighter palette."

I lagged behind the decorating duo. Who knew Ned would be interested in architectural styles? He was infallibly polite. But then, he was a kind of a renaissance man who kept surprising me.

We arrived at the bright kitchen that looked out onto our vegetable garden and flower borders, followed by a sea of apple trees stretching into the distance. I held back a gasp. Gone were the old cabinets and the clock shaped like a cut apple. And where were the curtains with little red apples Mom had made years ago? I knew she'd had a reno, but not that everything old would be tossed out.

Then I remembered she'd wanted this new kitchen for a long time and felt abashed at my dismay. Thomas

Wolfe had it right: you can't go home again.

A window over a large Belfast sink and a set of sliding doors leading out to the back porch let in copious sunlight. I could see Bob in the garden.

"Well?" Mom's eyes were shining. I couldn't disappoint her.

"You've outdone yourself. Look at this island."

Mom pointed out the shelves underneath with dividers that held rows of baking sheets and pans, with a large counter for stools for working and eating. The top was largely stainless steel with marble set in one end for rolling pastry dough. "It's exactly what I wanted," she gushed.

"Those are some ovens, Hildy." Ned had given me a glance and got into the spirit of things. "Two baker's ovens, and what must be the biggest fridge I've ever seen. And a separate freezer."

"There's a walk-in pantry here," Mom said, pulling open a door.

Then I saw something that made my heart soar. "I love that you kept the original cabinets on either side of the sink, but I did notice the apple curtains are gone." I hoped I kept the censure from my voice.

"Time for those curtains to go." Mom laughed. "I sewed those when you were in elementary school." She pointed to the cabinets. "I had those cabinets refinished and took out the center panels, put glass in." She beamed. "Saved my baking profits for a few years to get this kitchen. In the evenings I'd flip through decorating magazines and watch all the HGTV shows, making notes. It all came together."

"Mom is where I get my list-making tendencies," I told Ned. "She's a demon organizer." I felt a pang of remorse. Evenings alone must have been difficult for her for so many years.

"How are things in New York?" Mom asked Ned as she sent me a worried look. "I hope nothing too dangerous?"

Ned smiled. "Yes, your daughter can be a handful at times, but that's why I adore her." He sent me a meaningful look. "And work hard to keep her safe."

I bristled at that. "I think I've demonstrated I'm capable of taking care of myself."

Mom hugged me to her. "I'm glad to have you here for a while where I know you'll be safe."

I fought hard to keep the guilty look off my face. Would Mom still be happy I'm here if she finds out what I'm planning?"

"Bob's picking mint for our tea. Everything's ready out there." Mom ushered us to the porch, where a cheery vintage cloth with a design of a 1930s village topped the oak table from the old kitchen. "I'll get the chili and rice."

A basket of warm cornbread stood on the table. Bob

washed the mint at an outside hose bib and came onto the porch clutching a handful wrapped in a dishtowel. "Hello, Trudy." He gave me a warm hug. "So good to see my star pupil." He put the leaves in a small bowl on the table and dried his hands on the towel. "And this must be ace detective Ned O'Malley."

I introduced Ned and the men shook hands. I'd forgotten Bob's lively blue eyes, the color of the bachelor's buttons Gail grew, and how he could make you feel he was interested in everything you said. He hadn't changed much in the decade since I'd seen him. Maybe his hair was more salt than pepper, but he still wore it brushed back off his forehead. He looked relaxed in jeans and an oxford shirt with the sleeves rolled up, a far cry from the blazers and ties he wore when teaching at Schoharie High School.

Mom came out with a large tureen of chili she put in the center of the table. "Turkey chili to tide us over. The boys insisted on grilling steaks tonight. I have some chicken if you don't eat red meat, Ned."

"Steak is fine. I'm an easy eater," Ned said.

Mom returned with a bowl of rice.

"Save room for dessert tonight, Ned. Hildy's desserts are not to be missed." Bob winked at my mother, who blushed.

My mother blushing? This definitely took getting

used to. I remembered when I was much younger, and my parents would go to the movies or out to dinner with Bob and his wife before she died. These two knew what it was to be lonely.

Ned touched my ankle with his foot as Mom served us. I shook off my reverie and realized Bob had asked me a question. "Sorry, I was miles away."

"I said I want to hear about this mystery class at NYU and your book in progress. You were always one of my most talented writing students. And what a great job you scored at the movie studio, so different for a nurse. Hildy says you two met at the studio."

Over lunch I explained my work and the case that threw us together last spring, when the soap opera I consulted on lost several leads to murder. Bob asked about my writing and my decision to make my protagonist an American living in England. His questions made me understand I knew my main character more than I'd realized.

"You'll have to take a trip there at some point to nail down your setting," Bob concluded. "Did you bring your first chapters for me to read?"

"Already printed out in my computer bag. And yes, I have a trip fund started for the future."

"Trudy has always been a fan of *Masterpiece Mystery*," Mom said. "It was only a matter of time before she figured out a way to travel to England."

We shared a laugh and our conversation about where in England the series would open continued as we ate. I relaxed even more. Bob treated me as an adult who'd accomplished things in my twenty-seven years. He asked Ned about his precinct and the stress of a detective's life, too. As they chatted, I wished my father was around to see how I'd grown into a professional woman with good taste in men.

Suddenly, my doubts vanished, and I understood that for me, I was doing the right thing to investigate my father's death.

# CHAPTER FIVE

*ELEVEN MONTHS BEFORE*

It had been the strangest time in Greg Dietz's young life—and he still had at least another year to serve in the Troy Correctional Facility if he made parole on the first try.

Greg had been a promising third-year student at Albany Law, on a road leading to joining his father's law firm, when his cocaine addiction led to selling to friends to feed his habit. He'd been picked up for possession, and the amount he had on him led to a conviction for intent to sell. The Bolivian marching powder had cost him his career and his family's trust.

He'd finally knocked the addiction on its head, and regularly attended Narcotics Anonymous meetings at the facility, where all the drug users were lumped in together. In the prison library, he helped other inmates with legal forms and resumes. He even managed to avoid fights—being the cellmate of a known drug lord had given him a ring of protection. He also showed remorse, the key to an early release he'd found when he researched early parole. Greg kept his eye on doing everything he could to make it out on his first try to shave time off his sentence for good behavior in these crowded conditions, finessing every aspect to assure his release.

When he'd been shown to his cell the first night last year, overwhelmed by the noise and the shouting, a short man looked down at him from the top bunk. He had a wiry stature and a smug attitude Greg associated with a bantam cock. It was his eyes that froze the smile he'd plastered on his face. Those eyes were coal black and cold; eyes that had seen things Greg didn't want to think about.

He'd kept his mouth shut and been deferential to the older man, a talker. Years of dealing with his overbearing father had taught him how to hit the right tone of obsequious groveling. As Greg became used to the stale air and the meager portions of tasteless food, Bobby Costello stayed close to Greg, which helped keep the fear that haunted the new inmate in check. No one messed with the Big C, as some called Bobby. Older inmates called him the Mick, and while Greg wondered about the nickname, he knew not to ask. Nothing about

Bobby Costello, with his olive complexion and dark eyes, looked remotely Irish.

Greg quickly learned Bobby had been a middling drug dealer working the Schoharie-Cobleskill area for a big-time Canadian ring when he was picked up for trafficking pounds of cocaine in the spare tire of his car. Definite intent to sell in the eyes of the court. Bobby's goal to bump himself up to take over an entire upstate region had disappeared with his conviction and stiff sentence. Still, Bobby had too many ways to create havoc with anyone who crossed him inside. If the Big C wanted Greg to be his handmaiden, so be it. Greg could curry favor with the best of them.

Thankfully, Bobby hadn't wanted sexual favors like some of the men who groomed newcomers, but he did want Greg's skills to help him with legal paperwork on his appeal, unraveling those involved lawyer's letters and forms he didn't understand.

Despite his heavy Brooklyn accent, the man had a stilted formal way of speaking like a Damon Runyon character. "It is my belief, Gregory, and many New York lawmakers agree with me, that sentences for drug convictions are too stiff." Greg's eventual research for Bobby backed this up in a 1997 report from Human Rights Watch. "Drug offense sentences constitute cruel and unusual punishment when compared to similar sentences handed out to arsonists, rapists, and even murderers. This appeal I want for myself? You here, along with my lawyer, are going to ensure I get it."

Greg readily agreed to help when it came to research and forms. Many other inmates won their appeals on the same grounds and were being released for time served. Bobby's lawyer had encouraged and appreciated Greg's extra assistance, and over the past year, Greg deciphered all of the lawyer's correspondence for Bobby when it arrived. After already serving ten years, it looked like Bobby Costello might get out in another year, right around the time Greg, sentenced for a far smaller amount of cocaine and under the newer guidelines, was due for parole.

As the men grew closer and Greg gained Bobby's trust, they started a plan for going into business together. They would use connections Bobby had in the Sixth Family, the Canadian operation that encroached on New York's infamous Five Families mafia. "Together we take over this part of New York State, far and above the operation I had selling in rural towns like Schoharie. We run our entire operation through a legitimate business as a front to launder the money. We're two guys on parole keeping to the straight and narrow, my young friend. And we don't touch the product, ever."

Once Greg assured Bobby he was done with using drugs

but wanted to sell them, they'd tossed around ideas for what the front business might be. Bobby pushed selling used cars. "We go high end, Gregory. There's money there, but more importantly, we get a good bookkeeper, and I know just the person."

"Person" sounded to Greg like "poison."

One night Greg finally found the courage to ask, "Why do the guys call you 'the Mick,' Bobby? You have Irish blood somewhere?"

Bobby's laugh was rich. "You give me a kick, Gregory, I must stifle my laughter in my pillow to avoid attracting the guards." Then he sighed, his tone more sober. "It is for Mickey Mantle. Tell me you know him."

"The Yankee slugger?"

"The best, to my mind, after Babe Ruth. I am called the Mick due to my initiation to the Job." He paused.

In that pause, Greg heard the capital on "Job" and felt a tightening in his stomach as Bobby decided what, or maybe how much, to tell Greg about his initiation. Suddenly Greg didn't know if he wanted that information in his head. Before he could take back the question, Bobby cleared his throat, and in the darkness, started to talk.

"They pumped me up—alcohol, drugs, you name it my young friend, those were all in my system, running through my veins, making me feel powerful. Invincible, like the green man."

Greg cast his mind for the reference. "The Hulk?"

"That's it, the Hulk. That's how strong and big I felt, like one giant muscle. It had been made clear to me what I must do to join, and I did want to join, do not mistake this. This was my choice, this Canadian outfit, a step above the Sopranos-type that comes to mind when people hear New York mafia."

Greg heard the bed frame overhead creak as Bobby changed his position and continued, his voice a low rumble.

"They bring me this guy, sniveling, wetting himself. I cannot recall to this day what they told me he did to deserve getting whacked, but trust me, if they want you dead, you die. If I didn't do it, one of the others there would, and not only would my chance to join go down the drain, but I'd also probably end up like this poor slob 'cause by now I know too much."

On the lower bunk, Greg shivered and wished he'd never asked about Bobby's nickname.

"I had my choice of implements at hand, but I reach for this Louisville Slugger, the same kind of bat the Mick used, and I am that puffed up and unconquerable that I bring that bat down on this poor clown's head and watch it split wide open like a smashed grapefruit. And then I see before me my sonofabitch father, slapping my mother around, and right behind him, all the kids who bullied me in school. A red mist rises, along with a sickening sweet smell, and I keep beating him and bringing that bat down. By now his brains are all over the place but I keep swatting him, one direction and another."

Greg gulped down bile and felt it burn.

Bobby sighed. "Not my finest moment, and this I say to you sincerely. It scared the shit outta me, like some genie was let out of a bottle. Afterwards I shook like a baby. For days I wouldn't see anyone."

Bobby cleared his throat and Greg was glad he couldn't see his face. His own hands trembled at what he'd heard.

"After that I wanted nothing to do with hurting no one, but I didn't have to, 'cause the guys said I handled that bat like the Mick and the story went around like wildfire. The name stuck; everyone left me alone. Aside from a few broken fingers, I've never intentionally hurt or killed anyone again. But I always carried a bat, and that threat alone was usually enough."

Utter silence permeated the cell the men shared. Greg wondered at Bobby's use of "intentionally." His thoughts ran wild as he heard the *plink-plink-plink* of the faucet in the next cell, and the snores of the beefy guy across the corridor. He heard farts and moans, and down the hall, a man cried out as he masturbated into his hand over who knew what fantasy.

Greg now understood the meaning of "lost for words."

"Speechless, huh, kid? You asked. I owed you for helping me." Bobby turned over and a few minutes later Greg heard his regular breathing as he dozed off.

It took Greg a lot longer to fall asleep that night.

# CHAPTER SIX

I pointed out the red brick Schoharie High School on our right as Ned guided the car down the hill toward the center of town. A few students ran laps around the track, while two older teens used the basketball hoop to challenge each other, the way I'd insisted I could beat my brothers, banging the ball against our garage doors and never winning.

"See those bleachers?" I asked.

"Good make-out spot underneath?"

I shot him a look of surprise while I tamped down my reaction to the sudden memory of John Maydan kissing me after school, tongue and all, right before my sixteenth birthday. I'd had such a huge crush on him and couldn't believe he wanted to be with me. My first French kiss had been shocking yet made me feel mature. "You really *were* a kid at some point in life."

"Even private school boys liked to make out under the bleachers."

"As long as you didn't dirty your blazers, I'll bet."

Ned shook his head. "You have this idea about me —"

"That's totally true," I said. I counted off on my fingers. "Fencing awards, Honor Society, *summa cum laude* from Fordham."

He approached State Route 30, called Main Street in the village. "Let's see: Debate Club captain who still argues convincingly; captain of the volleyball team; editor of the school literary journal; played violin in the orchestra and sang in several choirs; oh, and your own scholarship to UAlbany nursing school."

"Huh, who told you that stuff?" My heart sped up as we neared the Schoharie Police Department. We were really doing this.

"Your mom, last spring when you were sleeping off your concussion."

"I'll be speaking with her when we get home."

Ned laughed and waited for traffic at the flashing red light to make the turn onto Main Street. "These are nicely maintained buildings," he said, as we drove past a collection of inns, restaurants, and shops.

"They're big on preservation here. Many had to be rebuilt after severe flooding from Hurricane Irene."

Ned nodded. "Changing topics. Bob Riley seems like a nice guy."

"He is. I'd forgotten how encouraging he could be. I'm

kind of glad Mom has him in her life."

"Whoa, that's a big change."

"Hey, small steps. I can be flexible."

"Sometimes."

I saw him smile. "You may think I'm fixated on my father being murdered, but if you'd known him, you'd know Mario Genova would never be involved in anything shady. I'm not looking at him through the rose-colored glasses of an adoring daughter, either. My dad could have a temper and he could brood with the best of them. But honesty mattered to him, and he instilled in us a strong sense of right and wrong. He believed in being a good friend, and had excellent manners." I looked out the window and swallowed hard. "He didn't deserve to have the life he worked hard to build with my mom cut short. It's why his actions immediately before he died are so out of character. Something was happening in his life we weren't aware of, which is why I've always been convinced his death wasn't an accident."

I took a breath and stopped talking as we pulled up in front of the small police station, aware I'd gone into a rant Ned didn't deserve. He was the one who was supporting me and had set up this meeting.

Ned parked and touched the side of my face with his hand. When I turned to him, he cupped my chin, making me look at him. "That's what we're here to find out, Trudy, as long as you're prepared for where this may lead us. Let's go find the truth."

When we exited the car, I noticed a tall, slim man with wire-rimmed glasses standing in the doorway. "Detective O'Malley? And you must be Trudy Genova." He stuck out his hand. "Lieutenant Paul Hoffmann." We shook hands, and after an admiring glance at Ned's car, he ushered us inside a small front office with two desks and pointed toward the back of the room, where several chairs were pulled up to a conference table. "You can work right here."

I tried not to let my dissatisfaction show. I'd hoped we'd be in a separate room where I could leaf through the file without someone watching over me.

"I understand you want to know more about your father's case, Ms. Genova." Hoffmann had a pleasant face and nice eyes and seemed to want to be of genuine help.

My mom always said you get more flies with honey than vinegar. I flashed him what I hoped was my most beguiling smile. "Call us Trudy and Ned. Thanks for your help, Lt. Hoffmann."

"Paul. Sorry for your loss. I wasn't working here then, so don't have any personal knowledge to share, but I've scanned the file, and it seems straightforward, if a little slim. The detective on the case, Larry Long, is retired and now lives in Saratoga Springs."

*DEATH in the ORCHARD*

Ned was all bonhomie, thanking Paul and guiding me to the table. My disappointment grew when I saw, despite everyone's warnings, that my father's file was indeed slender. Paul took a seat at the table with us. "Feel free to take notes, but I'm afraid I can't allow any copies of reports to go out of here."

"Understood," Ned assured him. "We appreciate you pulling the file for us."

"I'll take notes on my phone." I let Paul see me pull up the Notes app and muted the volume.

Ned opened the folder and I caught my breath. Stapled inside the cover was a portion of a photo from a family portrait we'd had done the summer before my father died. My father's olive skin, dark hair, and startling hazel eyes looked right at me; his face was creased in the sunny smile I remembered all too well. Next to it was another photo I'd never seen and immediately wished I hadn't. My father lay on the ground on his stomach. The hitch of the trailer he'd been found next to had blood on it, clearly visible in the photo. I caught my breath and felt heat rush to my face.

Ned quickly pulled the top sheet over to cover the photo of my father's body. "Sorry, Trudy." He touched my hand. "You want to continue?"

I took a steadying breath. "Absolutely."

"I'll get you some water." Paul disappeared into one of

several rooms in the back.

My hands shook while I tried to open the camera function on my phone while Ned was engrossed in reading the first sheet, which was the statement of the police officer who'd found my father. Ron Hanson had been to school with Ben and drew the short straw that day.

I heard a fridge door slam and quickly turned my phone face down as Paul returned. He placed two cold water bottles in front of us, and I thanked him as I twisted the cap off one and took a drink. The photo had upset me more than I realized, but it also firmed up my resolve to find justice for my dad.

"The next pages are statements taken from your mother about the timing when your father left home, and from the bank manager you spoke to when you went to the bank. You were there when Ron Hanson came to tell you he'd been found." Ned looked at me. "That's when you became aware your father had made significant withdrawals the day before he died?"

I nodded. "When we realized my father was missing, Ron told us to check with our bank, because financial irregularities often show up in these cases. The bank manager, Wynn Graham, told us my dad had closed out my parents' savings and retirement accounts. We were sitting with him, trying to absorb that news, when Ron showed up and told us they'd found Dad."

Ned flipped to the next sheet, and by the body outlines near the bottom of the page, I recognized the form. He glanced at me. "It's all right. I've seen autopsy reports before." But never my father's, which I'd always wanted to scrutinize.

He scanned the top page and frowned, which set my antenna wiggling. Ned flipped to the second page and I leaned closer to read with him, keeping my expression flat as I read through the report.

Ned sat back and looked around the office. A large map of the area was framed on one wall. "Paul, can you show me where this train station is? I'm not familiar with the area."

The two men moved off as Paul explained that trains hadn't run along that route for a long time. "It had become mostly for commercial supplies. There hadn't been passenger travel there since the 1960s."

"His drive that morning to Albany would have been here, along Interstate 88?"

"It's the quickest route."

Ned sat back down next to me with Paul at the head of the table.

"Based on Mrs. Genova's statement, backed up by the contents of their pickup truck, Mr. Genova left home around seven in the morning to drive to the outskirts of Albany for supplies for their lunch business, about a forty-minute drive from here. The paper supply store he visited first is nearby. May I?" Paul gestured to the file and when Ned handed it over, the officer flipped to the end pages where exhibits were listed. "Officers traced Mr. Genova's trip from these receipts, and both stores corroborated he'd been in. If he didn't stop anywhere else, he should have been home around 9:30 A.M."

"Exactly what my mom expected," I said. I flashed back to my mom sending Ben to town to hurry my father up an hour later when he failed to come home, thinking he'd stopped to talk to his friend at the hardware store. "My brother couldn't find my dad and drove around until he found our truck parked in the station lot. He called us, and Mom and I had a neighbor drive us down to the truck. Then the police told us to check the bank as they searched the area. If we'd stayed, we'd have been there when they found my dad." My voice shook as the day came flooding back. I swallowed and took a sip of water. "We were in the bank talking with Mr. Graham after eleven because I remember seeing the time on his desk clock. It was only a few minutes after that when Ron came by to say they'd found my father's body next to a trailer parked at the rear of the station."

Paul pointed to the last statement. "Your father was found at 10:58 AM and there were no signs of life. One officer stayed to await the coroner while the other notified your mother at the bank at 11:13."

"Ron and my brother Ben went to school together and he told us." I sat back in my chair. "The question becomes, what was my father doing from 9:30 to around 10:30? That missing hour tells a story I need to know."

*Eleven days earlier*

Greg Dietz scooped up the contents of the manila envelope he'd been handed, and then placed the meager bills and change in the pocket of the tracksuit he'd worn when he'd entered the correctional facility, his home for the past two years. As he'd hoped and predicted, he'd received parole once two-thirds of his main sentence had been completed. He gave the guard behind the counter a crooked smile and ran his hand over his buzz cut.

"Think I'll let this mop grow out a bit. Have to say I'm not sorry I won't see you again. Don't plan to return."

The guard grunted. "Heard it all before."

The tracksuit bottoms hung from Greg's waist, as he'd

slimmed down during his incarceration, but the sleeves and top strained across the bulge of muscles he'd acquired working out. He'd tackled the weight room in the same assiduous manner he'd worked in the library.

The guard had Greg sign a release and handed him two slips of paper: the name and time of his first meeting with his parole officer in Howe's Cave and the address of the Cobleskill halfway house he would live in for a few months to start.

He pictured his parents as he signed the release. Gerald and Cindy Dietz were well-known in their hometown of Cobleskill, where Gerald had a law practice and Cindy served on charity committees and volunteered at The Community Library. Greg's fall from grace had hit them hard and was a major embarrassment to his father. His father refused to allow him home yet, choosing to adopt a wait-and-see attitude after too many broken promises from Greg about staying clean. The man rarely spoke to him during his incarceration and never visited, preferring to remind Greg during his infrequent calls to "keep his nose clean." His mother congratulated him during those calls on getting sober and working in the prison library. Greg didn't need to have her spell out how difficult his father had made it for her to visit. As his release became imminent, Gerald Dietz told Greg he had to prove himself to them before he could move back to the family home.

*DEATH in the ORCHARD*

Greg supposed it a fair approach after what he'd put them through, but it stung that the people who were supposed to be his support system against all odds cared more for appearances than blood. His mother went along with what his father wanted, tired of the arguments and tension in the house. Gerald was a bully.

Despite his contacts in the legal system, his father constantly told Greg his criminal law bills had left them with a second mortgage on their house. So much for the fraternity of lawyers that his father claimed should be his aspiration. And he let him know it was Greg's fault that his younger brother's future college plans were changed to attending the local community college for the first two years since it was far less expensive, which was not such a big deal in Greg's mind. Doug could live at home, and maybe with fewer temptations, his younger brother would be stronger than he had been.

Doug was the only one in his family who hadn't deserted him. He'd shown up on visiting days, bringing him books and small treats. He would pick Greg up today, bringing the Ford Explorer Greg had used in college and law school, along with some of his clothes, his mother following behind to take Doug home. Greg realized he craved a warm hug from her and pictured himself inhaling the light flowery fragrance she always wore. He'd missed his mother and his brother.

He figured it was his mother who understood that he needed his wheels to get to work, and had convinced his father to keep the registration up on the car when Greg was inside. Their gift to him as he re-entered the workforce, as his father put it, was an agreement to pay the car insurance for a year while Greg established himself.

Greg had assured his counselor he would work hard to reintegrate himself into society. The words tripped off his tongue. He had the lingo down pat.

While he never planned to allow cocaine to get its hooks into him again, he'd learned other useful skills in prison, and with help from Bobby Costello, had a good line on how to get ahead and fund his future. He might never use drugs again after seeing how they controlled a person's life, but he would certainly supply them to others for his own financial gain. With the backing from Bobby to do it, he would be careful, cover his tracks, and after a little leg work, he could set himself up in the new life Bobby had left him as his legacy.

Twelve weeks ago, one of Bobby's nicknames became applied in a dreadful way. After a few months of unexplained weight loss, followed by bouts of crippling stomach pain, testing found the Big C in Bobby's pancreas and liver, a death sentence. Their plans to work together dissolved. What hadn't, Greg was surprised to hear, was

Bobby's determination for Greg to still have the future they'd planned together.

Each night before he was moved for the final time to the prison hospital, Bobby counseled Greg in hushed conversations. He'd never been tall, but now he was diminished, his arms and legs spindly yellowed sticks, his swollen belly giving him the appearance of a bloated tick. Bobby's once lustrous dark hair lay in scraggly strips across his scalp. He was running out of time.

"When I got in here, kid, my family abandoned me. My wife divorced me. Never had kids." Bobby wheezed and struggled to breathe. "Me, I got no one, my young friend, except my cousin Sal, and he's straight as an arrow. Everyone deserted me, and dying hasn't changed that. Good riddance to bad rubbish they're likely thinking. But you—you've been of significant help to me, Gregory, and we're not related. A total stranger has been kinder to me than my family. I want to leave you something to allow you to fulfill the plans we made."

As Bobby spoke, haltingly, he explained what had led to the day eleven years ago and this prison sentence, and laid out Greg's future.

It all started with Genova Orchards.

# CHAPTER SEVEN

After thanking Paul for his help, we left the office. The lieutenant said he would keep my father's file in his office for the next week during our visit in case we needed to refer to it again.

I slid into the Benz and asked Ned to drive up a road I knew would take us to a mountainside outlook with a great view of the area.

He followed my directions while I pulled up the pages of my father's autopsy report from the photos I'd taken while Ned and Paul Hoffmann consulted the map. My father had grazed knuckles on his right hand, with two depressed skull fractures, each with a subdural hematoma under them. There was an external cut from where the hitch on the trailer had caught his temple as he fell. The manner of death was "undetermined."

Ned parked. "You were right. It's spectacular up here. Look at the colors in those trees." He turned to me. "What are you looking at, instead of this view you supposedly wanted me to see?"

I glanced out the windshield. The hills undulated with Impressionist splashes of russet and amber, while in the distance, the higher peaks of the Catskills displayed the same colors as if an artist had dripped his palette. I swallowed back a surge of bile. Ned might be angry, but my deduction made me furious. "When you looked at the map with Paul, I took photos of the autopsy report."

"You what? As a serving officer—"

"You didn't know, so you can protest all you like, but it's done. You never have to look at them. I'll delete them once we're done with the case." I could tell Ned was uncomfortable and unconvinced. So be it. I hurried on. "There's an inconsistency which led the medical examiner to list the cause of death as undetermined, and I have no idea if my mother knew that." I frowned. How could I be sure of that? I was sixteen and she might have hidden things from me. "At least, she didn't tell me, but she might have wanted to protect me, protect all of us." I wondered what my brothers knew or thought. "I saw you frown over it, too, don't pretend with me." I started to show him my phone, but he held up a hand to stop me.

"Don't show me, just tell me."

"The *cause* of death was a subdural hematoma near the front of the skull and a second one at the back, with the rear one being worse. Bleeding in the brain, in this case from trauma to the head in two places. Often if the head is hit in one place, the brain hits the skull on the inside in a place opposite the first blow, to bleed in a contrecoup injury, but in this case, there are definitive fractures at both sites."

Ned nodded. "I understand a lot of whiplash injuries can be contrecoup, without a fracture at the bleeding site but opposite the forward motion."

"Exactly. But in my father's case, if he hit the hitch on his way down, that would account for one fracture and one bleed, which might be either right under the fracture, or opposite it in a contrecoup. Follow me?" At Ned's "Yes" I kept going. "That leaves the *manner* of death where the confusion occurs. If the ME was convinced this was an accidental fall and the hitch caused one bleed, then the manner would be accidental, but there's a second fracture in the back of the head and a second hematoma. This indicates my father fell with force after being hit in the back of the head, and the hitch likely caused the second fracture on his way down."

I paused to catch my breath and align my thoughts so they made sense to Ned. "If someone hit Dad hard enough to cause his fall and fracture his skull in the back, the investigation was unable to prove that without a witness. A defense attorney would call that supposition, which forced the ME to call the manner of death undetermined, because he couldn't distinguish between an accident and homicide."

"Hmm." Ned sat back. "You're saying this report and the manner of death as unknown is evidence that at least one other person thought your father's injuries could be the result of a deliberate act."

"Yes. And it seems there was no follow-up when the evidence was fresh." At Ned's frown I backtracked. "At least nothing in the file says they did. Now eleven years later we're trying to read between the lines and figure out what's become a cold case with skimpy documentation."

Ned stroked the back of my hand. "It's not as cut and dry as we'd originally thought. This is going to be tough to decipher, Trudy."

"We'll figure it out. We need to establish how this was pursued by reinterviewing anyone who was around then."

"Without letting your family know, too." Ned tapped his fingers on the steering wheel. "It may be it *was* followed up, but there was no other evidence found to support a murder. We have to stay calm when we talk to the detective who handled the case originally. I think I should conduct that interview."

"Agreed. We need to talk to this ME, too." I checked the typed name and scrawled signature at the bottom of the page. "Dr. Frank Bozzelli." I clicked off the offending photos and shoved my phone into my jacket pocket.

"There's something else upsetting me, something I don't want to linger on, but can't help thinking about."

"I'm sorry if the photos upset you."

I shook my head and looked at Ned directly in the face. "A subdural hematoma builds pressure in the brain as it bleeds, and Dad had two of them. Still, that pressure takes time to cause death. Even if he were unconscious after the fall, my father would have been alive while his brain swelled. If he'd been found sooner, or if the person with him had only called 911, even anonymously, Dad might have had a fighting chance to survive. Instead, my father died there on the ground, alone. He lost any possibility he had of being saved because of someone's inaction." I set my mouth in a firm line. "To me that's a clear-cut case of murder."

*Two hours ago*

Greg took a sip of cool water and checked his watch. Lunch break would soon be over. The crew at one of several picnic tables behind the big red barn ranged in ages and ethnicities. The Genovas were certainly equal opportunity employers. He wondered if the father who'd started the business had operated in the same way.

When he started work two weeks ago, Aidan McCarthy had introduced him as "Greg Dietz, our newest recruit" and left it at that. It would be up to him to tell his history if he wanted to, but so far only one of the men, Vince Russo, recognized him from the hostel, where the crimes that brought them there were not spoken about. Vince had mentioned that Greg's last name was the same as "some hotshot lawyer" in Cobleskill. He'd kept his anger in check and brushed the comment off with a shrug and muttered "distant relation."

When he'd thought about it later, Greg had realized that his father had always believed himself to be better than everyone else. Why get into a fight at his new job over someone telling the truth? Since then, he'd kept an eye on the weather-beaten, muscular guy, and knew if he was going to have trouble with anyone, it would be Vince. Vince, who liked to tell the others how to handle the equipment. Vince, who told everyone they were doing things wrong if they weren't done his way. Greg had already noticed Vince only showed off if Aidan or Rick Genova weren't nearby.

But it might be a simple matter for Vince, or any of the others, to Google his father's name and find out he had a son named Greg who'd been inside. There had been a lot of press at the time of his arrest. He watched and waited to see if he had to nip something in the bud before anyone blew it out of proportion. The last thing he needed was to lose this job before he'd found his hoard.

He'd plotted his release carefully, explaining to his counselor he'd worked summers for a landscaper and knew trees and shrubs; he yearned to be in a job where he could be outside as he decided his future pathway. They liked words like "goals" and "pathway" in the parole office.

Then he crossed his fingers there wouldn't be too many outside jobs involving trees on offer in autumn. He acted supremely grateful when Rick agreed to give him a shot at this job, stopping short of groveling, although he had a feeling Rick's husband, Aidan, was largely responsible for his hiring. A policeman named Ron Hanson did the background check, and when he'd interviewed him, Greg had stressed his feelings about being out in the open air, being near his family, and his love of trees and knowledge of pruning. He already knew the landscaper he'd mown lawns for in high school had retired to Florida. He figured he was safe elaborating the accuracy and depth of his knowledge.

Rick and Aidan had interviewed him together. Aidan seemed more enthusiastic about hiring an ex-con from the restorative justice program at Greg's halfway house, a program Genova Orchards not only participated in but supported, as it had with Vince Russo. It helped that this past summer they'd hired a couple of kids working off their community service after stealing a car. Both teens had done a decent job and were back in school without further incident.

But bringing a drug addict, even a reformed one, on their premises seemed tougher for Rick to swallow. He'd stressed their strictly enforced zero drugs policy at the orchard, and that there would be no second chances if Greg was found with so much as a roach in his pocket.

Greg looked him right in the eye and assured him he'd left that all behind him.

The job was physically demanding at times but working in the fresh air felt wonderful. It had a smell all its own, a mix of loamy soil with the sweet and tart scent of apples. He came to appreciate the pervasive scent of the fruit, rich earth, and green leaves that now seemed as fresh as the breeze that ran through the orchard.

Best of all, the job gave him the opportunity to scout out his surroundings. He was often the last to leave at night, sniffing around the orchard, eyes peeled for any sign he'd found the right place. He might have to play the ace Bobby Costello had told him about, that personal connection still in town, if he didn't come up with the goods soon. He felt frustrated when he considered the size of the orchard.

"Chocolate chip?" The worker who sat across the table from him held out a large homemade cookie. "My wife always packs too many for me." He patted his stomach. "Need to keep my figure." Vince and another guy at the next table hooted at this, and the man cheerfully raised his middle finger. "You two are jealous of my tight bod."

"Of your wife and her cookies, maybe!" Vince laughed.

Greg took the proffered cookie. "Thanks." He bit into the fragrant snack, filled with chips and a hint of something he didn't associate with cookies. "Coffee in these?"

"A touch. My wife says it brings out the chocolate flavor. She adds a pinch of cinnamon, too."

"It's very good." Greg took another bite and looked around the neat rows of fully-grown apple trees as he polished off the cookie. It must have taken the senior Genova decades to plant and maintain all of these apple trees in different varieties.

It was hard to imagine that the treasure Bobby Costello had gifted him lay buried under one of these trees. The motherlode would be the start of his new business, more than ample seed money to set him up, buy him a new car and wardrobe, and hire the bookkeeper whose name was in the little journal he'd given to his brother for safekeeping.

His future was tantalizingly close at hand.

*DEATH in the ORCHARD*

# CHAPTER EIGHT

Mindful of the animals and children. Ned turned the car slowly into the orchard compound and drove past the closed café. The flurry of activity from earlier in the day was gone and the parking lot empty, except for a blue SUV parked head-in to the side of the big red barn. Its parking lights came on and suddenly the driver reversed quickly in a huge arc across the drive. Ned heard Trudy inhale sharply as he slammed on the brakes, coming to rest six inches from broadsiding the other car.

The driver shrugged and waved as he threw his car into gear and drove around Ned up the drive and out onto the road.

"Phew!" Ned checked Trudy. "You all right?"

"Due to your quick reflexes. What an idiot."

"It helped I was going slowly. Any idea who he is?"

"Probably one of the seasonal workers." She blew out a breath.

Ned reached the house and parked where he'd been

before in front of the second garage. Bob's car was gone, but a large electric golf cart stood in his spot. "One of your brothers'?"

"Based on the level of dirt, it's the one Rick and Aidan use," Trudy said as they exited the Benz. "Ben is over the top on neatness. They must have stopped by after closing up the barn."

"We have to grab our bags." Ned opened the trunk and retrieved both cases as a sharp whistle made them turn their heads. A man with dark blonde hair like Trudy's walked up the drive toward them.

"Rick!" Trudy ran to meet her brother halfway.

Ned watched Rick grab Trudy and lift her off her feet. He twirled her around, eliciting a screech, before setting her down and enveloping her in a bear hug. The two walked toward Ned, Rick's arm slung across Trudy's shoulder, while she wrapped her arm around his waist. Ned could see and feel the affection between them.

Trudy introduced the men. Rick's handshake was firm; he had the same green-blue eyes as Trudy.

"My sister showing you the sights of Schoharie?" Rick asked.

"We had a look around after the lunch. Your mother's a great cook."

"Wait 'til dinner. I heard a rumor there was apple crumble for dessert. Mom makes it with extra crumble.

*DEATH in the ORCHARD*

Decent drive up from the city?"

Trudy interjected. "It was fine until just now. Some jerk backed out too fast from the barn and we almost hit him broadside. Who drives a blue SUV?"

Rick frowned. "Must have been Greg Dietz, our newest hire. He's always the last worker to leave. Wants to make a good impression so I'll keep him on for the winter. Sorry, I'll speak to him." Rick noticed Ned's car. "Say, this is a beauty." He ran his hand approvingly over a rounded fender. "What year is she?"

"1960. It's my father's. You need to see how he restored the interior." Ned opened the driver's door and Rick sat right down, asking questions. Ned felt immediately at ease with a fellow car guy. One brother down, one to go.

Turned out Ned was right about the Benz being an icebreaker. I grabbed my suitcase and pushed it across the porch where it rolled to a stop near the front door, then put my backpack on and threw my computer bag over one shoulder. Ned could take his own bag when the newest episode of *Car Talk* petered out.

As I crossed the porch, the front door opened, and

Aidan stood there. "The Trudster returns." I loathed the childhood nickname my brothers gave me, but I liked Aidan, and gave my brother-in-law a peck on his cheek. He divested me of my computer bag and carried my suitcase inside. "Good to see you, Trudy."

"You, too, Aid. Leave those at the foot of the steps, please. Mom hasn't given out room assignments yet."

He laughed. Aidan's good looks with his pointed chin and startling blue eyes had always caught my attention, and his hair still had summer's flaxen highlights. The first time Rick had brought Aidan to supper, by dessert I'd told Rick that Aidan was a keeper, since his personality matched his looks. He was as funny and thoughtful as he was handsome, a winning combination.

"You barely know him," Rick had teased as he helped me load the dishwasher. Mom and Ben took turns getting to know the man my brother had brought home, a fact which let us know this was a serious relationship. Rick had come out in high school, and while my parents had always been supportive, Mom seemed relieved to see Rick happy. She'd worried about him being alone.

"I always wanted a brother-in-law who looked like Bradley Cooper," I'd teased Rick. Aidan had truly become a part of our family after their simple wedding at the orchard three years ago.

Now Aidan asked, "Where's this guy of yours I've yet

to lay eyes on? He needs my stamp of approval."

"Outside talking to Rick. You'll like him. His last name's O'Malley and his father is called Paddy."

"No kidding. Kindred spirits then." Aidan strode back to the door and stood on the porch. "I like him already." I watched his eyes gleam as he took in the Benz. "Sweet ride."

Another convert; two for two. *Job well done, Ned*, I telegraphed. Ned had popped the hood, and he and Rick were deep in conversation.

Rick noticed Aidan and yelled out: "Test drive! Come on, you've got to see this. You won't believe the restoration."

Ned slammed the hood shut and raised a hand in greeting while directing Rick to the driver's seat.

Aidan moved Ned's suitcase to the porch, then slid into the back seat. I watched Rick carefully back up and turn the car, then pull away down the drive, and wondered if all men could be bought so easily.

I moved Ned's case next to mine at the bottom of the stairs and went in search of my mother. The room at the front of the house with the bay window overlooked the drive and was used as an office. My mother had changed the furniture around when she took it over. Now my father's desk stood facing that window. She'd recovered the window seat recently, I noticed. The burgundy, green, and gold colors echoed the view outside the window. I recalled time spent lying there, pillows propped behind my head, reading and trying to be quiet while my father did his accounting. I was a voracious reader by seven or eight, and the window seat became a safe haven where my brothers couldn't terrorize me, fearful of Mario Genova's wrath. After hours spent supervising in the orchard, Dad spent most afternoons before dinner at his desk, whistling lightly, a background to my reading.

One day when I was nine, the tune he whistled sounded so lyrical it took me out of my fictional world, and I put my book down. "What's that song, Dad?"

My father looked up from his accounts, his dark eyes gleaming. "It's an aria called 'Vissi d'arte' from an opera titled *Tosca*. Why do you ask, *mi cucciola?*"

"My little puppy" was my father's nickname for me. He loved operas and had a stack of CDs he often sang along with as he worked. "Tosca's the name of the pear tree you showed me, the one you planted in the yard for Mommy. A Tosca pear you said."

"You are so smart. Yes, I planted that particular type of pear tree for your Mommy before you or your brothers were born, because *Tosca* is my favorite opera."

I tilted my head. "The music is pretty, but it sounds sad. What's the story about?"

"Come here, *cucciola*." My father pulled up the visitor

chair and told me the story of Tosca, a fiery opera singer, who fights to save her lover from a sadistic police chief. "Her beautiful singing is her offering to her God. One line of the song is, 'I sang to the stars and the heavens shone more brightly.' She sings of feeling betrayed. At the end, the three main characters—."

"Mario!" My mother stood in the doorway. "Are you filling our girl's head with gory opera tales?"

My father gave one of his classic shrugs. "She asked, and if she's old enough to ask, she deserves an answer."

My mother shook her head. "Trudy, get your bike and play in the fresh air until dinner." I did as my mother told me, but the haunting story took hold. The next time I went to the library, I took out a book on classic operas and found what my mother wanted to hide from me: all three main characters die in *Tosca*. I was hooked. My brothers thought it a hoot I grew to love classical music, another source of teasing, but it led to me playing the violin in the school orchestra. I still played it on occasion. Both things grew out of the day my father sparked a young girl's imagination.

A wave of sadness rushed over me. Mario Genova would never be able to tell his stories and capture the imagination of Ben and Gail's child, or Rick and Aidan's, or my own one day. None of his grandchildren would ever know the man who loved opera.

*M.K. GRAFF*

"Trudy?" Mom found me standing at the office door, lost in memories. "Thought I heard you come in. Where's Ned?"

"He took Rick and Aidan for a drive in the Benz." I pictured the desk in its former spot and me sitting on my father's lap, while opera played in the background. I shook off the past. "What can I do to help you?"

"I could use another pair of hands in the kitchen."

"Sure." We passed the dining room table, pushed back to the windows for tomorrow's buffet, and decorated for the shower. Mom and Bob had been busy while Ned and I were out. A banner stretched between the windows read WELCOME BABY GENOVA! There were stacks of large disposable plates and baskets with utensils standing ready on one corner of the table. The napkins had Winnie-the-Pooh on them and a stuffed Pooh bear sat in the center of the table.

I followed my mother into the kitchen, where its appearance still took me by surprise. The island held small jars of honey wrapped in clear film, with rolls of green and yellow curling ribbon nearby. A large basket lined with yellow gingham held jars already wrapped and beribboned. "The dining room looks great."

"Bob's a good helper. Follows directions well and is always happy to lend a hand. We've had fun decorating." Mom pointed to the island. "These are favors for the shower—I've cut the ribbons for the rest. If I tie, can you curl them?"

We worked with an easy rhythm, the scrape of the scissors against the ribbons punctuating our conversation as Mom shared details of the Pooh-themed shower and the evening ahead.

"We'll eat dinner on the porch tonight. I have a heater if it cools down too much."

"Where's Bob?"

"Gone to Cobleskill to pick up paints for the mural we're doing for Gail in the nursery, a woodland scene with Pooh and his friends. We want to get started on Monday. He'll be back for dinner." Mom handed me another jar.

"Honey's the perfect favor. I'm excited to see Gail tonight. We've been friends for so long, but texts don't always cut it." Thinking of texts reminded me to contact Meg in a few days and see how Wilkie was settling in.

"She's looking forward to seeing you. She'd be over here already but she's been taking an afternoon nap after the café closes. The honey was Gail's idea. I piped Pooh on the shower cake, too." She handed me another jar. "Have a nice ride?"

I almost spilled our real destination but kept my counsel. "I told Ned the history of the school." This was true. "We went up the side of the mountain, such a glorious view."

"No details, please," Mom said with a laugh.

That's when I remembered that the overlook was a favorite parking spot for teens, and blushed. "I'm too old to go parking." But her comment made me think of the silk teddy I'd packed in case Ned and I seized an opportunity to be alone together.

Mom met my eyes. "Trudy, you're never too old to enjoy the company of the man you love."

It felt like Mom was sending me a message, despite my not having used the L word with Ned yet. "Like you do with Bob?"

Now it was Mom's turn to blush. "Hush. We don't need to act like teens in a car."

"Not when there are comfortable beds around." I smiled but grew pensive as I curled another set of ribbons and placed the jar in the basket with the others. "Mom, do you still miss Dad?"

Mom leaned on the island. "I do, but by now I'm reconciled to him being gone. It took me years to get used to being without him after the uncertainty about things when he died. I try to focus on the good parts of life now. Bob and I have that in common. He lost his wife, remember, to a heart attack a few years ago." She picked up another set of ribbons and started to tie them. "We don't always talk about our spouses, but we can if we choose. Being together doesn't take away our past lives.

We both understand that tie, and it's nice."

I thought it wouldn't be long before Bob and Mom started to live together. It seemed silly to run two households when they were probably together often. "I knew Bob retired from school, but he's still working?"

"He teaches creative writing at SUNY Cobleskill once a week. He writes articles for writing journals, and is working on a book for English teachers, too."

"Ambitious guy." My respect for Bob grew, but thinking of him and my mom having a future together brought me right back to my father.

Our talk had made Mom think of him, too. "Talking about your father brings up the way he died and everything surrounding it."

"Sorry." It seemed like a good time to ask a question. "Do you still wonder what happened that day?"

Mom pushed a lock of hair streaked with silver behind her ear. "I spent years thinking of nothing else, Trudy, trying to get over my anger toward him, even while I was missing him. I still can't understand why your father withdrew all our assets without telling me. He wasn't a closet gambler, or planning to run away with a mistress I knew nothing about. Maybe he cracked, mentally." She shook her head. "There were many possibilities I considered until I discarded them all, and you know why?"

"Tell me."

"I finally decided Mario Genova was none of those things. The man I married must have had a good reason, even if he never shared it, even if I've never been comfortable with the way he died." She looked up at me, searching my face. "Still, it would be a great relief to know what happened to him—and to all our money."

# CHAPTER NINE

Greg Dietz grabbed a cart at the Cobleskill Price Chopper and mentally prepared a list of the items he wanted to pick up. His room was modest and his storage space small, but he needed drinks and snacks for the evenings when he watched television, and maybe some instant oatmeal to line his stomach before work. His room had an apartment-sized microwave and an electric kettle he could use to boil water. He needed more cold cuts and bread for the lunches he took to work, too. Doug had brought him his old dorm fridge stored in the family garage; it was big enough for a few things. Seeing the Post Malone and Drake stickers he'd plastered over it brought him back to another time in his life.

His frustration at the incident in the orchard driveway hadn't left him. He had no idea who was driving the vintage car he'd cut off, but he'd seen it parked earlier up at the Genova family house. Why did he always have to show off? A cowboy, his father used to call him.

He needed to stay in this job to cement his future. He tossed a loaf of wheat bread into his basket, hearing Bobby's voice in his head, reminding him to eat healthy. "Kid, your body needs good fuel." Despite being a life-long smoker, Bobby had eaten whole grains and organic crap before being locked up, and look where it had gotten him. Didn't stop cancer from eating him up from the inside out. But Bobby's words stuck, and Greg felt he owed the Mick for giving him a future, so he heeded his words.

Greg lingered by the grapes and remembered how Bobby's stomach had blown up, while his wiry arms and legs became toothpicks. His smoker's cough hacked worse than ever as he deteriorated, and their nightly plan talks dwindled. Greg had memorized each of their conversations, repeating key details like a mantra. Bobby told Greg he'd left him his prison income, too, several thousand dollars that had accumulated over his sentence. "Never had much to spend it on," he said, with a grimace as a wave of pain swept over him. "Hold you over while you search."

When the pain took serious hold, Bobby had been moved to the prison hospital to die under a miasma of morphine. As he was wheeled away, Greg clasped his friend's bony, cold hand, and gave it a squeeze. There was a promise in that squeeze he meant to keep, and when

*DEATH in the ORCHARD*

their eyes met as he was wheeled away, Bobby had raised one hand in a salute, winked at Greg, and mouthed, "Remember."

Greg waited at the deli counter while the woman in front of him ordered from a long list. She either had a huge family or was hosting a party tomorrow. He'd bet her husband was having guys over to watch the Giants game. The thought made him feel sorry for himself for a moment. He'd work in the morning, Sunday be damned, because he took any overtime offered if it gave him a chance to look around. Then he'd either watch the game alone in his room on the small set from his childhood bedroom or if he wanted to see the game on a huge TV, he could watch in the common room while surrounded by the other jerks at the hostel.

There was one idiot who liked to think that because he'd been there longer, he should control the remote and always have the best chair, and they'd had words over it twice already. Scary guy he'd keep an eye on. Greg knew he could always go to a sports bar, but he didn't need to tempt fate by drinking and getting stopped for a DUI after too many beers. And he had an appointment after the game. When he'd set it up earlier, he'd loved how the voice on the other end of the line had quavered before consenting to meet him.

Greg looked around to see if this store carried fresh

flowers, then decided there must be a florist in Cobleskill. It was finally his turn at the counter, and in Bobby's honor, Greg ordered a half pound of Genoa salami, which kept well. As the butcher sliced it, Bobby's instructions came to him as if the man stood next to him, whispering in his ear.

"The prize is there, my young friend, you just have to find it. Keep your eyes and ears open, look around. I don't care how long it's been, there would have been a news report if it had been found. There must be some kind of sign where the jerk buried the stash. Once you find it, it's all yours. You won't even have to share it with me now."

# CHAPTER TEN

Ned turned down a second helping of Hildy's excellent apple crumble. "I couldn't. Those steaks were perfect, guys. What a meal."

They were ranged around the porch table, two to a side, everyone but Gail helping to finish the second bottle of the good cabernet Ned had brought. Bob had his arm around the back of Hildy's chair. With a heater pumping warm air around their feet, they were cozy and satiated from the steaks Ben had grilled, served with a huge Caesar salad and baked potatoes Aidan and Rick made.

"Simple but filling." Ben Genova grinned at the praise. Trudy's oldest brother had his father's dark hair and olive complexion, with a smile highlighted by a dimple on his left cheek that gave him a rakish air. "We do some things well for hicks."

His wife elbowed him. Light to his dark, Gail was heavily pregnant, a tiny blonde with curly hair and lots

of sass. "Stop. Accept the compliment with a thank you.'"
Gail pushed her chair back and put her swollen feet in
his lap. "For that you can rub my aching feet." She looked
around the table. "If no one minds."

"Go right ahead," Trudy said. "He's the one who put
you in this position."

While Ben rubbed her feet, Gail said she was counting
down the weeks before the baby came. Ned asked, "Do
you know if it's a boy or girl?" He saw a mischievous look
pass between Gail and Ben.

"Gail wanted to know, but Ben wanted to be surprised,
so we don't know." Hildy said, then frowned at the smirk
on her son's face. "What am I missing?"

Trudy broke in. "Don't tell me you found out and kept
it from the rest of us."

"Relax, Trudy," Ben soothed her. "I did want to be
surprised, past tense, but I couldn't hold out. Since Gail
really wanted to know, we asked the sonographer to tell
us at last week's checkup and she showed us."

Rick chimed in. "You know the sex but we can't?"

"We plan to announce it at the shower tomorrow,"
Gail explained, "after the Giants game. That way you'll
all know at the same time."

"Sounds reasonable," Aidan said and received scathing
looks from the rest of the Genovas seated around the
table.

*DEATH in the ORCHARD*

Ned was sorry he asked and stayed out of the discussion.

"Tomorrow is almost here," Bob said firmly. "More coffee, anyone?"

"None for us. We have to get home and start the ice cream for tomorrow." Rick turned to Aidan. "Hey, your charity guy almost killed Trudy and Ned today."

Aidan dropped his spoon. "What? Greg Dietz?"

Ned explained how Dietz had swung his car in an arc in front of them without looking to see if anyone was on the drive. "It was careless, but an accident, and I have good brakes."

"And good reflexes," Trudy threw in.

Aidan shook his head. "I'll speak to him tomorrow. He needs to be more careful. Sorry, guys."

"Do I detect a hint of hostility about this guy?" Trudy asked.

Rick waved away the topic. "We didn't agree at first about hiring him, but Mr. Softy here insisted we give him a chance."

"Sometimes people need an opportunity to prove themselves reformed." Aidan closed the subject by asking Gail, "Vanilla bean, right?"

Ned tried to recapture the pleasant mood. "Is this the famous Genova homemade ice cream I've heard about?"

"It is, and I fully intend to take any leftovers home," Gail said with a cheeky grin. "Better get some with your cake when you can, and then leave your mitts off my ice cream."

"The Queen Bee hath spoken." Ben ducked as Gail threw her napkin at him.

Ned turned to Hildy. "I'm impressed with the businesses you've grown."

"Mario and I didn't take vacations; we planted trees," Hildy said. "After he died, the boys stepped up to fill his shoes and help me run this place. I couldn't do it without them."

Ned wondered if Trudy felt left out of what the rest of her family had created but it had been her decision to go to nursing school and later move down to the city.

Hildy continued: "And now Gail is an integral part of the family business, too, and expanded the café and shop. Everyone helps out."

"Everyone but Trudster, who couldn't wait to get away," Rick teased. "The Big Apple called and Trudy ran."

"I get my independent streak from Mom and Dad," Trudy said.

"I can attest to her independence," Ned said. At Trudy's look of consternation, he added, "What? Did you listen to me when we first met, and I told you to leave the investigation to the professionals?"

"I know human nature and I knew those studio people better than you," Trudy asserted.

"Which almost got you killed. I still remember Ned's call to come to the hospital." Hildy grabbed Bob's hand. "It's a mother's nightmare to hear your child is in a coma."

"And yet here I am, totally fine, Mom."

"The jury's still out on that one, Trudster." Ben ducked as Trudy threw her napkin at him, too.

"Hey, by the way, I think we might have an issue with woodchucks," Rick said to Aidan. "I saw disturbed ground in a few places. Not tunnels though."

Aidan frowned. "Weasels, maybe? I'll have one of the wildlife guys take a look next week."

"Monday's fine," Rick said, draining his glass. "I only have one guy coming in tomorrow for the last of the cider apples."

Hildy's face showed her dismay. "Tomorrow? You're working tomorrow?"

"Relax, Mom. Only half a day. Plenty of time for me to show up with my appetite for the shower."

Gail leaned over and swatted her brother-in-law. "You better be there on time. Your first niece or nephew only comes once and you're in the running for godfather."

An hour later, when the brothers and their partners had departed for home, Ned stood in the kitchen drying the salad bowl Trudy handed him. She'd insisted that since her brothers cooked, she and Ned should clean up. Only their four wine glasses remained on the small kitchen table under a window, where Bob and Hildy sat at the banquette finishing the last of Ned's wine.

"I can't believe Ben has known the baby's gender for days but we have to wait until tomorrow," Hildy fumed. "Mario would have taken him to one side and made him tell his Papa."

"Who would have then told you," Trudy laughed.

Bob put his glass down. "Does one day more matter? They could have stuck to their original plan and made you wait until the baby arrives. A lot of couples still like to be surprised, you know."

Ned hung the damp towel over the dishwasher handle once Trudy started the machine. He let Trudy slide into the banquette by her mother and sat on the end next to her and raised his glass. "Here's to Baby Genova, boy or girl."

Hildy laughed and raised her glass. "You're right, Bob. As long as it's healthy, it won't change a thing when I find out."

"It won't affect our mural, either." Bob reached for Hildy's hand.

Ned watched them and wondered if Mario Genova had had the same calming effect on Hildy. He liked this couple—he liked all of Trudy's family, for that matter— and for a moment, felt guilty about not letting them in on the investigation he and Trudy had launched.

*DEATH in the ORCHARD*

He looked at Trudy, who seemed lost in thought as she sipped her wine, and wondered if she was thinking the same thing. It felt disingenuous not to tell them. For now, though, he'd go with Trudy's wishes. They'd see when the time was right to let everyone know they were investigating Mario's death.

Harry Holland hated how Saturday afternoon meetings with his parole officer ate into his free time, but he needed to keep his job on the construction crew renovating an Albany office building. A large, burly man, Harry was used to getting his way, whether choosing which jobs he'd do on a work site or taking control of the remote in the common room at the hostel where he stayed, selecting what the others would watch.

If he'd pulled his punch, he might never have received a custodial sentence, but his fists were almost a lethal weapon at his size, with the strength to do serious damage. It didn't help that he carried a baseball bat with him for leverage. Jostling that bit of wood from hand to hand would often discourage anyone from trying to change his mind. The idiot who'd tried to stand up to him at the old job site had hit his head on the way down after Harry thumped him.

To Harry's mind, the guy's brain had already been damaged, but that jerk of a judge had called it a Class B felony and given him three years in Troy Correctional. Such bullshit. At his sentencing, chafing under the stiff collar of the button-down shirt his public defender had brought him, he'd pictured grabbing the judge off his high leather chair and squeezing his meaty hands around the asshole's neck until he turned blue.

His lawyer may have sensed Harry's thoughts because he put a restraining hand on Harry's arm as the judge read his sentence. The lawyer had been afraid of Harry. He'd seen it in his eyes, in the way he stuttered whenever Harry roared at him, and in his refusal to visit Harry unless a guard was present. Another weakling. Harry had no use for weaklings.

He'd done his time and had kept his nose clean for a while now. He looked forward to getting out of this hostel once he'd saved enough for his own place.

Harry hadn't met Greg Dietz at Troy; despite their time overlapping, they'd been in different units. But word gets around a prison, and when Bobby Costello took a new guy under his wing, Harry heard about it. Dietz spent hours in the prison library, working with other inmates on legal stuff. Harry hated libraries. Who needed books anyway? Pussy stuff. Give him a few beers and a good workout, a football or basketball game to watch, and he was good to go.

But what interested him was why a drug runner like Costello, a hard-nosed guy after all, would want a patsy like Dietz to be his sidekick. Maybe they had a thing going, sexual like. Hey, not for him. But he knew tons of guys who gave in to that in prison. Not Harry, who only needed a drizzle of baby oil and a slick magazine, and he got himself off fine. Safer, too.

No, the thing that interested Harry was when he'd heard stories in Troy of how Costello had earned the nickname "the Mick." He couldn't figure out why Costello allowed a two-bit dealer like Dietz to hang on him and thought maybe Dietz had kept some kind of ongoing drug business going while he was inside. When Dietz was released to the same hostel, Harry saw his chance to look into Dietz on a whole different financial level. Snooping in the guy's room would be the place to start. A little blackmail to keep his mouth shut would bring that apartment closer a lot faster.

He had to find a way to get in there without being seen.

A wave of fatigue washed over me, and I yawned. "Time for bed. Tomorrow's a busy day."

"We'll see you in the morning," my mom said, while Bob poured her the last inch of the wine.

I tamped down the feeling that she and Bob wanted to discuss me and Ned out of earshot, but maybe my imagination ran rampant. "Where do you want us?"

"I turned Ben's room into a craft room this summer, but yours and Rick's are still set up as guest rooms." Mom's eyes twinkled. "Ned, I gave you Rick's room, but I'll leave things up to you to decide. In any case, Bob is staying here tonight to help out tomorrow. We don't need to be listening for the patter of night-time feet."

I refused to blush. I could give as good as my mom. "We won't be listening, either."

We all laughed, and I gave my mom a goodnight kiss, then Ned and I headed to the staircase, where he insisted on carrying both cases up so they wouldn't mar the woodwork. "Why is it my clothes are much bigger than yours, but your case is much heavier than mine?"

"A girl has to be prepared for any outing. And you don't carry makeup or hair products. Maybe I packed something to surprise you." I fluttered my eyelashes in a coquettish parody. He smiled and shook his head, but I caught a pensive look.

We reached the landing and I pointed ahead to the hall bath. "Mom has her own bathroom. We'll use this one. Come see my room."

Ned left the bags by the door of what used to be my refuge, with its curved wall that followed the turret and windows that looked down the drive. But things had changed in here, too, even more than when I'd been home last Christmas. Then I'd found my high school awards and memories had been packed away in the attic, where Mom had assured me there was a labeled tub waiting for me any time I wanted it.

While some of my favorite books were still here, the bookshelf had been pared down and held fluffy towels alongside them, and now the walls were painted a celadon green that complemented the airy down comforter. Gone was my tattered old comforter; this new one had lilac flowers with deep green leaves on a white background. My old night table had gotten a coat of white paint, too. Change this past year was everywhere I looked. I wasn't certain how I felt about it at all.

Ned whistled from the doorway. "This is a spacious room."

"Dad said the only girl had to have the turret room."

"I bet your brothers were jealous." He brought my

suitcase into my room. I followed him as he brought his across the hall into what had been Rick's, a smaller room with wood wainscoting and cranberry and beige plaid curtains.

"Rick slept with Ben in bunk beds for years until he insisted he had to have his own room. Mom gave up her sewing room then." I opened the closet door. "Plenty of hangers if you want to get wrinkles out of anything." I sensed an awkward moment was upon us.

"What's the dress code for tomorrow?" Ned lifted his case onto the double bed and opened it to reveal a few neatly folded shirts, more jeans, and a pair of chinos.

"Casual. The men will be in jeans and any kind of shirt you'd like." I watched Ned pull a flat package from his suitcase. A hand-drawn infant hanging from a blanket held in a stork's beak filled the front of the brown wrapping paper. "Thanks again for stopping at Monica's to pick this up."

We'd already sent Gail and Ben the car seat listed on their registry. This was a special gift for my friend and sister-in-law.

"Gail will love it," Ned said as he gently pressed the parcel into my hands. "Lots of bubble wrap under there to protect it, Monica said."

I'd recently worked with Monica Kiley, an actress who painted charming watercolors. Monica had sold me one from her collection of Central Park settings at a nice discount. The one I'd chosen depicted the bronze statue of Alice and her kitten, Dinah, sitting on a giant mushroom, surrounded by Wonderland friends like the Mad Hatter and the White Rabbit. Children climbed over the statue, their bright clothing and the greens of the terraced Conservatory Water gardens behind them a colorful counterpoint to the dark metal. When I'd told Monica about Gail's Pooh theme, she'd painted a stuffed Pooh in the hands of one of the children.

Ned cleared his throat. "Trudy, don't be upset but I feel uncomfortable sleeping with you right under your mother's nose, despite her disclaimers. It feels awkward. Can we leave it for tonight?"

I was stung, but nodded before he could see I'd hoped otherwise. "Sure, I get it. We've had a long day, and I was already at the studio this morning when you were probably waking up. You go ahead and use the bathroom first while I unpack."

Ned planted a kiss on top of my head as he took his kit and the gym shorts he slept in with him across the hall to the bathroom. "Thanks for understanding."

I closed the door to my bedroom and managed not to slam it. Ned had kissed my head like I was a small child. And he didn't want to sleep with me—so much for my slinky nightie.

He didn't say that, I chided myself as I unpacked. He said he felt uncomfortable sleeping together in my mom's house. I thought of how I would feel if we were to sleep over at his parents' New York apartment and realized we probably would be given separate bedrooms. How would I feel sleeping with him there? Our intimate relationship was fairly new; we were still adjusting to each other and our expectations. And Ned could always be counted on to be the perfect gentleman, darn him.

I heard the bathroom door open and Ned's footsteps across the wood floor before he closed the door to Rick's old room. I nipped into the bathroom and a few minutes later, makeup off and teeth brushed, I slipped into my soft yoga pants and a t-shirt.

I looked around the room that used to be mine and now bore the stamp of what it was: a lovely guest room, but one I would sleep in alone, while Ned was only across the hall but a world away.

Turning out the light, I stood in the darkness by the curved window. The night was filled with shadows and shapes. Anyone could be out there looking at me, I realized, but I sensed only a few chipmunks and squirrels were my companions tonight.

I tamped down my disappointment and thought of the childhood years I'd spent in this room, dreaming I'd fall in love one day with a handsome stranger, the stuff of fairy tales. Then I recalled my last years of high school, fraught with grief and worry about finances after my father died and took with him the feeling of security our home had always represented. It had all worked out, thanks to Mom and my brothers, but nagging thoughts of what had actually happened to my father had always tugged at me. He wouldn't have knowingly thrust insecurity upon any of us.

I shook my head to clear it as I slipped between the cool sheets. No sense wallowing in past loss or new disappointment. There was time for attending to death on Monday. Tomorrow was for the living. I hoped when Ned and I came clean about our search for the truth, my family would be happy we'd pursued this, especially if we'd solved the mystery of my father's death.

# CHAPTER ELEVEN

*Sunday*

Greg Dietz rubbed his eyes after he turned off his alarm. He used the shared bathroom at the end of the hall and dressed quietly, trying not to disturb the others on his floor. All he needed today was to wake that giant bully, Harry Holland. One guy who always had his nose in a book called the big man "Harry Hole" after a character in a Norwegian crime series he read. The others snickered at the nickname, but not one of them, Greg included, had the temerity to use it to his face. Not that Harry would get the reference. Harry's goal after work was to hog the big screen TV. There were tables for playing cards or working on a puzzle in the common room, but raise your voice too loud, or try to suggest a program other than the one Harry wanted to see, and a murderous look came over the large man's features, chilling to experience. No one wanted to be the target of that look, especially Greg.

At the bottom of the stairs, he paused to pull on his work boots and headed out to his truck. He sighed in relief when he opened the door. The temperature dropped into the 40s last night, cool enough to turn the interior into a fridge. It kept the flowers he'd laid across the passenger seat fresh but not frozen. He resisted turning on the heat as he left the parking lot and rode into Schoharie and Genova Orchards.

When Rick had told him earlier in the week that Sunday's overtime would only be until noon, he'd mentioned the reason: a family baby shower in the afternoon. Greg had never been the most patient person and was frustrated with his hunt-and-peck system of searching the orchard. When the opportunity rose in front of him to move things along quickly, he'd taken it. Knowing no one would be near the cabin at the back of the orchard, he'd made the call last night to set up this afternoon's meeting.

Greg slowed sedately into the yard and parked in his usual spot by the barn. No sign of Rick or Aidan. His bosses would be here soon, but he'd beaten them today, which was another way of staying in their good graces. He was so close to his goal he could taste it.

Last night he'd made notes in a little journal, a duplicate of the one he'd given to his brother, Doug. He listed the things he would need to do on his upcoming day off, like scouting a rental property for the front business. Staying in this general area would allow him a close ride to the Canadian border while keeping him in a rural area away from police attention. He still had to work out his parole for a few months to get a clean slate, but then he would be free to start up the business he and Bobby had envisioned.

Next week he'd see if he'd be welcomed home for Sunday dinner. He already had Doug planting those seeds. He would bring his mother a bouquet like the one on the seat next to him, while he let his father know of the plans for his future business, the clean part. Those didn't include moving back home, not with his father's treatment after he fell from grace. Maybe he'd find a business property with an apartment overhead, so he could live and work right there. Yeah, that sounded good. Save on rent and always be on the spot. It made sense to be careful with his funding when he was getting his enterprise off the ground. He needed to use Bobby Costello's legacy wisely.

Greg grabbed the flowers, fluffing up the bow around the paper holding the large bouquet together, and hurried up to the main house. All the workers knew not to bother Mrs. Genova. Her house was off-limits. He'd break that rule this morning, but hopefully it would pay off for him.

Greg mounted the steps, crossed the wide porch, and knocked on the purple door with a glass oval in its center, several sharp raps anyone downstairs could hear. He could see a shadow behind the lacy curtain. A moment later the door was jerked open to a young woman his age, wrapped in a thick robe, wet hair piled on top of her head. She was short and had piercing green-blue eyes and a questioning look on her face. The scent of breakfast spilled out behind her: coffee, bacon, and a sweet scent, maybe maple syrup.

"Can I help—oh . . ." Her voice trailed off as she recognized him from yesterday's near-crash.

Perfect. It was the gal from the Mercedes Benz. Greg held out the flowers and launched into his prepared speech. "I'm Greg Dietz. Please take these as an apology for my hotdogging yesterday. I was anxious to get home and didn't look up the drive, but that's absolutely no excuse for being careless, and I'm truly sorry." Nicely done.

She took the proffered flowers as a tall man with light brown hair and a craggy face appeared behind her. This was the driver from yesterday. "What's up, Trudy?"

"Mr. Dietz brought these flowers as an apology for yesterday."

The man's eyes narrowed. Her boyfriend, maybe, or a friend of one of the brothers? Greg could see he wasn't buying the apology.

"I was explaining I take total responsibility for being reckless yesterday. I was hungry and tired, and eager to get home after a long day, but I was completely in the wrong." He gave them his most charming smile. "Saturday dinner at the halfway house is spaghetti, and those jokers snarf it up if you're not on time to dig in."

The man frowned and spoke to the woman. "Why don't you put those in water, Trudy?"

Her gaze flicked between the two men. "Sure." She turned and walked away.

"Halfway house? May I ask what your offense was?"

*No, you may not! Whoever you are, it's none of your fucking business!* Greg screamed in his mind. Outwardly, he grimaced, dipped his chin down, and shifted his weight around as if embarrassed, then met the man's look. "All my friends took stuff in law school to stay awake to study, and I got hooked. Naïve, I guess, but all behind me. I've been clean for a while, go to my meetings, and won't allow that to ever happen again. Ruined my legal career chances."

The man stood silently appraising Greg, wanting more.

"My parole officer approached Aidan McCarthy when I said I wanted outside work and had experience gardening. I've always enjoyed being out in the fresh air."

The man nodded. "I hope you'll make good use of that

opportunity, Mr. Dietz."

Now Greg's smile was genuine. "I intend to, believe me."

I brought the flowers into the kitchen, where my mother was taking a tray of bacon out of the oven. Two huge baking dishes of lasagna stood on the stovetop, coming to room temperature for baking later.

"French toast is almost ready, Trudy. Oh, aren't those lovely? Was that the florist at the door on a Sunday? I wonder if Ben sent them to Gail."

"They're from Greg Dietz." I unwrapped the bow and paper around the extravagant bouquet.

"Who?" Mom blotted the bacon with paper towels and put the slices on a platter.

"The orchard worker who almost creamed us in the drive yesterday. He brought them as an apology."

"Very nice, dear." Mom was distracted by Bob's entry into the kitchen. "Use Grandma's cut glass vase from the dining room cabinet."

"How can I help?" Bob rubbed my mother's arms. "Smells wonderful, Hildy."

"You can get the French toast out of the warming oven."

Bob grabbed potholders while I put the flowers in the sink and left the kitchen to retrieve the vase. I was on my way, hefting my grandmother's tall, heavy pitcher, when I met Ned in the hallway. I muttered to him, "Am I the only one who thinks this is creepy?"

"What's creepy, the guy or the flowers?"

I waved the vase. "Both. His look was so intense."

Ned agreed. "Something felt off about him. Don't be alone with him."

"Trust me, that won't happen."

I filled the vase with cool water and grabbed a pair of kitchen shears to cut the stems. I usually enjoyed arranging flowers, but these gave me the willies. It was a showy collection of yellow sunflowers, orange mums, deep red dahlias, and even a few coral roses. A few strands of pale freesia and eucalyptus added a spicy scent.

"Put those on the dining table for the buffet later, Trudy. Come everyone, let's eat while it's warm."

I left the flowers on the table and had to admit it was an appealing and probably expensive offering. Then why did I have this nagging negative feeling about Greg Dietz and his glitzy flowers?

# CHAPTER TWELVE

Ned found he enjoyed the afternoon, surrounded by people he'd just met. After being introduced to Gail's parents, then waiting politely for the women to serve themselves at the buffet, the men loaded their plates with lasagna, meatballs, garlic bread, and salad. Ben carried a large foil-covered platter with more of everything for second helpings, and they headed to his house to watch the game. Ned was glad he didn't have to miss the game. He hoped the Giants would make the playoffs this year and had a small wager with Tony on that. Rick and Aidan had a good-natured debate about the merits of the quarterback, Ned chimed in, and even Bob had an opinion. There were shouts of glee and groans of defeat as the game progressed.

Ben was an easy host, pointing out the cooler stocked with soft drinks and beer, entreating them to help themselves, then settling down to watch the game as they inhaled Hildy Genova's excellent meal. Ben's father-in-law was a realtor, who told Ned he'd promised to help Ben assemble the crib during the next week, and the spouses of the women at the shower were a mix of local friends, including a fireman and a dairy farmer.

Once the game ended, the men trooped back to Hildy's to find the women chatting in the living room in a ring of folding chairs, exclaiming over the honey jars and talking about babies. Gail sat with her feet up, surrounded by mounds of unwrapped gifts.

Rick voiced Ned's thoughts. "Who knew a tiny baby needed this much stuff?"

"This is just the start," said the fireman, who had told Ned he and his wife had three kids at home.

Ned sidled up to Trudy, busy stuffing used wrapping paper into a large garbage sack. "Did Gail like the painting?"

"Loved it." Her smile was wide.

He slid an arm around her shoulder. "Looks like the party was a success, Trudster."

She gave him a horrified look and whispered, "Not you, too. First and last time, please."

He lowered his voice. "I heard Aidan and your brothers call you that. I thought it was a term of endearment."

"It's a label to terrorize me." Her eyes blazed greener. "You do not get to use it. Call me honey, sweetheart, or plain Trudy."

"If you insist, honey."

"I do." She flashed him a warning look until they both laughed.

Ben raised his voice over the chatter. "I need you guys in the dining room for the cake and the big reveal," he announced and started to usher people across the hall while his friends brought over the folding chairs. The others followed and Gail was given a seat at the table as everyone gathered around. Aidan brought over the box from the car seat for Gail to prop her feet up.

The table had been cleared of food and set with cake plates and plastic forks and spoons. A coffee urn bubbled away in one corner, and the sheet cake Hildy had made stood in the center of the table, Winnie-the-Pooh painstakingly picked out in colored icing, complete with his "Hunny" jar.

Ned stood next to Trudy and held her hand. She must have been tired from helping her mother all day, but her face glowed as she waited to learn if she would have a niece or nephew by Christmas. Next to the cake stood a small white box tied closed with pink and blue ribbons.

Ben shushed them and Gail cleared her throat. "Most of you know I wanted to learn the baby's gender, but Ben didn't. Then he changed his mind recently, and before he could change it back, we found out last week and have kept it a secret to share with you all now."

"About time, too," Gail's mother said to a round of laughter.

Ben picked up the box and handed it to Trudy. "We decided to let the baby's only aunt do the honors."

Trudy looked surprised but took the box and fumbled with the ribbons in her eagerness to open it. The lid finally came off and she reached inside. With a giant smile she held up a gold Christmas ornament with "IT'S A BOY" painted in blue. People cheered and started talking at once. Several of Ben's friends slapped him on the back, while Gail's mom hugged her. Ned saw Bob squeeze Hildy's hand as people called out.

"What will you name him?"

"Ben Junior?"

"Knew it was a linebacker in there!"

Trudy looked at Ned, her eyes dancing. "A little boy. You can teach him how to fence."

He grumbled in resignation. "Payback for the Trudster comment already."

"I warned you." She smiled and left his side to congratulate Ben and Gail, leaving Ned next to Rick and Aidan.

"Congratulations on your nephew," Ned said.

"I'm thinking a basketball hoop for Christmas is in order," Rick said.

Several people started to get their coffee. Rick asked

Aidan, "Where did you put the ice cream?"

Aidan groaned theatrically. "I left it in our freezer."

"I'll run home and get it, but you'd better save me some cake." Rick left the room and through the window a minute later, Ned saw their golf cart fly by the side of the house.

"Where's Rick off to?" Bob asked Ned.

"Off to get the ice cream I forgot," Aidan said.

"Good, because I was just looking for it."

"Everyone expects our homemade ice cream," Aidan explained to Ned.

"Especially the mother-to-be," Gail chimed in, eliciting more laughter.

Gail and Ben cut the cake and Trudy helped them place generous slices around the table, waiting for the ice cream to arrive.

Bob helped Hildy pass out coffee. "There's hot water on the kitchen island for tea drinkers," she said.

A few minutes passed; then a few minutes more. People sat down in both the living and dining rooms, nursing their drinks and waiting for the ice cream. Ned took a seat and saw Aidan glance at the grandfather clock in the corner of the dining room as he sat next to Ned.

Aidan tapped his fingers on this thigh. "How long does it take to zoom down to the cabin and grab one thing?"

Trudy plopped down on his other side. "You always

say Rick takes twice as long as anyone else to accomplish anything."

"Yes, but—" Aidan was cut off by his cell phone. "Where are you?"

Ned could hear urgency in Rick's voice down the line but not what he said.

Aidan frowned. "I don't understand." He stood and looked at Ned. "They're right here. We're coming now." He spoke to the waiting crowd. "Sorry, folks, there's trouble with the freezer—no ice cream today. Please help yourselves to cake." He turned to Ned and Trudy. "I need to see you in the kitchen."

Ned followed Trudy into the kitchen, closing the swinging door behind him. He'd seen the stressed look on Aidan's face. "What's happened?"

"Rick needs us at the cabin and asked for you to come."

"As a cop?"

The color fell from Aidan's face as he nodded. "He called the police after finding Greg Dietz on our front steps—dead."

# CHAPTER THIRTEEN

I pulled my mother aside and told her we had to go to Rick's cabin. "Rick's fine, but there's an, um, emergency there. We'll explain later." Mom raised an eyebrow but didn't ask questions. I knew we'd be grilled later, but efficient hostess that she is, when I left she'd already turned back to help Bob hand slices of cake around.

Ned waited next to Aidan in Ben's golf cart. As I ran down the steps, Aidan turned the key. "Wait! I'm coming with you guys." I threw myself in the back seat as Aidan backed out.

"Trudy, this is a crime scene," Ned said. "The fewer people the better."

"Just go, Aid. If nothing else, Rick needs us, and we can keep him company."

Aidan took off, the electric cart eerily quiet as he careened around the side of the house to a track along the garden, running back through fields of varieties of apple trees. The scent of ripe fruit permeated the air, while leaves from trees passing their prime littered the track. I noted the cloudy sky and hoped it wouldn't rain. My stomach tightened as I held on to the frame. The anxiety was too reminiscent of the day my father died and our world irrevocably changed.

"What exactly did Rick say?" Ned asked as we bumped along the path.

"He said he found Greg on our front stairs, bleeding from a wound in his side. He checked for a pulse and realized Greg was cold, then he called 911 and me." Aidan seemed breathless while he hurtled us toward the cabin.

When the log home came into view, Rick raced to meet us. A white sheet covered Greg Diez's body, whose head and shoulders lay on the first two steps. His torso and legs were sprawled on the gravel walkway.

"Looked like rain so I covered him with a clean sheet, but didn't touch him again," Rick babbled. "All right, Ned?"

There was a tremor in Rick's voice, and I worried he was in shock. I'd keep a close eye on him. Finding a dead body on your doorstep would make anyone freak out. I hoped having Ned here would bring a small amount of comfort to Rick and Aidan right now. I also hoped Rick wasn't flashing back to Dad the way I had.

"It's fine," Ned answered. "I won't ask you to go through it all again, but I'll stay with you when the police arrive."

*DEATH in the ORCHARD*

He turned to me and Aidan. "We should stay clear of the scene." Rick climbed into the seat next to me and I grabbed his hand.

We heard a car on the road that ran behind the cabin and out to the back road and saw red strobe lights come into view. The police car pulled around the side of the cabin and stopped. Paul Hoffmann got out of his squad car, accompanied by a deputy I recognized. This was Ron Hanson, the friend of Ben's who'd been a new officer when my father died. Eleven years later he had braid on his uniform and a few lines on his face but looked remarkably the same. I'd wondered why he hadn't been at the shower, but it must be his weekend to work. In contrast, Paul was dressed in chinos and a golf shirt and looked like he'd been enjoying a day off before Rick's call came in. Paul knew my brothers from town, and the orchard always participated in fundraisers for the police department.

Paul waved to us and told us to stay where we were. He took clear plastic stepping plates from his trunk, doled them down on the ground from his car along his route until he was next to Greg Dietz's sheet-covered body, and pulled on a pair of gloves. He stood on the plastic squares and squatted next to the body as he lifted one corner of the sheet to survey under it.

Ron unwound a roll of yellow and black crime scene

tape and cordoned off an area from one edge of the porch to the other, enclosing the body, using a thick rhododendron bush as the apex. Paul let the sheet drop and walked over to us.

"Not a nice way to spend your Sunday, guys," Paul said. "Did you all find the body?"

"Just Rick," Ned explained. "He called Aidan after calling 911. We just got here."

Rick introduced Ned to Ron, who took out a small notebook. Paul leaned against the golf cart and asked Rick to explain the sequence of events while Ron jotted notes.

"We're having a baby shower for Gail and Ben this afternoon, and I came back here to get ice cream we'd made," Rick started.

"My fault," Aidan volunteered. "I forgot to bring it over earlier."

"Go on." Paul turned as a loud squawk from Ron's radio startled us all. Ron walked farther away to answer.

Rick blew out a breath. "I saw someone lying across our steps as I pulled up to the cabin and ran over. I recognized him as I got closer. Greg Dietz is our new worker Aid hired through the prison rehab program. I thought at first he'd fallen and hit his head on the step, until I saw the blood coming from his side." Rick paused and gulped in a breath.

*DEATH in the ORCHARD*

"What did you do next?" Paul's voice was smooth and calming. "Try to recall each step."

Rick nodded. "I leaned down to check his neck for a pulse, but didn't find one, and his body was cool, so I didn't try CPR. I backed away and called 911. The dispatcher told me to wait here for you." He exhaled.

Ron walked back to our group. "The coroner's almost here and said he called out a forensic crew."

Paul turned his attention back to Rick. "And the sheet?"

"Sorry, yeah." Rick sounded flustered. "It looked like rain, but I didn't want to step over Greg, so I went around to the back door and took an old sheet from our linen closet, then came back here and threw it over him. Then I sat in the golf cart until the others arrived."

"You didn't go in through the front door at all?"

"No, it's probably still locked. I had to unlock the back door when I went for the sheet, too. Nothing inside looked disturbed."

Paul motioned with his head to Ron, who climbed up onto the porch from the side, away from Dietz's body, and tried the front door. He called out, "Locked."

Paul turned back to Rick. "All right. What can you tell me about this Dietz fellow?"

"Not a lot. He's only worked here a few weeks."

Paul looked at Aidan. "Anything to add?"

Aidan shook his head. "We hardly knew him. He'd

been in Troy Correctional on a drug charge, but his parole officer showed me he'd tested clean consistently for more than the past year. He had to stay that way to keep his room at the halfway house and meet his parole requirements. It was my idea to give him a chance after his parole officer told me he had gardening experience and was looking for outside work. He'd mentioned an orchard and the officer thought of us right away."

I'd watched this entire interplay between my brother, his husband, and Paul Hoffmann, wondering if it was important Greg Dietz had appeared at the house today with flowers to apologize for his behavior of the day before. It might explain why he was at Rick's cabin. Maybe he'd gone to apologize to him, too.

But no, that didn't make sense. He'd worked all morning with both men and would have had ample time to apologize then. My mind whirled and I thought of the young man who lay on my brother's step. At least both Rick and Aidan had been with plenty of people when Greg had been killed. No way could I believe either of these men I knew and loved were capable of murder.

*DEATH in the ORCHARD*

Ned looked on and let the lieutenant do his job. He was deciding if he needed to mention Greg Dietz's visit to Hildy's when Paul's questioning led to it.

"Did either of you see this guy earlier today?"

"We both did." Rick explained Dietz had worked overtime until noon. "He left right at noon as we had to get ready for the shower. I have no idea why he came back."

"Trudy and I saw him this morning, too," Ned said.

Paul turned his attention to him and Trudy. Ned saw Ron's head raise in surprise. "When?"

"He came to the house about 7:45," Trudy said. "I'd just gotten out of the shower and answered the door. He brought flowers and apologized for being an idiot yesterday."

Ned explained about the incident on the drive the day before. "I sent Trudy to put the flowers in water and spoke to him for a minute alone. He admitted his previous prison time and drug use, said he'd been clean for a while."

"He creeped me out," Trudy said.

"I agree he seemed intense," Ned said.

Paul had Ron make a note of the make and color of Dietz's car. "We passed one with that description pulled off on the shoulder near the back entrance. I'll have Ron run the plates and secure it." He looked at all of them.

*M.K. GRAFF*

"Anything else?"

"He apologized to us about the incident, too, when we met at the barn," Aidan admitted. "He was already there when we opened. He didn't mention any flowers to us."

Wheels spinning on the gravelly back road announced the arrival of the coroner. Paul sent Ron around the cabin to direct the man to the body. "You four please stay by your carts."

Aidan and Rick climbed into theirs, while Trudy moved to the front seat with Ned in Ben's. A man short in stature wearing round glasses and carrying a medical bag appeared, using the stepping plates. "Thanks for coming," Paul called out.

"At least you had the decency to wait until the Giants won," the coroner said. He stopped by the side of the porch to don a white forensic suit and shoe covers, then gloved up and approached the body and knelt.

Trudy leaned forward to get a better view when the doctor carefully folded the sheet covering Greg Dietz to one side and busied himself examining the body and taking his temperature. She whispered to Ned: "George Zimmer. His daughter Kim was in my class at high school."

Paul walked over to the two golf carts. "I'm afraid we'll have forensics here for a while. You'll have to stay somewhere else tonight, guys. Rick, you'll need to come to the station to make a formal statement, but tomorrow morning is fine. Let me get Ron to check your hands for gunshot residue, and we'll need the shirt you're wearing."

At Rick's horrified glance, Ned hastened to reassure him. "All part of the process, Rick," he said, hoping to calm him. "Helps to eliminate you."

Rick looked uncomfortable but told Paul he'd come into the station the next morning once he had set the crew to work. "Can we get some clothes and things like phone chargers?"

"Use the back door, one bag each, and Ron will go with you. Shouldn't be more than a night or two." He called Ron, who was watching the coroner work. "Go in through the back door while these two get some stuff for tonight. Bring me his shirt and do the GSR first, please."

Ned stopped himself from nodding in approval. He would have handled things the same way.

Ron met Rick and Aidan at the corner of the cabin. The three men disappeared around the back.

Dr. Zimmer stood and peeled off his gloves as he came over to Paul at the carts. "Okay to talk?"

"Go ahead. This is Trudy's friend, NYPD homicide detective Ned O'Malley. Ned, this is our coroner, retired GP George Zimmer."

Dr. Zimmer greeted Trudy and the men. It seemed to Ned everyone in Schoharie knew Trudy and her brothers.

"I won't shake hands but suffice it to say, Paul may welcome your presence," Dr. Zimmer told Ned. "Looks like you've got a murder here, Paul, unless this young man managed to shoot himself and throw the gun away. Up to the ME to ascertain manner of death, but I'm giving you a heads up."

Paul said, "I saw the wound and figured a gunshot. I'll have forensics scour the grounds for a gun in case it was tossed." He looked at the hundreds of trees surrounding the cabin at the back of the property. Ned knew he was not only thinking of the chores ahead of him but how the gunshot wouldn't have been heard this far away from the other houses.

"Only one shot, but gauging from where it went in, it likely hit his spleen and he bled out." Dr. Zimmer pointed to drag marks with a thin blood trail Ned saw in the gravel when he looked carefully. "Guess he tried to pull himself up the stairs to get help but didn't make it far. And I know your next question." The doctor checked his watch. "Close to six now. With the ambient temp, I'd say he's been dead for several hours, so earlier this afternoon, sometime between one and four. Just a ballpark—ME will give you his idea."

"Any idea what time Rick and Aidan arrived at the house, Ned?" Paul asked.

"They were there as the first guests arrived a little

before two, so at least a quarter of . . . Trudy, you have a clearer idea?"

Trudy nodded in agreement. "I was in and out of the kitchen helping Mom, but that sounds right."

"Time of death without a witness is tough to determine," Dr. Zimmer said. "Still, I'd say if he wasn't here when the boys left, that narrows our window down even more." He clapped Paul on the back. "Good luck with this. Beats me why anyone would want to meet this guy in an apple orchard and shoot him." Dr. Zimmer waved and walked away to take off his forensic suit.

"Small time window," Ned noted.

"Which may be helpful," Paul agreed.

Ned heard Dr. Zimmer's car start up as Ron Hanson came back around the other side of the cabin with Rick and Aidan, who each carried a backpack.

Ron carried a large envelope and a smaller kit. He stopped Rick at the corner of the porch and proceeded to open the small kit and swab Rick's hands, putting each swab into test tubes he'd labeled. Rick had changed his shirt and handed Ron the one he'd been wearing. Ron slid it into the large bag without folding it and again labeled the bag. "All done, Rick."

Trudy ran to her brother and gave him a hug. "You all right?"

Ned saw Trudy's concern for Rick and mentally girded

himself for a second investigation on his plate. Trudy would want to clear her brother as quickly as possible, which he understood, but his main concern had to be to protect Trudy with a murderer running loose.

"Let's get out of here. Hopefully the guests are gone."

Trudy held up her phone. "Mom texted to say everyone's gone, and Bob and Gail's dad helped Ben take the gifts to the nursery. Gail's parents are over there but leaving shortly. Mom's wondering where we all are."

Ned looked at Trudy. "Who gets to tell your Mom these two need a room for the night due to a dead body?"

# CHAPTER FOURTEEN

"Oh, no!" Mom sat back heavily in her seat after Ned explained what had happened. "That poor man's family." She shook her head. "I know what sudden death is like." Bob put his arm around her shoulder, and I was even more glad she had him to lean on.

We sat around the kitchen table, an awkward silence upon us. We were all shaken by the events to different degrees. Death had found the Genovas once again.

Ned explained the next steps: statements, investigating while the autopsy was carried out, and soon after, an inquest. His calm, matter-of-fact tone let us know what would happen over the coming week.

Mom rose to the occasion as I knew she would once Rick explained they couldn't sleep in their own home tonight. Her hand might be shaking a little, but my mother channeled her strength and resolve.

"Trudy, help Ned move his things into your room when you go upstairs. Rick, you and Aidan can share your old

*M.K. GRAFF*

room." She lifted an eyebrow. "Bed's only been slept in one night if that. We'll manage; you two stay as long as you need."

I reheated the lasagna and took out the rest of the leftovers while Ned and Rick told Bob and Mom in more detail what had happened. Talking about it seemed to help my brother calm down, and then Rick and Aidan took their backpacks upstairs. By the time Mom placed the casserole on the table, they'd returned. "Greg Dietz is the new hire, right?" she asked. "The careless one on the driveway yesterday?"

Bob brought out the salad dressings I'd forgotten. "Who would have wanted to kill him?"

I didn't think any of us would have much of an appetite, but we picked at our food to keep Mom happy. If you didn't eat, you were ill in her book, no matter the circumstances. Food was comfort.

"No idea. None of us knew him well." Aidan pushed salad around his plate and forked an olive.

Rick scowled. "We wouldn't be in this position if you hadn't insisted on hiring him."

I shot Ned a look before plunging in. "You disagreed about hiring this guy?"

Aidan lifted a shoulder. "When his parole officer contacted me, I felt we should give him a chance, especially after I saw he had clean blood work. Rick didn't agree at first."

Rick's face had a sour look. "Until you talked me into it." He pushed his untouched plate away. "Sorry, Aid. It was upsetting to find him, knowing he was beyond my help. It isn't your fault."

"Of course, it's not Aidan's fault," my mother snapped. Everyone's nerves were frayed. "Certainly not. We have to let the police figure out what happened."

"Like they did when Dad died and we had no real answers as to what happened? And what about the orchard and business? Will customers want to come here after someone's been murdered on the premises?" Rick's comments hung over the table for a moment; then he had the grace to look abashed. "No offense to police, Ned. This whole thing is worrying, from the loss of business to bringing back bad memories. We didn't get resolution then and I don't want to live through another unsolved crime."

Apparently, I wasn't the only one who thought there was more to my father's death. Why hadn't Rick ever talked to me about this? It made me wonder how Ben saw the situation.

"I can appreciate your feelings, Rick." Ned sipped his coffee. "Can I ask why you weren't in favor of hiring Dietz?"

Rick shook his head. "I felt he was trying too hard to

ingratiate himself, talking about how well he knew trees, blah blah blah."

Ned nodded and I knew Rick had observed what Ned and I both felt this morning. "Grandiose, while pretending to be sincere?"

"To be honest? I thought he was a fake who pulled the wool over the big-hearted one here." Rick leaned into Aidan.

Aidan gave Rick a playful push. "What does that say about me marrying you?"

Our smiles broke the tension, but I knew I hadn't heard the last of Rick's dislike of Greg Dietz. I hoped the police didn't focus on it.

Bob must have decided it was time to change the subject and reminded me he wanted to read the draft chapters of my English mystery with the working title *A Death in Oxford*. Not terribly original, but I'd change it after I finished the first draft and found a better option. The topic of Greg Dietz and his murder was shelved—for now. "I'll get those pages for you, Bob."

"I'd better give Ben a call and update him," Rick said as Ned and I rose from the table.

Ned came with me as I went upstairs to retrieve the copy I'd printed of my fledgling mystery, along with the brief synopsis of notes on other characters I planned to introduce as the book advanced. I hadn't thought out the

entire plot, but enough to outline the opening chapters
and sketch out a rough frame for the rest. Ned packed
up his stuff and rolled his case into my room; his eyes
met mine and we both smiled. "Guess we'll be sleeping
together after all."

"I could always get one of the boys to put a bundling
board between us like they did in Colonial times."

"I think we'll manage." Ned touched my shoulder.
"Sorry this happened, Trudy."

It was like Ned to understand how chilling a new death
on our property would make me feel. When we returned
downstairs, Rick was still talking to Ben.

". . . so we'll stay here tonight. Please tell Gail we're
sorry we didn't see her at the end of the shower, but
I know she'll understand. Her ice cream is still in the
freezer." He clicked off the call. "Ben said Gail had a
wonderful time but was exhausted and already in bed.
He'll tell her tomorrow and maybe have her stay home
from the café to avoid any journalists who show up."

"Journalists?" Mom's voice squeaked in worry. When
my father died, the newspapers had haunted our café and
barn for days, hoping for information or interviews.

Once again it was Bob who calmed her down. "Hildy,
they're doing their job, and yes, it's news and there's a
chance it will bring out journalists. Tell your staff at the
café 'no comment' is their buzzword, and the reporters

will quickly go elsewhere for a story."

Mom "humphed" and rose to load the dishwasher. Rick and Aidan said goodnight and Rick hugged her. Her face was drawn.

I had a hasty thought as I handed Bob the pages I'd brought him. Was there a connection between my desire to write a mystery and to solve my father's death? Maybe the attraction was that the resolution I sought and hadn't yet found could be put on the printed page. But while that might have been a part of the reason, I'd enjoyed reading mysteries as a girl since the days of Encyclopedia Brown and Agatha Christie, and now read Val McDermid, Elly Griffiths, and MK Graff. I was drawn to the idea of a puzzle being solved, but I could see that a part of that was also to the justice I'd been denied.

"Thanks, Trudy." Bob took the pages and gave them a cursory glance. "I'll read these before bed tonight." He stood up. "I can help Hildy clear up here. You go rest. You've had an eventful day." He met my eyes and I saw the message there. He wanted to comfort Mom.

Ned and I trooped upstairs and sat on my bed, waiting for Rick or Aidan to vacate the bathroom. I took out the small notebook I carried in my backpack and sat cross-legged on the bed. "Let's plan our day tomorrow." I headed a clean sheet "Monday" and drew a line down the center, heading the columns *Trudy* and *Ned.*

*DEATH in the ORCHARD*

"Always the organizer," Ned teased as he moved closer to me.

I felt the warmth of him radiating from where our bodies touched at the hips and tamped down my urge to throw my arms around his neck. "When Rick goes to the station to give his formal statement, I should go with him. We can use Rick's truck and leave you the car."

"Good idea. See if you can keep him on an even keel."

I sighed. "People think Ben's the short-tempered one because he looks like Dad, those Italian drama genes, but Rick's temper comes out when he's frustrated. Dad could be fine for weeks, even months on end, usually sweet, and then suddenly be set off by some injustice he'd rave about, and we'd know to stay out of his orbit for a few hours until he calmed down." I thought back to those flashes of what my mother called Dad's hot Italian temper. "He had a fistfight once with an old foreman who made disrespectful comments about Mom, and he flew off the handle. I do know that guy was checked out when Dad died, but the man had moved to Canada years before."

"I didn't know Mario had a bad temper." Ned rubbed my arm.

"It would only flare on occasion, and looking back, usually with good reason, a matter of unfairness or disrespect. Then it would pass, and he'd be super nice to us to make up for his black mood." I made a note in the left column. "Ben is more even-tempered like Mom, who lets things roll off her back until they build up and she gets cranky, but that's rare." I shook off the mood and flapped my notebook at him. "What will you do?"

"I'm going to try to find the ME who did your father's autopsy, and the retired detective who handled the case, if he's still around here."

"Dr. Frank Bozelli and Larry Long." I added those names to Ned's column. "Maybe I should try to find background on Greg Dietz?"

"Trudy . . . let the locals do their job, as your mother said. It's not our case."

"It could be." I avoided looking at him directly, tracing the outline of a lilac on the new comforter with my finger.

"*Trudy*. We have enough to do this week."

"I know." I put my notebook away and my pack on the floor, then pulled Ned to me for a light kiss so he couldn't see my expression. "It's just that you and I know if it comes out Rick wasn't keen to hire Greg Dietz, my brother will be an automatic suspect."

Ned smoothed a wave back from my face and returned my kiss with more force before breaking away. "He already is, simply by being the person who found the body. Better to be upfront than try to keep that a secret or it assumes more importance."

*DEATH in the ORCHARD*

"Don't remind me." I snaked one arm around his neck to pull him toward me when a knock on the door pulled us apart. "Come in."

Aidan stuck his head around the door. "Bathroom's up for grabs. Rick is using Mom's."

"Thanks. Hey, Aid, I was thinking I'd ride along with Rick tomorrow when he gives his statement. Let you keep working here."

Aidan stood in the doorway, his smile the first genuine one I'd seen since Rick had found Greg Dietz. "That would be great, Trudster. I don't want him to go alone, but one of us needs to be here. He's talking about going to see Greg's parents after, to give our condolences. Would you be up to ride with him there, too? They live in Cobleskill."

"I don't see why not." I couldn't look at Ned. A way to look into Greg Dietz had fallen right into my lap.

Aidan started to leave and then turned back. "Thanks for your help tonight."

"We didn't do anything," Ned said.

"Yeah, you did. Your being here was a calming influence on us both. We need to make sure the police know there's no way in hell Rick had anything to do with Greg Dietz's death."

# CHAPTER FIFTEEN

*Monday*

At breakfast, Ned tackled the plate of scrambled eggs, bacon, and toast my mom put in front of him. "Less for me, please." I finished texting Meg to check on my cat and watched him shovel in the food like he was starving. We'd both fallen asleep quickly, tired from the long day, facing out on our respective sides of my bed. Sometime during the night Ned rolled toward me and I woke with his arm thrown over my waist. The little intimacy reassured me we were all right.

**Wilkie loves it here, says he may not go back. How's home?** Meg replied.

I texted back: **Changed. Big happening, too. Call you later.** I sipped my coffee while Ned reached for more toast.

He caught my eye. "What? A growing boy needs sustenance." Bob thought this was hilarious.

*DEATH in the ORCHARD*

"The boys at work already?" The aroma from the ovens told me Mom had been awake for a while. I spotted scones and cinnamon buns puffing up through the glass windows.

Bob answered as Mom handed me a plate and filled her own. "They called the workers together in the barn for a meeting to explain what's happened and make sure they all stay away from the cabin end of the orchard today."

Mom started to eat. "Rick said you were going with him to the police today, Trudy. Good idea. I keep thinking about that young man's family." A timer dinged and she took two large baking sheets out of the oven to cool, then warmed up her coffee and sat back down to finish her breakfast. "I guess they've been notified by now, Ned?"

"Paul Hoffmann had their address and was headed over there when he left us. Greg's identity was backed up by Rick and Aidan, plus his driver's license was in his wallet. One of his family still had to go to the morgue for a formal identification last night."

Mom cleared her throat, and I reached over and squeezed her hand. She'd insisted she bear that burden when my father died, and I knew this dredged up painful memories for her. "Keep an eye on your brother, Trudy." Mom put her fork down and moved the trays to cooling racks.

I could see Mom was disturbed and felt guilty about

our investigation. But it must pale in comparison to this new death.

Bob said, "Trudy, I read your pages last night and was impressed. You've planned a nice setup with a good inciting incident with the murder at one of the Oxford colleges. Your main characters are well drawn, and especially your protagonist, Kate. Interesting to make her an American."

Ned reached under the table to take my hand. This was high praise from someone who taught creative writing. "Thanks, Bob. The classes at NYU gave me the groundwork."

"My class at the community college is later this afternoon. Would you like to come along and talk about what you've learned? They're all beginners and would be interested in hearing how you found your way to this point."

"Trudy, do it for Bob, please." Mom beamed at me. "He's always saying he can't find good speakers to talk to his students." She took the lid off a bowl of creamy frosting. "Help me ice these, Trudy."

We heard a car engine and I saw Ben bring his SUV to a stop near the back door. He bounded up the steps, through the porch and into the kitchen. "Here for the goodies."

"Perfect timing, Ben. Have a cup of coffee while we

finish icing these." Mom handed me an offset metal icing spatula and poured the icing in stripes over each row of the cinnamon buns, while I followed with the spatula, spreading the white frosting to cover each bun. I remembered doing this when I was still in high school.

"I'm good." Ben leaned against the counter. "Had breakfast with Gail. She's going to stay home today. We've already had a journalist try to doorstep us. I got rid of him fast."

Mom frowned. "I'd forgotten journalists would try that."

"Like bees to honey, they're drawn to any story with blood." Ben shifted his feet. "I remember chasing them off the property when Dad died."

"I didn't know you did that," I said. My brothers must have protected me from a certain amount of the ugly side of things. Mom's sister had flown up from Florida, and she and I spent time with Mom after the funeral, going through Dad's clothing to donate. Then we set up his office for Mom to manage the orchard. Those activities kept me away from the café and the roadside. When I returned to school the following week, the principal hadn't allowed anyone to bother me, either, and until things died down, Mom or one of the boys drove me to and from school.

"It's a good idea for her to stay home. She needs to start cutting back now, anyway." Mom cut a row of cinnamon buns off and put them on a plate and handed Ben a stack of leftover cake plates from the shower. "For the house. Help yourselves."

I could see by her distracted look Mom was bothered by the thought of journalists at our gate once again. I hoped they would leave sooner than later.

"Gail's looking forward to a quiet day," Ben said. "She was already in the nursery putting away the new baby clothes when I left."

Ned put our plates and utensils in the dishwasher after thanking Mom for cooking breakfast. He refilled his coffee mug and took a warm bun. "I need to call the office, Trudy."

"Going out today, Ned?" Mom asked.

I put my own plate in the dishwasher and avoided looking at him as he answered. "Might set up a meet with a detective who retired to Saratoga."

"Nice town. Lovely architecture. You'll enjoy it."

I gave him a light kiss. "Text you later." I refilled my mug. "Stay in touch."

Bob held the back door for Ben as he took the trays of baked goods out to his car. He'd no sooner left when I heard the front door open and close, and Rick came down the hall and into the kitchen.

"Ready to go, Trudy?" He looked flushed. It couldn't have been easy to tell the crew Greg Dietz had been

*DEATH in the ORCHARD*

murdered on his front steps.

"How did it go, dear?" Mom asked.

"They were all shocked, but none of them had known Greg long. My manager ate lunch with him most days, and he seemed the most upset." Rick looked at the coffee cups and then at me. "This yours?" We were the two who took our coffee black. When I nodded, he took a slug from my still-warm cup. "Vince made some wiseass comment about good riddance to bad rubbish, but Aidan shut him up."

"Trudy, what about visiting my class today?" Bob reminded me I'd never answered him. "We wouldn't need to leave here until close to four."

"We should be back way before then," Rick said, "even if we visit the Dietz family."

"How many do you have in the class, Bob?"

"Six, and you know one of them—Ron Hanson, Ben's friend."

Ron Hanson, the officer who'd found my father and arrived for yesterday's crime scene. "Why yes, Bob, I'd be pleased to speak to your class today."

Ned sat in Trudy's bedroom and consulted his phone. Detective Larry Long did indeed live in Saratoga Springs, home to the oldest racetrack in America, a gambling and sports hub that endured along with its famous spas. Long's name came up as a partner with his husband, Wayne Baar, as owners of an antiques shop called Veronica's Vintage. As he consulted the most direct route on Google Maps, he heard the front door open and shut, and the voices of Trudy and Rick fade away as they headed out.

When he called the shop, the man who answered said, "Wayne at Veronica's Vintage, how can I help?"

Ned explained who he was and asked if Larry Long was around. "It's in relation to a cold case of his."

"Right up his alley," Wayne said, and called, "Larry, it's for you."

Long agreed to meet Ned at his shop at noon and gave him directions. Ned next Googled the New York State Medical Examiners listing and found Dr. Frank Bozzelli had also taken retirement and lived in the old town of Cohoes, where the Mohawk and Hudson rivers merged. A second call set up an appointment for the afternoon at the doctor's home. He'd be able to easily drive from Saratoga to Cohoes on his way back home.

Once he had his day sorted, Ned called his partner in the city. Besides wanting to check in, he'd capitalize on Tony's excellent research skills. With Paul's limited resources, he had no issue using some of his own. He heard phones ringing and the noise of their busy precinct house in the background when his partner answered.

"Boss, how's cold case stuff?"

"Lots going on here. I'll fill you in, but first, how goes it there?"

"I don't want to jinx things, but we haven't caught a big one, although you've only been gone two days. The other team had a good drug bust. I'm using the time to catch up on reports."

"When you finish, you're welcome to start on my pile on the corner of my desk."

"How's Trudy's family? I liked her mom when she was down last spring."

"The family's been warm and welcoming." Ned filled Tony in on their appointment with Paul Hoffmann on Saturday, then explained about yesterday's murder. "Need a favor with all your free time. Small outfit up here. See what you can dig up on Gregory Dietz, D-I-E-T-Z. He's in the system, recently out of Troy Correctional." He gave his partner what little he knew of Dietz's background. "Check who was his cellmate, too. Text if you find anything interesting."

"Sure thing. Does this mean I get to sit at your desk?"

"Don't even think about it."

# CHAPTER SIXTEEN

I sat next to Rick as he drove his pick-up and looked over at him to gauge his mood. Next to my jeans, shirt, and sweater, he'd made more of an effort, and wore a button-down shirt and chinos with a quilted vest, instead of his work clothes. His dark blonde hair shined as it dried from his early shower. "Did you get any rest last night?" Dark circles under his eyes spoke of little real sleep.

He raised his shoulder. "Aidan gave me some melatonin he takes when he can't sleep, but I kept replaying finding Dietz. I watch crime shows, too, so I know the person who finds the body is automatically top of the suspect list."

"You were with our family when he was killed. That should clear you."

"My alibi's a baby shower." Rick shook his head. "Unless I suddenly found a gun and decided to off Dietz for some unknown reason when I ran home to get ice cream. You can't make this stuff up."

*DEATH in the ORCHARD*

"When you put it like that, all bets are off." My brother gave me a half-hearted smile.

"I was happy to see there weren't many reporters hanging around yet."

"*Yet* being the operative word." I told him about the one who tried to doorstep Ben and didn't get far. "Let's hope he's a one-off."

I patted his hand when we pulled up in front of the station. "The autopsy should give a clearer time of death. I'm thinking it will put you squarely at Ben's house, yelling at the Giants game."

"From your mouth, as Mom says." He parked and we entered the small office, where an officer I didn't know sat at the front desk talking on the phone. A receptionist typed on her computer at the second desk. She nodded to us and called out, "Hoff!"

Paul Hoffman came out of the back room, drying his hands on a paper towel he tossed in a garbage can. "I was making a fresh pot of coffee. Can I get either of you some?"

We passed on the coffee and he directed us to the same table where Ned and I had reviewed my father's file.

"Be right back." Hoffmann disappeared into the break room, and we took seats. He reappeared a moment later carrying three mugs of coffee, put one on the table for himself, and distributed the other two to the front desks.

It was a nice touch that he'd poured for his staff; he rose in my estimation.

Paul sat across from us and opened his laptop, then hit the keys with his index fingers as he spoke. "Not every day you stumble across a body. I'm sure you know the old chestnut about the person who found the body being a suspect, so let's get your times down pat to clear you and get you off my list."

Rick and I shared a look. At least Paul wasn't pretending with us. Rick said, "Sure."

I kept quiet and watched the proceedings. Each time I'd been involved with Ned in a case, even peripherally, I counted it as a learning experience for my writing. Now I was upset for my brother and wished we were anywhere but here in these seats.

"All right, Rick. Let's go back to yesterday. I'll type up your statement as I go, but I may interject to clarify or ask a question. You saw the victim earlier in the day at work?"

Rick nodded and blew out his breath, a nervous tic for him.

"Then tell me about your actions from when you woke up."

"I got up around 7:15 and made coffee. Aidan was dressed by then and he packed us a handful of tangerines and put the coffee in a thermos while I threw on work clothes. We knew we were having a big meal at the shower at 2." Rick sat back in the chair. This was the easy part. "We left in the golf cart for the barn where we met Dietz, who had volunteered to work half a day."

"You don't usually work Sundays?"

"Depends on the month. In October we're usually open till 4 and have more staff, but we closed early for the shower, so I only needed one person for the overtime we pay on Sundays. He volunteered first."

"All right, you met Dietz and then what?"

"Aid took him in our golf cart with three empty crates to the rows of Cortlands left to pick for cider before they were too ripe to use. I kept the pumpkin patch and apple sales open at the barn. When two crates were full, Aid drove back and exchanged the full crates for two empties, while I graded the apples for cider-making and discards and handled sales. Dietz kept picking into the third crate while Aid was gone, and we kept swapping when two were full. We stayed at it until the apples were picked and graded. I sent Dietz home around 11:45."

"What do you do with the discards?" Paul's question, probably meant to keep Rick composed, mirrored my own. I'd forgotten the workings of the orchard since I'd been gone.

"We put them aside at a discount for people who buy them for their animals or other wildlife. Horse owners love them."

"To clarify: each time Aidan came back to the barn with two full crates, Dietz would have been left alone in the orchard, correct?"

"Yes, but Aid wouldn't have been gone more than 10 to 12 minutes on each trip, and he would have seen if Dietz had quit picking."

"All right. You said Dietz left before noon and as far as you know, went where?"

"I have no idea. We talked about the Giants game when we were packing up. He sounded like he was going to watch it. I assumed he went back to his hostel, but I don't know if he did."

Paul pecked at the keys. "And after you closed up the barn?"

"Aidan and I went back to our cabin to shower and get dressed. We left for Mom's right after 1:30 and were there a few minutes before the first guests arrived." Rick briefly described the events of the shower, taking food to Ben's to watch the game, and coming back to the house for the gender reveal and cake. "We realized we'd left the ice cream at home, and I said I'd get it."

"Any reason you went and not Aidan?"

Rick shifted in his seat. We were coming to the part where he'd found Greg Dietz's body. Tension showed in his rigid posture; his hands gripped the arms of his chair.

*DEATH in the ORCHARD*

I wished I could save my brother this part of it.

"Aidan tends to take longer than me to do things. I thought I'd zip there and get back faster."

"It also would give you something to hold over his head later." Paul smiled. I appreciated him trying to relax Rick.

"There is that. I drove to the cabin and saw what I first thought was a bundle of clothes. As I pulled closer, I realized it was a person." Rick started to talk faster to get past this part. "I jumped out of the cart and ran over, recognized Dietz as I came closer." He swallowed. "There was a trail of blood from his side on his shirt."

Paul's voice softened. "Tell me what you did."

"I knelt next to him and put two fingers to the side of his neck. I couldn't feel a pulse, and his skin was cool. His eye—" Rick faltered, and I put my hand on his arm. "The eye I could see had this blank stare, clouded over, and I knew he was dead, beyond saving." Rick shook his head to clear the memory. "I backed away and called 911. I've seen enough crime shows to know I shouldn't do more and mess things up."

"You're doing great, Rick. What happened next?"

"I called Aidan and told him what I'd found, asked him to bring Ned, being a cop and all, to wait with me." Rick swallowed. "Then the clouds darkened, so I ran to the back door and let myself in. I took a clean sheet from our linen closet and came back and covered Greg. I'd just sat back in our golf cart when Aid arrived with Ned and Trudy. They'd only been there a minute when you and Ron arrived."

Paul nodded. "I understand you didn't know Dietz long, but would you know of anyone who might have wanted to harm him?"

"I didn't know much about him outside work at all."

"All right, this will do." Paul read the statement aloud, fixed a few typos as he went, cut unnecessary details, and concentrated on Rick finding the body. "Does that sound like what happened accurately?"

"Yes." Rick sat back, relieved to have this over.

A second later we heard the printer spring to life and the receptionist brought the form over. Paul thanked her and checked the form before handing it to Rick. "Read this over again, make sure I've gotten your words and the details right, then sign it with the date and time at the bottom."

I didn't think Rick could read so fast, but he skimmed the report, then signed the form with the pen Paul offered.

"We found Dietz's car outside your back entrance, parked down the road about a hundred and fifty feet away. It's been towed to our garage, but a quick look didn't throw up anything of note. We did find a crumpled receipt for the flowers he brought Trudy, and another

*DEATH in the ORCHARD*

from Price Chopper, but not much else."

"He hadn't been out long enough to mess up his car," I said, thinking how at this time yesterday Greg Dietz had been picking apples and today he was lying in a morgue.

Paul stood up and so did we. "All done?" Rick asked.

"For today. I'll let you know if there's anything else. At some point, you'll be asked to testify at the inquest unless we find a suspect and get a confession."

I hadn't mentioned an inquest to Rick, but if he was surprised, he didn't stay to ask questions. Paul showed us out, wished us a nice day, and suddenly we were on the sidewalk where the cars swished by on Main Street, people passed us with barely a glance, and life went on.

Ned looked at the time. He should leave for Veronica's Vintage in half an hour. He gathered up his mug and the empty paper plate and made his way downstairs. He'd heard sounds of the kitchen being cleaned. When he walked in, only Trudy's mom remained, sitting on a stool at her island, consulting an iPad while the dishwasher ran. He rinsed his mug and put it in the drain.

"Terrific cinnamon bun, Hildy. No wonder they sell

out at the café."

She looked up and smiled. "Glad you liked it. I enjoy baking for people who like to eat."

He motioned to her iPad. "Checking out dinner?"

"No, comparing recipes for a German butter cake I want to try. Mondays when Bob teaches, he brings Chinese from Cobleskill. I'm off duty until morning baking."

"Good plan." He was interested to know if Trudy had been holding out on him. "Did Trudy inherit your baking skills?"

Hildy laughed. "She's decent but has a lot to learn. She's aced cookies, though."

"Nice to know."

"How's your father, Ned? It must have been scary when he collapsed."

"He's doing great, thanks for asking. The stents work well, and my mom does all of his cardiac rehab exercises with him, no skirting those."

"I'm glad to hear it. Ned, thank you for keeping us calm yesterday. After the way Mario died, our family didn't expect to have death literally on our doorstep again like this."

"It's fine, Hildy. I'm sorry you're involved at all."

"Once you've been touched by sudden death, it brings back old memories in a flash. I know Trudy has been haunted by the way things were left." She pulled out another stool. "Have a seat for a moment if you have time."

"I have time." He slid onto the stool and waited for Hildy to continue.

"When Mario died, it was shocking, but not knowing why he was there when it happened affected us all the most. We, and I mean me and the boys, were angry with Mario for a long time. It's common with grief to feel anger—how could you leave us, that kind of thing. But Trudy was never angry as much as she was dazed, "knocked back for six" my father would have said. She was bewildered by her father's actions. It was bad enough he'd died, but with the bank accounts cleared out, it raised so many unanswered questions."

"It must have been a difficult time."

"It was awful, to be frank. I suspected my husband of all kinds of things he'd never been involved in before. Did he have a gambling habit he'd hid or a mistress? He spent his days here at the orchard under my nose, so a secret life seemed impossible. Then I thought he'd gotten into something illegal." She shook her head. "I finally let go of all of those ideas, but the questions surrounding his death remain. Trudy—she's the kind of person who won't let things go until she ferrets out the truth. Since she was a girl she's loved mysteries. Here's a serious one that affects our entire family, and has a huge emotional component on top."

Ned had a feeling he knew where this was going. He hoped Hildy wouldn't ask him anything outright.

"Since nursing school, Trudy's only been home for visits around the holidays or a few days over the summer. Too many memories here, I guess, and too many unanswered questions. When she said you two were coming for a week—" Hildy shrugged. "I know my daughter, Ned. She's corralled you into helping her figure out what happened to Mario."

Ned hesitated. "You should talk to Trudy, Hildy."

She nodded. "I won't ask you to break a confidence. And I will talk to her soon. Right now, Ben is wrapped up in his baby, as it should be, and Rick's got enough on his plate with this murder literally on his doorstep. I think if you are investigating and there's a breakthrough, you'll share it with us."

"We would certainly do that."

"Agreed." Hildy stood up. "I should get over to help Gail and give Bob a hand with that mural. Do me a favor, Ned?"

"Just ask."

"Keep an eye on Trudy if she does try to ferret out what happened to Mario." She looked him in the eye. "Keep my daughter safe."

*DEATH in the ORCHARD*

"I'll do my best."

Hildy left the room and the front door closed. Ned checked his watch. He hoped he'd handled things the right way. He knew Trudy was worried about her mother after this new murder. He also knew she wasn't prepared to tell her family yet that they were investigating her father's death.

He checked his watch. Time he left to meet retired Detective Larry Long. While he drove, he'd have to figure out how to tell Trudy her mother had known all along what they were doing.

# CHAPTER SEVENTEEN

"Would you like me to drive?" I asked Rick as we left the police station.

"Nah, I'm fine. Glad that's over." He slid behind the wheel and pulled away from the police station, then reached in his shirt pocket and handed me the slip of paper Paul had given us with the Dietz home address, along with his phone. "Stick it in here, Trudster."

Cindy and Gerald Dietz had a Cobleskill address. I turned on Google maps and glanced up at the sky as he drove. The clouds were fleecy wisps in an otherwise pale, clear sky of the kind of blue I associated with home and crisp fall days. No sign of rain today. It should be a perfect autumn day, but our thoughts were mired in murder. "Are you sure you want to see the Dietz family today?"

"I feel like I should, and then that's over until the funeral. There's an apple pie from the café in the back seat to bring them."

"Good idea." We drove east along Route 30 toward the

Dietz home. Rick avoided the interstate and took local roads toward a neighborhood called Mineral Springs, one of the better areas. While he called Aidan on speakerphone to check on work, I called Meg to catch up and see how Wilkie Collins liked his new digs.

"He's made friends with the schnauzer next door. How're things by you?"

"The shower was great. Gail and Ben loved the outfits you sent. Don't give Wilkie too much catnip." I felt awkward talking over Rick and explaining about Dietz. "Rick's talking to Aidan about work on speakerphone so I'll text you the details about what's going on here." We hung up and I texted her a summary about our last two days, from the initial interviews on Dad's file to Rick finding a dead body lying across his steps. I told her Ned would be calling Tony today, and he would fill her in. I added I was starting to think Bob Riley was good for my mom. That should hold her for now.

Rick ended his call with Aidan. "Things are fine there."

"Good. Paul Hoffmann seems nice."

"At least he didn't overtly treat me like a criminal." Rick turned the radio on low. "But things can change."

"You'll soon be cleared," I said with more confidence than I felt. "You were with plenty of people all afternoon."

Rick grunted in response and switched the radio to the oldies rock station he'd favored in high school. Pink

Floyd sang about walls as I looked out the window to the hills on our right. I thought back to the times I'd been with dead bodies. As a nurse, sudden death happened regularly in the ER, but sometimes on a floor unit, I'd held the hand of a seriously ill patient so they weren't alone as the light faded from their eyes. Then in Manhattan, I'd seen several actors die right in front of my eyes on the set of a soap opera where I worked, and another at the famed Dakota apartments when we filmed a TV movie. The finality of death had felt the same, despite the circumstances, and I was someone who was supposed to be inured to death.

I could only imagine how finding Greg Dietz had affected my brother. I ticked off points on my hand to reassure him. "One, you had no motive to kill Greg. You hadn't known him long enough to hate him. Two, you don't own a handgun, only hunting rifles. I heard Paul question you yesterday."

Rick butted in. "Three, I found him. Four, I didn't want to hire him. Even odds at this point."

"Nonsense." We pulled into the curved drive of the address of the Dietz family home, a two-story white colonial with dark green shutters and a small front portico held up by pristine white columns. The grounds were immaculately landscaped with precisely clipped hedges separating the house from its neighbors. A row of golden mums ran along the front of the house on either side of the door. The drive split off on one side and continued to a three-bay garage in the rear.

I grabbed the pie and smoothed my sweater over my jeans. We mounted the two brick steps and when Rick rang the bell, a dog immediately barked. A moment later, the door opened a crack, and a young man with brown hair falling over his brow looked out at us. He held the collar of an orange and white spaniel that leapt and shook in its determination to greet us enthusiastically.

"I'm Rick Genova and this is my sister, Trudy. We stopped by to pay our respects."

Before the young man could answer, a voice boomed from deeper in the house. "No reporters, Douglas! Shut the door on them."

"It's not reporters," he yelled back, and rolled his eyes at us as he opened the door wider, holding the dog back so we could enter. "Don't mind Rusty. He's super friendly. I'm Doug, Greg's brother." He wore a UAlbany sweatshirt with his jeans and stuck out his hand.

Rick shook his hand and I shut the door behind me while Rusty sniffed us both. I held the pie high in one hand while I offered the dog my other, opened, to get my scent. "We're sorry for what happened to Greg."

Doug nodded and his lips thinned as he controlled his emotions. "My parents are in the sunroom. This way."

Rusty fell into step next to the young man, his fluffy tail swishing.

A tall staircase faced us. I could see a huge dining room on the left, but Doug took us to the right, past an equally large formal living room. The dog's nails ticked on the glossy wooden floors as we walked down a hallway with pine wainscoting halfway up the walls. The wallpaper above it had a pale gray background with clusters of bushy peonies that added spots of bright pink flowers and glossy green foliage.

The room behind the stairs was a kitchen spread across the back of the home, large enough for two granite-topped islands, both covered in foil-wrapped casseroles and plastic cake carriers. Doug saw me notice and whispered, "You should see the fridge. Filled with food we'll never eat."

I gestured to the pie box I held. "People mean well," I whispered back.

"I know." He paused at the opening to a sunroom, a step down, Rick and I behind him. I tucked the pie under one arm while I took in the room and its occupants. It functioned as a den, with a stone fireplace separating floor-to-ceiling windows. French doors allowed access to the sprawling yard, where I saw the edges of a flower border in the process of being tidied for the winter. A huge television hung over the mantel, turned to a replay of a World Series baseball game. "Strike two!" rang out. The incongruous noise made me flinch, even as it took me back to the many nights I'd watched my father coach Little League while my brothers played.

Two sofas and two recliners easily fit in the space. Cindy Dietz sat on the left sofa dressed in a loose caftan, paging through a photo album, lost in a world of happier days. She didn't appear to notice us.

Gerald Dietz had the sandy coloring of Greg. He wore cargo shorts, a short-sleeved shirt, and hiking boots with thick socks that exposed muscular arms and long legs. I could picture him hiking one of the many trails in our area. He had a leather briefcase next to his recliner and sat reading from a file. Perhaps work never stopped for a busy lawyer, or this was his way of coping with his loss. He saw us and muted the ball game but didn't turn it off.

Gerald Dietz put his file in his briefcase, then stood while Rick introduced us. "This is Rick Genova, Greg's boss, and his sister, Trudy."

For all his youth, and I pegged him in his late teens, Doug was socially adept. Rusty had decided to sniff our crotches and Gerald's instructions were terse. "Get that god-damned dog out of here."

His words and tone made Cindy Dietz raise her head. She looked surprised to see us standing there and patted her brunette hair into place.

*M.K. GRAFF*

"Thank you for coming. C'mon, Rusty." Doug dragged the exuberant spaniel away and we heard the front door slam. Silence.

I felt awkward and placed the pie on the coffee table. "We're sorry for your loss."

Gerald sniffed and pointed to the empty sofa. "Have a seat."

Cindy caught my eye and patted the seat next to her. "Sit here, Miss Genova." Her voice was low and she sounded hoarse, from too much crying if her swollen eyes were any indicator.

"Trudy, please." I sat next to her and saw the glassiness of sedation in those red-rimmed eyes.

"I was looking at photos from when the boys were young. Look, here's Greg and Doug at our cabin. They're both good swimmers." Two reedy boys in wet bathing suits, arms wrapped around each other, smiled for the camera. It was clear Greg was years older than Doug, a difference I estimated at seven or eight years. Maybe Doug was a surprise second baby?

I admired the photos as Cindy flipped the pages, but had my ears peeled to hear the stilted conversation between Gerald Dietz and my brother. Rick had taken a seat on the empty sofa nearer Gerald.

"We wanted to offer our condolences," Rick began. "I didn't know Greg long, but I know he was trying to turn his life around and—"

Gerald had pursed his lips and abruptly stood again. "Turn his life around by working in an orchard?" He walked to the hearth and put one foot up on it, accentuating his height by drawing himself up. "Greg was supposed to be studying for the bar, getting ready to join me in my practice. He'd been given brains and he squandered it all." Gerald shook his head as if to clear the ugly thought away. "And you think manual labor was going to help him turn his life around? He didn't need your charity."

Rick's mouth gaped open. Whatever reception either of us had thought we'd get, this wasn't it. Beside me, Cindy Dietz stiffened while her husband built up a head of steam. She must be used to his temper.

Gerald continued. "The cop said you found him?"

Rick had become still, and I knew by his clipped response that his own temper was gathering. "Yes."

"Don't worry, I won't be suing you for negligence leading to a wrongful death." The man waved his arm as if to shoo us away.

"Gerald!" Cindy Dietz looked as shocked as I felt.

Rick stood and I did, too. Rick made a great effort to control the timbre of his voice. "I hardly think a stranger coming onto my property with a gun is a situation I could have anticipated or prevented. You're way out of line." He turned to Cindy. "Please accept our condolences on your loss." He stalked out of the room.

I gripped Cindy's hand a moment and left to catch up with my brother, throwing Gerald a dirty look while I walked past. When we reached the front door Rick started to slam it. I grabbed it from him and closed it quietly.

Out on the front patch of lawn, Doug threw a ball for Rusty. Rick walked past him to his car. "I need to call Aidan."

I stopped to speak to the young man to give Rick privacy to vent. He was gesticulating with one hand as he told Aidan about our condolence call, and I left him to it.

Doug looked at the house and then at me. "Dad drove you out, too?"

"Let's say it wasn't the visit we expected. I think his anger at your brother's death made his attitude . . ." I searched for the right inoffensive word. This young man was grieving, too, and his father's behavior wasn't his fault.

"Obnoxious? Despicable? Offensive?" Doug's suggestions were said in a rueful tone of someone who had years of experience dealing with Gerald Dietz.

Here was a chance to gather information and I plunged right in. "Is that your father's usual way of dealing with people?"

Doug gave an ironic laugh as Rusty panted by his side.

*DEATH in the ORCHARD*

"It depends if you're one of his wealthy clients or a golfing or range buddy. He has plenty of time and charm for them. Not so much for the rest of us these days, especially since Greg disappointed him."

I focused on one word. "Range? As in shooting range?"

Rusty dropped the wet saliva-coated ball at our feet and looked from one to the other to see who would pick it up. Doug obliged and threw it down the drive toward the back of the house. The dog raced after it. "Yeah. He shoots handguns and rifles there. He's good, won several marksman's tournaments."

I filed this information away. "How did he react when your brother went to prison?"

"He was furious. Greg had 'sullied our good name' was how he put it. He refused to visit him the entire time. Mom wrote and spoke to him, and I visited when I could." He paused. "When I brought him to his hostel some of those guys looked downright scary. I keep thinking if Dad had let him come home, maybe things would be different now."

I smiled at the young man. "I'm sure your visits meant a lot to him, Doug."

He shrugged. "He wasn't perfect, but he was my brother, you know?"

I looked at Rick, still talking on his phone. "Yes, I do know." I shook his hand. "Take care of yourself and your mom."

"I will. Thanks for coming. Your pie is one I'll eat." Rusty returned and Doug ran off to the backyard with the dog to hide the tears I'd seen forming.

I walked to Rick's truck and slid into the passenger seat, wondering how many handguns Gerald Dietz owned, and how I could find out their models.

Rick clicked off his call. "I'm glad you were there, Trudy. Some nerve! I wanted to deck that guy."

"Which is why it was good we left when we did. You did the right thing there."

Rick started the car and steered us back toward Schoharie. "Let me buy you lunch for sitting through that."

I checked my phone. Plenty of time before I had to think about getting ready to go with Bob to his class. "Sure. And let me share what you need to tell Paul Hoffmann this afternoon."

Ned set the cruise control and relaxed as he turned off I-88 and headed north onto I-87, which he knew could take someone all the way into Canada, making it a popular drug runners' route. The last thing he needed was a speeding ticket from a vigilant trooper. The Benz gave him a comfortable ride, and it was too easy to have the speedometer creep up. Once he loaded his destination on the GPS and set the speed, all he had to do was steer.

Despite the days of GPS being second nature, Ned liked to check an online map and have a visual idea of where his route would take him on a trip. He prided himself on a good sense of direction and would instinctively know if the friendly voice in the car took him in the wrong direction.

He'd learned to trust his instincts, the sixth sense a detective needed. It came from watching people and reading body language and gestures, even facial expressions, in an innate way that led to other things, like his directional sense. At least that's what he told himself.

Trudy had good instincts, too. He'd seen hers over the months they'd been together and the cases they'd been involved in, honed from years of taking care of different personalities at their worst: ill-tempered patients in pain, sometimes dying, and dealing with their family members, too. She'd also worked in a hospital emergency department, where injuries and sudden loss were apparent on every shift. After they'd started dating, she'd told him it was one reason she'd jumped at the movie studio job when a broken engagement left her raw on too many levels. She'd needed a break from death. And now she was surrounded by it again, partly of her own choosing. And partly not.

The landscape changed to the foothills of the pointed Adirondacks with the same show of rust and gold colors in the nearer foliage. He knew once the snow season started, both the rounded domes of the Catskills and the sharper Adirondacks were havens for skiers. Not yet though. Today the sun was out in full force, fingers of light playing across the hood of the car.

He took the exit for Saratoga Springs, an area with a rich heritage as a health resort in the 19th and 20th centuries, and a gambling mecca with the renowned racetrack six minutes out of town. Ned followed the directions down Broadway. This north end was residential, and he passed several in the Queen Anne-style of the Genova homestead. The southern end of the main street was more commercial, and he parked behind a row of shops, then walked back to Veronica's Vintage.

A large burgundy awning stretched over the front window and door, providing a perfect spot for window shopping in the shade, or keeping out of the elements on a rainy or snowy day. The window display was tastefully chaotic, a mix of furniture, linens, toys, and old books. A sign in one corner read:

*Jewelry inside.*
*Browsers welcome.*
*Dogs and children on leash, please.*

When he pushed open the door, a tinkling bell announced his presence. He was a few minutes early and worked his way past jumbled clutter up a center aisle to two long counters, where the cash register and wrap desk took up the right side. The left was a workspace, spread with several thicknesses of toweling. Both glass-fronted cases held trays of jewelry and other small items easy to shoplift.

Ned heard water running behind a curtain. A voice called out: "Be right with you."

"Take your time. I'll browse," Ned called back, switching his gaze to inspect the goods for sale. He realized the crammed shop had a sense of order to its muddle. The walls were chock full of framed paintings, mirrors, and stained-glass windows in varied states of disrepair. There were old medicine cabinets, a tall Hoosier in need of refinishing, and too many chairs to count. Thin metal bars suspended from the high tin ceiling held an assortment of lighting, from pendants to chandeliers, from gaudy to industrial. A handsome round table with barley twist legs caught his eye, its top gleaming with the warm patina of the aged wood he could see between baskets holding hinges and doorknobs. He stopped to take a photo of it to show Trudy.

A lanky man with a full beard and mustache emerged from the back, carrying a tray with jars of jewelry cleaner, two small plastic tubs with water, one soapy, and tiny brushes and Q-tips. He placed the tray on the towels. "One of New York's finest, Detective O'Malley, I presume?" He wiped his hand on the towel and stuck it out. "Wayne Baar."

"Ned, please. Off duty this week." In his jeans and sneakers, Ned thought he looked like any other browser, but then he had made an appointment to see Larry Long. "Nice shop you have. Who's Veronica?"

Wayne pointed to a large ginger cat sleeping on a chair behind the desk. "Veronica, in all her chubby glory. Great mouser. See anything you can't leave without?"

Ned pointed up the aisle. "That barley twist table caught my eye."

"A honey. Local estate sale, English oak. Nice gateleg, probably late 1800s. Apartment dwellers like it 'cause it folds up when not in use."

Ned could picture the table in his sitting room, having an intimate candlelit dinner with Trudy, instead of in his tiny kitchen. "It might fit perfectly by my fireplace."

"Always happy to negotiate the price for a colleague of Larry's. He's washing up after painting a set of bookshelves. Gotta keep him busy in his retirement, right?" Wayne took a small box from under the counter and opened it to reveal a layer of cotton strewn with brooches he carefully spread on the towel. "Bought this box at a sale yesterday. Stuff someone's grandmother loved but the kid didn't want."

"They're colorful. What do these pins go for?"

Wayne picked up a swirl of blue and green stones and examined it with a jeweler's loupe. "A piece like this from the 30s was meant for a coat or jacket. This one's signed by Eisenberg, a top designer. Even though the stones are artificial, the setting is silver and will bring several hundred dollars. Now this one." He picked up a small enamel pin. "There are plenty of this enamel kind, probably get twenty for it." He cast his eye over the other pieces. "The thrill of the hunt."

"You're giving me an education," Ned said.

The curtain parted. "Don't get him started. He'll fill your head with nonsense and soon you'll be spouting phrases like Art Nouveau or Art Deco like they make sense." Larry Long shook hands with Ned. His dark tortoiseshell glasses matched his dark hair, while his wide smile gave him a genial air.

"Too late," Ned said. "My mother's an antique maven. I'm already ruined."

"Let's get lunch and figure out if I can help you." Larry

turned to Wayne. "You coming along?"

"You guys talk shop while I clean these. Bring me some of that five-cheese mac to go."

Larry saluted, and he and Ned left the shop. "Salad and sandwich place down the block all right with you?"

"I'm easy. You're doing me a favor meeting with me."

"I like to talk cop shop. Wayne doesn't get the allure."

The men walked to the entrance of Druthers Brewing Company in an alleyway off Broadway and were seated. They checked the menus and specials, then talked about their careers until they ordered, while light music played in the background of the upbeat venue.

Ned ordered a baby kale Caesar salad with salmon. Larry ordered chicken and waffles.

Once the waiter moved off to put their order in, Larry got down to business. "When you called, I didn't have to think hard to remember the Genova case. You know how some of them don't sit right and stay with you?"

Ned nodded. "My girlfriend is the victim's daughter, sixteen at the time. She's always felt she needed more of an explanation for her father's actions and death. The events leading to it seemed out of character." He worked his approach delicately. He didn't want the retired detective to feel he was questioning his work. It was too easy to look back after the fact and think you would have handled the case differently.

*DEATH in the ORCHARD*

"I remember her. Bright as a shiny penny and inquisitive to go with it. Kept asking me questions I couldn't answer."

Ned smiled as the waiter put their lunches down. "Sounds like Trudy."

Larry drizzled maple syrup over his waffle and chicken strips. "Genova's actions, plus the place he was found, gave me more questions than answers."

Ned forked a bit of salmon and let Larry talk about the case.

"Here's the thing that stood out to me. I couldn't find anyone in town who had a bad thing to say about Mario Genova, other than his temper sometimes got away from him when he met injustice, but there was nothing recent or unresolved. He didn't abuse his wife or alcohol. He ran his business well and was raising his sons to learn it. You know the story of his orchard?"

Ned paused in eating to think and couldn't recall Trudy telling him much of the early days of the orchard. "Just that whenever he could, Mario would plant trees on the raw part of the land. Not much about the early days."

"The land had a small grove of apple trees left unattended when the previous owner went bankrupt. Genova and his wife were getting married, and he used their wedding money to scoop up the land at a bank auction. They restored the house and turned a cottage near the road into a café. They owned the land outright and he plowed any profits back into the business, restoring the barn and adding cider making over the years."

Larry paused to cut up his waffle. "He knew how to run a business, which grew and expanded. Every person I spoke to said he was genial and fair."

"So the missing money . . ."

"Doesn't make sense. Something else was going on. There were no leads on anything to follow; it was all negatives. I tell you, when I saw the photos of the truck bed with all those paper goods for Trudy's birthday, it hit me hard. This man loved his family. I found no mistress and no shady dealings. He was a local Little League coach. Nothing about his death or the missing money made sense."

Ned sipped his water. "Trudy's a nurse now, and we thought the autopsy might have indicated someone else was there due to that second fracture."

"What I thought, too, but with no evidence of another person found and no witnesses, we were stuck to prove it. His blood was found on the trailer hitch parked at the station right next to his body. Say he fell off that platform and hit head on the way down, that would account for one of the fractures and his blood on the hitch, right?" Larry gesticulated with his fork. "But how did he get down there? And what about the second fracture? And then there's the money."

"I saw the second fracture led the ME to leave the

manner of death open."

"Yes. But nothing else was ever found to account for it, no weapon, or where his money was or even why he withdrew it. I mean, you don't take out that kind of money, over a hundred thousand, wipe out your family's future, and not put it *somewhere*."

Ned could see Larry was still troubled by his inability to figure out what had happened to Mario Genova. They finished their meals and walked back to the shop with Wayne's takeout.

"Larry, I appreciate your thoughts and your time. If you think of anything else, anything at all, please give me a call." Ned passed him a card with his cell number.

"You know, there is one thing. I kept all of my notebooks, kind of compulsive, I guess. Wayne wants to know if I'm planning to write a memoir one day. Let me pull out that year's notebook."

"If it's not too much trouble, that would be great."

"Hey, you never know what one small detail that didn't go into a formal report might mean years later." They entered the shop, passing two women leaving. Both held Veronica's Vintage shopping bags. Larry handed Wayne his lunch. "Looks like you had a few sales while we were gone."

"They were looking for vintage baby clothes for a doll collection. Sold that whole box I'd washed and pressed."

Wayne looked at Ned. "He teases me when I do stuff like that but I'm convinced having things in good condition increases sales."

Larry laughed and held up his hands in surrender.

"Was the old detective any help?" Wayne opened his takeout container and dug in. "God, I love this stuff."

"Larry's getting me one of his notebooks."

"To take to the garbage dump?" Wayne waggled his eyebrows.

"Hah! You're surrounded by other people's junk and you object to a few old notebooks stored in our closet?"

Wayne pointed his fork at Ned. "Ask him how many there are. Go ahead."

"What's a few rows of—okay, maybe eight or eighteen boxes, I don't know."

Wayne nodded in satisfaction. "Maybe I should thank you, Ned O'Malley. If he looks through and sees how little he uses those notebooks, he may toss some of them."

A grandfather clock chimed the hour and Ned looked up. "I've taken up enough of your time. Thanks again, Larry."

"Hey, it was fun."

Ned hadn't learned anything useful, but at least he could tell Trudy that Larry Long had tried hard to find evidence that wasn't there. He could only hope he'd glean useful information from his next interview.

*DEATH in the ORCHARD*

# CHAPTER EIGHTEEN

Harry Holland waited for the halfway house administrator to head to the showers before he left his room. He pocketed the small penknife he wasn't supposed to have and set off down the hall.

He'd been signed off work for three days after a gash on his arm became infected. The pills the clinic gave him were giving him the runs. No way could he work on a building site having to run to the frigging porta-potty every half hour. He'd told the foreman his arm hurt so badly he was afraid he'd drop a piece of lumber on someone's head, and the man had told him to take some sick days.

He waited for the squeal of air in the water pipes and left his room, tiptoeing down the hall to Dietz's sealed-off room. Dietz had been inside for selling drugs, but maybe he didn't take them himself or hadn't had time to establish a contact. Harry hoped to score a little weed to make his days off worthwhile and maybe find Dietz had hidden money in his room. He could see that apartment already. A dead man couldn't use anything left behind.

Police tape didn't bother Harry. He carefully removed one corner and entered the room, closing the door behind him. It had been turned over but not left in a mess, and he was surprised there was so little to see. 'Course, Dietz hadn't been out long enough to gather too much good stuff, but there wasn't any privacy in a place like this except in your bedroom.

Harry surveyed the room and shifted a few things to look where cons usually hid stuff. No sense checking the communal toilet in the hall. Dietz would have kept anything important close to him, not in a place with public access. He examined the lining of the denim jacket hanging in the closet. A portable CD-radio player caught his eye, but the family would expect that to be returned. Not good if it was found in his room.

Harry became frustrated. This was a waste of time. He lifted the stripped mattress and inspected it carefully for slits in the covering. Nothing but old stains. The air vent was empty, too.

He studied the floorboards, in case one had been pried up, but struck out there, too. While old and worn, it was clear they hadn't been tampered with at all. It was when he was leaving the room that he noticed the irregularity at eye level in the doorframe. One of the side boards let in a smidgen of light, and when Harry looked closer, it appeared looser than the other side. He used his penknife to carefully pry it away from the wall. That's when he struck gold.

A small piece of lined paper, torn from a book of some kind, was stuffed in the crack between the wall and the framing board. Harry teased it out with his fingernail.

He opened the paper carefully. It was so creased the scrap would easily tear. He squinted hard to decipher the penciled writing. It made no sense to him.

The shower water squealed as it was turned off. No time to waste. Harry tucked the paper into his pocket, quietly closed the door, and pressed the tape back into place. He'd be taking a nap when the administrator walked past. Later on, he'd check into this in the privacy of his room.

Rick and I finished lunch at the Cobleskill Diner and returned to the orchard. He'd quickly brought his seething at Gerald Dietz under control. We talked about growing up with such an exacting bully for a father.

"Dad might have lost his temper once in a while at

some unfairness, but he was usually supportive and patient," Rick said.

"He had to be to coach you and Ben all those years." I punched him lightly on the arm. "That would have been a trying experience for a saint."

"Hilarious." But he smiled at the memory of our dad talking earnestly to the players in the dugout.

I wondered if Ned's meeting with the Saratoga detective had garnered any new information and shot him a text. If I called, Rick would be all ears and have questions about what Ned was up to that I wasn't ready to answer at the moment.

Rick went straight to the barn to assist Aidan. I'd been relieved to see no reporter lurking by the gate. Either the papers hadn't made a big deal of the story yet, or murder didn't rate as much as it used to. I walked up to the house, which was silent. My mom and Bob must be over at Ben's.

Ned had replied with **"call me when you're home."** I went to my room and opened my closet door, looking through the clothes I kept at home for a warmer jacket while I called him.

He answered immediately. "I didn't want to talk if you're still with Rick."

"We're back and I'm in the house alone. I want to make some notes for Bob's class."

"Good thought."

"How was Larry Long?"

"Nice. Professional but willing to talk. He remembered you asking questions, and called you a 'bright penny.'"

"I suppose that's a compliment?"

"You made an impression on him."

"At least he didn't say 'relentless questions.'"

"Nope . . . but look, he confirmed what we've found, agreed with our assessment, and said it was what he thought at the time. It wasn't that he ignored evidence. There was never any evidence trail for him to follow. He couldn't add anything."

"Oh." My shoulders dropped in disappointment; a dead end already.

"How did Rick do?"

"Paul Hoffmann was professional, too. He said the timing on the autopsy should clear Rick, hopefully by tomorrow."

"That's great."

"We went to see the Dietz family and brought a pie. Not so great."

"That must have been a tough visit."

"You have no idea." I related the visit: the younger brother, the grieving mother, the irate father. "Gerald Dietz told Rick he wouldn't sue him for Greg being killed at his house on our property."

Ned whistled. "That's a new one. It's not like Rick or

Aidan had a gun hanging out on the porch, and Greg picked it up and shot himself."

"It was awkward, to say the least. But here's the thing, Ned." I took a breath. "Gerald Dietz has handguns and rifles and is in a shooting club. Doug says he's a great marksman."

"Which I'm sure Paul will discover if he hasn't already."

"You don't think Rick needs to tell him?"

"In the spirit of cooperation, I suppose Rick could let him know. Paul will see Rick is trying to be helpful, even if Paul's already aware."

"All right. I'll call the barn and remind him." My gloominess must have come through because Ned's next statement was designed to cheer me up.

"Larry and his husband have a neat vintage shop. We should go there before we leave and check out a table I saw for my apartment. I want your opinion on it."

That perked me up. "I like field trips." I also liked that Ned wanted to consult me on a piece of furniture for his apartment. "I'm in."

Almost forgot." Ned explained about Larry Long's notebooks and how he was going to comb through his notes around my father's case.

"You're saying a margin scribble may hold a clue we need?"

"Stranger things have happened. Hold on." I heard the

noise of a car blinker. "On my way to see the medical examiner. Trudy, there's one more thing."

"Uh oh . . ."

"It's not bad. Your mother asked if we were investigating your father's case."

I sighed. "I should have known. She's got this weird sixth sense about things. What did you tell her?"

"Non-committal—I told her to talk to you. But she sounded fine with it and agreed that if we did happen to be investigating, unless we found new information, we should hold off telling Rick and Ben. You might want to speak with her."

I sighed. "I guess that's a good thing." I felt a sense of relief that I didn't need to hide this investigation from Mom any longer. "I'll talk to her before we go to bed tonight."

"My exit's coming up. Good luck at Bob's class. You'll nail it. I'll see you later for Chinese."

"How do you know we're having Chinese?"

"I'm a detective, remember?"

Ned drove through the old town of Cohoes, past the spectacular waterfall that had made the town famous for its cotton and knitting mills and foundries. Now rundown areas with abandoned warehouses were being renovated into gentrified apartment complexes.

The GPS directed Ned to a boxy white Italianate villa, two stories tall, with gold and black trim on the windows and overhanging corbeled eaves. A small widow's walk in the center of the roof had been plunked down like a square bishop's hat. The porte cochere on the right side led to the back, and Ned parked under it as instructed when he'd set up this appointment. A man sitting at a small table in the shade provided by the leaves of a Glory Maple rose when Ned exited his car and beckoned him over.

"See you found us, detective." He held out his hand for a firm shake. "Frank Bozzelli. Please, have a seat and give me a minute for my after-lunch *bevanda*."

"Ned O'Malley. Thanks for agreeing to see me."

The ME walked toward the side door, calling over his shoulder. "Call me Frank" as he disappeared inside.

Ned took a seat at the wrought iron table and looked around. A grapevine in fall colors ran along the side border of the property toward the backyard. He could see the edges of a vegetable garden in raised beds, with squash and a few large pumpkins on the ground. A prime specimen stood on the steps leading to the side door, already carved into a jack o' lantern.

*DEATH in the ORCHARD*

Frank returned from the house carrying a tray across to the table. He unpacked a small silver espresso pot, two tiny ceramic cups with saucers, glasses of sparkling water, and a bottle of Sambuca. Alongside these, he placed a plate of iced cookies. "Espresso?"

"Thank you." This was obviously the man's afternoon habit and Ned wasn't going to dissuade him.

Frank poured carefully, preserving the floating crema on top, and passed the cup to Ned. "A bit of dolce?" He offered the Sambuca.

"No thanks. I'm driving, but please go ahead."

Frank nodded and added a dollop to his cup, stirring it before raising it in a toast to Ned. He took a sip. "Perfect."

Ned repeated the ritual stir and found to his surprise the bitterness he'd associated with espresso wasn't present. Instead, a deep, earthy coffee flavor permeated his mouth. "That's excellent."

"That's the Italian way." Frank sighed with delight. "Have an anisette cookie, go ahead. My Josephine makes them. You can even dunk if you like."

Ned chose a cookie but didn't dunk.

Frank took a second cookie. "For my sweet tooth." He sighed contentedly. "What more could I ask for? An espresso under the shade of this magnificent old tree, and a chance to talk about an old case with a detective."

That was Ned's cue. "I explained on the phone I was

looking into the death of Mario Genova for his daughter."

Frank's head bobbed. "Yes, I called up the file in my archives, but I thought I recalled the case when you mentioned his name."

"Can I ask if you remember why you termed the manner of death 'undetermined?'"

"The man had two fractures and two bleeds that caused his death. One fracture is explained by the trailer hitch he apparently hit when he fell, as his blood was recovered from that. Due to the force exhibited, I'd say he fell off the platform and hit the hitch, not fell from a standing position next to it."

Ned finished his cookie, which suddenly felt dry in his mouth. He took a last sip of his espresso to wash it down. "And the second fracture?"

"Was likely the first and the reason for the undetermined manner. There was no evidence and no implement found at the scene to account for it. As such, I couldn't term the manner outright homicide. 'Undetermined' meant I didn't have enough substantiation to say that."

Ned sat up straighter in his chair. Trudy had understood the situation. The afternoon sun had dropped in the sky, bringing a golden glow to the yard that opposed the topic the men discussed. A chill ran through him. "Then you believe Mario Genova was murdered."

"Unless someone can explain how a man could have

two skull fractures in different places, I'd say yes."

"Any idea what this implement might be?"

The doctor drained his cup and took a drink of water. "Your proverbial blunt object that the culprit took with him. Nothing like a hammer—those leave a distinctive circular mark." He looked into the distance as he searched his mind. "This was something broader, like a chunk of wood, say a 2 x 4, or a baseball bat."

# CHAPTER NINETEEN

After Ned rang off, I leaned back against the pillows on my bed, thinking over our conversation. Then I called Rick and explained Ned felt he should let Lt. Hoffmann know about our visit to the Dietz family, and Gerald Dietz's shooting experience. He seemed reluctant at first until I said, "If he already knows, Ned says it won't matter. If he doesn't, it bears looking into."

"Ned's right. I'll call the station now."

"See you guys at dinner." I hung up and made my way downstairs. I checked the hall closet and found the barn jacket I'd been searching for and brought it with my laptop case to the office. Coming into the room again nudged a memory. First, I sat at the desk and jotted down bullet points for the impromptu talk I would give later. I needed some kind of framework to sound organized. Satisfied, I sat back and looked around the office.

I remembered my mother had received a box of the effects from my father's truck a few weeks after he died.

She'd been given his watch and wedding ring after his autopsy, and for the first years after he was gone, she wore his ring on a chain. The box had arrived once it was deemed it contained no evidence related to his death that needed to be kept on file.

Right on top had been an old blanket Dad kept in the backseat for when he took our beloved cocker spaniel for a ride. Blondie had been young then and had lived until last year. Mom used the blanket to pad Blondie's basket next to her bed after that tragic day. But what had she done with the box? It had to be either in the attic or this office.

I opened the double doors of the closet to find two cartons of printer paper on the floor, with a tray of ink cartridges on top. Mom hated to run out. A narrow shelving unit placed inside held various stacks of forms, warranty folders, and repair manuals for the equipment the orchard used. At first glance, all I saw on the original wood shelf along the top of the closet were two large baskets that held my father's opera CDs and a retired adding machine. But I couldn't see into the far corners of the floor. I grabbed the flashlight my mom kept in her lower desk drawer and looked past the shelving unit into the left corner. Nothing.

Then I turned my attention past the stacked cartons of paper to the right corner, where there were several cartons covered in dust. I placed the basket of inks on Mom's desk and had to remove the heavy paper cartons, one by one, to get at these boxes. I lifted the top one and blew off the dust. When I removed the lid, I saw it held the Little Golden books my brothers and I had loved that I'd insisted be saved for future generations. I left that carton on the desk for Gail. The second carton had a label, "Schoharie PD." My heart beat faster.

I took my find to the window seat and opened the box.

Then my heart sank. Inside I found the usual detritus that accumulated in people's vehicles after years of ownership. Outdated road maps that wouldn't be in use these days; a tire pressure gauge; an old gray Schoharie Volunteer Fire Department sweatshirt with an oil stain on the front. I remembered my father wearing that when he changed the oil on his truck or worked on a piece of orchard equipment. I pressed the sweatshirt to my face and inhaled a faint lingering scent of my father, a mix of the Aramis cologne my mother bought him every Christmas, plus oils from his tools. I felt a hitch in my breath as a wave of grief enveloped me.

There was a manila envelope. I undid the clasp and poured the contents onto the padded seat beside me: a few coins, a stiff, crumbly packet of Wrigley's gum, the truck's registration and insurance cards. It held the truck's handbook and a handful of salt and pepper packets from the local Stewarts where Dad pumped his gas. The last thing was a small burlap drawstring pouch that held a jumble of gold golf tees, stamped with the initials "MG."

Those must have been a gift from someone who didn't know my father never played golf. I sighed and put everything back in the box. Mom could dispose of it when she wanted. I replaced it in the corner of the closet and left the book carton out on top of the printer paper.

After I washed my hands, I walked over to Ben and Gail's, inhaling the scent of fall in the air, dispelling my memories. My friend loved to decorate for any and every holiday. Now her front picture window sported a row of "Boo!" plaques and signs she'd collected. Hanging over the front door was a wreath of fall leaves with berry vines fashioned around a witch's black hat. I found Gail sitting in the dining room, already writing out thank-you notes for the shower gifts. "Girl! You're certainly on top of things." I pulled out a chair and sat next to her.

"Your mother's rubbed off on me. I keep thinking I need to be ready in case this guy makes an early appearance. I want to have things done so I can devote my attention to him." When she smiled her dimples crinkled. "Most first babies are late, I know, so then I'll have bought time to myself to sit around and be fat and sassy."

We both laughed. "Who would have thought when we

played volleyball, you'd marry my brother and be having a baby together?" I reached out to touch her belly. "My god, you look like you have your own volleyball in there but from behind you don't look pregnant."

"Really? I feel like a blimp most days."

"My bro is in for it when this baby arrives. He hates having his sleep interrupted."

"Tell me about it." Gail swished her feet. "I've stopped seeing my toes."

Then another thought hit me. "Please don't tell me he wants to name the baby Mario?"

"No, and no juniors, but I agreed to Benedict for a middle name. My father's middle name is Lucas, so we're leaning toward Luke."

"I like it. Today I came across a carton of our old books in Mom's office. I'll clean them up before we go home and bring them over."

"Sweet. Oof." Gail rubbed her side. "Check this out—" She took my hand and held it to the side of her distended belly.

A moment later I felt the distinct kick of an infant's foot, twice in succession. "That's amazing, like he's trying to stretch out."

"Wouldn't you?" She rubbed her lower back. "Say, this week we need to take our selfie  by the pear tree. I've been a slacker."

"Should we pose with smokes, like we did in high school?"

"We coughed through every single one, probably why neither of us took it up."

"But we looked good doing it!"

"Say, have you seen John Maydan since you've been home? You know he—"

Mom appeared in the doorway. "Hi Trudy. Thought I heard you talking to someone, Gail. Come and see our progress."

"We'll revisit that later." I helped Gail out of her chair while I wondered what she'd been about to tell me about my high school crush.

I noticed Mom didn't ask me about our visit to the police station or the Dietz home, and I didn't comment. Plenty of time to talk later. Rick could fill everyone in over dinner; it was his story to tell. I followed Gail down the hall to the bedroom she and Ben were using as a nursery, next to theirs. Bob yelled hello from the bathroom, where he cleaned paintbrushes. A drop cloth spread in front of the right-hand wall held tins with various bright paints for the mural Bob had designed.

A large tree trunk along one side sprouted a long branch into the center of the wall with stippled bark, while shades of greenery for leaves and the forest behind it spoke of bushes and more trees. A path was penciled in, as were the outlines on the trail of Pooh, holding Tigger's hand, as they headed into the forest.

Bob joined us, wiping the brushes on a rag. "Early days, but it's a good start."

Gail stood closer and pointed out where smaller characters and animals would be painted in, including a bird in the tree. "You made tremendous progress today. I love it already."

"With Hildy's help." Bob put an arm around my mother's shoulder.

"These two need to get to Bob's class," Mom told Gail.

Bob checked his watch. "Let's run back to the house so I can change my shirt and we'll head out, Trudy."

While Bob changed his shirt, I gathered my laptop case and notes and pulled on my barn jacket. In a pocket I found a crumpled leaf from the pear tree from my trip home last year when Gail and I had taken our selfie in front of it.

As I brushed my hair, I thought Ned would probably be talking to the medical examiner. What would the man say? As a nurse, I'd always thought a pathologist's duty was to learn what story the body in front of them could tell. I hoped this doctor had seen my father's story and could shed some light on what had happened to him eleven years ago.

In Bob's truck on our way to SUNY Cobleskill, we

talked in more depth about my storyline. He asked pertinent questions, and I scribbled down ones I didn't have answers for but realized I would need to address for the plot to come together.

"This is very helpful, Bob."

"It's an added challenge to set the book in England, Trudy. Why did you choose the UK for your setting?"

"Probably read too much Jane Austen and Agatha Christie as a teen." He had the good grace to laugh, but I knew I wasn't off the hook. "I've always had an affinity for the area, this notion I would love it there. I like movies set there, too, even though I haven't been—yet."

"It would make a good honeymoon, for sure."

I blushed and looked out the window. "Ned and I are still fairly new together." Even as I said it I realized I could picture a future with Ned in it. The thought pleased me.

Bob turned into the campus and cruised for a parking spot. "When it's right, you feel it."

"You mean like you and Mom?"

"Your mom and I were friends who found love after we'd each lost our first great loves. One of my favorite quotations is: 'All, everything that I understand, I understand only because I love.'"

"Tennyson?"

He winked at me. "Tolstoy."

Ned thanked Frank Bozzelli for his time and insights and left with a promise to let the medical examiner know if he learned anything that would change the way Mario Genova's death had been left.

"Please tell Miss Genova I hope she finds resolution, and keep me in the loop."

"I will."

On his way back, Ned hit traffic. Resigned to the slower journey home, he reviewed what he'd learned today. Both the detective and the medical examiner felt Trudy's father had been killed, but there hadn't been evidence or witnesses to prove that had happened, and hunches didn't play well on things like case reports or death certificates.

Tonight, he would talk to Trudy about letting her family know what they were doing. He saw Schoharie was truly a small town, even if it was spread over a large rural area. Someone was bound to tell Rick or Ben that he and Trudy were asking questions about her father's case. Since Hildy already suspected, it might be time to put them all in the picture. What had been accepted before could very well need to be changed as they unraveled

*DEATH in the ORCHARD*

more and more.

With his years of experience, Ned knew murder brought implications with it for the family, from initial shock waves at the time of the event, to regrets and anger at being left, even though the victim could rarely have controlled his or her death. Years later, those feelings reverberated, and he could see why Trudy hadn't wanted to bring those emotions to the surface without justification.

Trudy admitted she'd never looked at her hometown the same way after her father died. What would their investigation reveal about Mario Genova and his dealings before his death? While Trudy insisted she was ready to hear whatever the truth might be, there was still a tendency to put a dead person on a pedestal and forget their shortcomings. What if Mario's were difficult to hear? How would her family react, and would he and Trudy bear the blame for unearthing things that could have been left dormant?

Still, he knew Trudy was determined to get to the bottom of things. It was as if a part of her couldn't move forward until she knew the truth. He appreciated and even understood it, or he wouldn't be here with her now.

He changed lanes as the traffic opened ahead. He hoped Trudy's family would see their investigation might bring them closure, even though he'd come to hate the word. What kind of closure could there be when they would still feel the absence of a loved family member?

His main goal at the end of the day was to protect Trudy—not from the truth she sought that she claimed to be prepared for, but from anger from her family if they found out from someone outside their circle. And there was always the thought in the back of his mind that if Mario Genova's murderer had never been brought to justice, poking about would put Trudy in physical danger. Her father's killer had struck once before and might not hesitate if they felt their freedom was in jeopardy.

"Time for one more question." I'd been surprised my talk had kept these people interested. Bob's class had been interested in how I'd gotten to the point where I was writing scenes for my book. I discussed the stages I'd taken, deciding on a setting, creating the main character and a few sidekicks, and beginning a storyline.

Bob had arranged the desks in a small circle for the five adult students of varied ages who'd shown up. An older woman wanted to write a story about life growing up on a farm. One young man was leaning toward an action novel, maybe graphic in form, as he was artistic and could be his own illustrator. The middle-aged woman who sat next to me was writing what she called "a domestic cozy with cats" and had already sketched out her main character, who ran a cattery and owned a Siamese whose thoughts she could read. Hey, stranger things had worked.

Then there was Ron Hanson, who wanted to write a detective story set in a small town, but instead of Schoharie, he was taking his young detective out west. We'd chatted briefly when I arrived before class, casual stuff, and I collared him to wait for me after it was over.

The remaining student was a young woman with a thick green stripe in her hair who was having trouble choosing her project. She raised her hand. "How did you get over your fear of looking at a blank page and feeling overwhelmed?"

Ah. "It *is* daunting to face that sea of white, especially when you're sitting there alone, which is why it's important to be part of a writing community, like the one Bob has created here. But to answer your question, first ask yourself what kind of story appeals to you most. You have so many options. Maybe a poem would be more up your alley, or a short story, which is a snapshot of a particular event and easier to imagine finishing. Once you start, you can always make the story part of a novel if that's what you choose."

The young woman's face brightened as I continued.

"Whatever you decide, all writers play the 'What if?' game to get you started. What if a woman who runs a cattery could hear her own cat's thoughts, and they solved mysteries together?" The group chuckled. "What if a young girl raised on a farm becomes a vet and dedicates her life to taking care of animals?"

"What if a New York detective finds himself sent to a small Montana town?" Ron threw in.

The graphic writer catcalled, "Yippee, cowboy!" We all laughed good-naturedly.

I tucked my hair behind one ear while I continued. "Once you've decided on a project, be flexible, and most of all, be kind to yourself. Do your research, take plenty of notes, keep your eyes open for descriptions, and your ears as well, for dialogue that catches your interest. Maybe today's a day when you can't advance your story, so take a walk instead. But bring your notebook!"

Bob stood. "We have to wrap it up for today. Let's give Trudy Genova a big hand for speaking to us." A round of applause ran around the room and people gathered their things, thanking me as they left the room. Ron stayed behind, as did the graphic novel guy, who had a question for Bob.

"Trudy, meet you at the truck in about fifteen minutes," Bob said. "Tim and I are going to the library for a bit of quick research."

*DEATH in the ORCHARD*

"Sounds good, Bob." I sat back down and Ron did the same. "Thanks for staying behind."

"No problem, Trudy. I'm on nights, not due in until much later. But you know I can't discuss an ongoing case."

Ron thought I wanted to talk about the Greg Dietz murder. I hurried to correct his impression. "I know. What I wanted to ask you about was the day my father died."

"Shoulda figured. I knew the lieutenant asked for the file from the archives."

I wondered how much to tell him about Ned and me investigating on our own. He'd been on the original team, and I didn't want to put his back up by implying they hadn't done a good enough job. There was the chance he'd tell Ben, too.

I chose my words delicately. "I'm trying to put things in the right order, you know? I mean, I was sixteen and it happened out of the blue. Could you maybe walk me through the day from your perspective?"

"Dating a detective brought it all back, huh?"

"Sort of—I have a lot of unanswered questions in my mind."

Ron nodded. "I was fairly new on the force then. When Ben called in and said he'd found your father's truck in the station lot but there was no sign of him, I headed right out. The truck was there, all right, at the far edge of the lot, loaded with supplies. Ben said your dad was to bring those things home and hadn't showed up. There was no sign of Mario at first. You and your mom pulled up after getting a ride from a neighbor to help bring the truck home."

"I'd forgotten Mrs. Dunbar drove us." I hadn't, but it sounded good. Contrary to what I'd said, every moment of that day was emblazoned in my memory.

He shifted in his seat. "I remember Ben was upset with me when I told him we wouldn't automatically issue a missing person report yet. Mario could have taken off and left his truck behind. He was an adult with no known medical issues, and free to come and go as he pleased."

I cast my mind back and could see Ben gesticulating at Ron. Once he established we hadn't found a note at home, and saw the supplies bought but left in the truck bed, the young officer had frowned. It was his suggestion we visit the bank. "You told us to check the bank while you kept looking for him."

Ron agreed. "Yes, to see if there was any activity that would suggest this was a planned disappearance. Another officer showed up and we scoured the area. I was the one who found your father, on the opposite side of the station. His, um, body was hidden from first glance by a parked trailer the fertilizer company left there."

I asked what had been on my mind, steeling myself

for the answer. "Ron, there was no chance my dad could have been alive when you found him?"

"No, Trudy, I'm sorry, but there were no signs of life, and believe me, I tried. No pulse, no breath sounds, pupils . . ." He trailed off when he realized that, despite my medical knowledge, this was still my father we were discussing.

"Pupils fixed and dilated," I finished for him.

"Sorry. There was nothing I could do for him. The other office stayed to set up a cordon and called the detectives, so I could be the one to find you at the bank and break the news."

I remembered being ushered into the bank manager's office by his assistant, then sitting with Mom and Ben in the office of my father's good friend, Wynn Graham. His eyes widened at the news Mario Genova was missing. He pulled up my parents' accounts at his desk computer, frowned, then spoke into his phone with a teller. He seemed upset with her, and when he hung up, told us my father had left the business accounts and my mother's checking account intact, but emptied their savings and retirement accounts the day before. Mr. Graham had taken the morning off to play golf and hadn't known about the withdrawals, or he would have questioned my dad. The men had been friends since I could remember, with my parents and the Grahams going out on occasion with Bob and his wife, but my dad and Mr. Graham were especially close and coached baseball together. The banker had obviously been troubled by what he had to tell us.

We'd been absorbing these revelations when Ron appeared at Mr. Graham's door. I'd known immediately my father was dead from his expression of deep sorrow.

"You called Ben out of Mr. Graham's office and told him you'd found my father," I said.

"One of the toughest things I've ever done. Ben and I were on the same basketball team at Schoharie High, and we're still friends. Mr. Graham had been friends with your dad as long as I can remember, too, and they'd coached together at all those games when we were kids."

I stood up and held out my hand. "Thanks, Ron. I appreciate you going over this with me."

Ron's handshake was firm. "No problem, Trudy. I hope you'll be able to put the past to rest."

"Me, too, Ron."

We walked out together into the twilight. The sun's pink fingers lit the horizon. The temperature had dropped, and I shuddered, whether from the chill or the thought of my father lying dead on the ground.

I did know the next stop for me and Ned. Tomorrow, we would visit the First Citizens Bank of Schoharie and speak to Wynn Graham.

*DEATH in the ORCHARD*

# CHAPTER TWENTY

Ned waited politely, despite Hildy's urging, as the extended Genova family piled their plates with the Chinese food Bob had brought home. They settled in couples around the kitchen table as they had last night. He filled his, and when he put his plate down next to Trudy, gave her shoulder a squeeze as he sat. She seemed subdued. When they were alone in her room later, he would ask her what Ron Hanson had to say.

"Chinese food is supposed to be good for bringing on labor," Gail said. Ned noticed she had chosen chicken with steamed vegetables and a piece of egg foo young. "These are the lowest in calories and salt. Six weeks and counting."

Hildy showed off a photo on her phone of their progress on the nursery mural, and Bob told them how well Trudy's talk had been received.

"My students learned a lot from the pointers Trudy gave. I could tell they were impressed." Bob bit into an egg roll.

Ben leaned over and patted Trudy on the back, breaking her reverie. "Good going, Trudster. You must be doing something right."

Trudy narrowed her eyes and waited for a punchline. When none came, she said, "You're being sincere? Since when?" There was a ripple of laughter.

It seemed to Ned everyone was judiciously ignoring the Dietz murder. Then Ben spoke up.

"How'd your interview at the station go, Rick, or should I call you jailbird?" Gail thumped him on his arm. "What? I'm kidding and he knows it."

"Still not funny, Genova," Gail said, rolling her eyes. "You see what passes for humor with this guy?"

Rick took his brother's question in stride. "It was all right. Paul Hoffmann didn't put the cuffs on me, so I think I'm good for now. Weird being considered a suspect, though." He shoveled in a huge mouthful of fried rice, chewed, and swallowed. "But Dietz's father— what a lousy guy."

Rick recounted the meeting, giving them details of the grieving brother, his dazed mom, and then explaining the angry confrontation with the father who was a gun club member. "He's arrogant and rude, grieving or not. Trudy had me call Paul after we left. He was on his way to do an in-depth interview with the parents and appreciated the heads up."

*DEATH in the ORCHARD*

"Always good to help the police when you're a murder suspect." Ben's irony earned a glare from his wife and a stern look from his mother.

"Not cool, Ben," Aidan said, leaning into Rick. "A man died, killed at our house, and clearing Rick is a priority."

Ben held up his hands. "I give. Just trying to lighten the mood. No one thinks Rick is involved, Paul Hoffmann included, I'll bet. The timeline is too tight, and we all know Rick might talk big but wouldn't hurt a fly. He won't even bruise an apple." He chewed a sparerib and used it to point to Rick. "Don't forget Ron Hanson is my pal. He knows Rick well enough."

Ned wondered if Ron Hanson had been speaking to Ben about the case or if that was only the impression Ben wanted to give. As far he knew, Ron had been at Bob's class with Trudy, but there was the entire day before it when the policeman could have spoken with Ben. But would Ron really talk to Ben about the case?

Still, they had been friends for years. If Ben had called him, the officer might have offered reassurance without giving out details of the case, which would account for Ben's ability to tease his brother. Ned had the sense for all his comic bluster, Ben Genova was a deeper man than he liked to show.

❦

I didn't have much appetite at dinner. Ben's casual teasing of Rick took me right back to numerous family meals, only with a key person missing from the table. I realized delving into my father's murder, seeing his autopsy photos, and speaking with Ron Hanson about his death, coupled with the death of Greg Dietz right on our property, had left me saddened, with good reason.

Mom stood to clear the table and I rose to close containers and put items together to fit into the fridge. She started to lay out pantry items for her morning baking on a large cookie sheet. Gail opened our fortune cookies and read them aloud.

"Bob's reads, 'Ten small steps make one large one, but the smaller are required.'" She looked around quizzically. "What does that even mean?"

Bob replied, "It means I need tinier brushes for your mural."

We all laughed as she continued. "Hildy, yours says, 'Sunlight shows the scars as well as the truths.'"

Aidan leaned toward Bob. "That's the new light she wants in her sewing room, Bob. Better get on it."

More laughter ensued. I watched everyone enjoying themselves and felt my mood lift. This was my family, and Ned was a part of it. My father would never return, but the Genova clan had survived his death, and if Ned and I were successful and the truth about Dad's passing was finally exposed, we could all rest a bit easier in his absence.

"This is yours, Ned." Gail cracked the cookie and read aloud: "'A light that illuminates the present also shines into the past.'" She looked up. "That sounds profound."

Mom murmured "Mmm . . ." and refused to look at me. Ned took a drink of his iced tea. Bob gathered used napkins. I waited for the moment to pass.

Rick broke the silence. "That's perfect for Ned, what with him and Trudy looking into Dad's death." Aidan's quizzical look matched Gail's.

It was Ben who turned beet red and slammed his fist on the table as he roared, "What!"

"Come on, Ben." Rick had a look of surprise. "Tell me you've forgotten Trudy as a kid, always thinking she was Nancy Drew, making up mysteries to solve. Now she's writing one, for God's sake. And she and her detective boyfriend—nice as you are, Ned— visit and he disappears all day to talk to 'old colleagues.'" He used air quotes for emphasis. "She hasn't been able to let the mess with Dad's death go." My brother looked right at me. "I happen to agree with her. It's about time we knew what happened." He gentled his voice. "Am I right, Trudster?"

I looked at Ned and saw acquiescence in his eyes. Time to stop hiding and come clean.

"You're right, Rick."

Ben stood abruptly; his chair fell back with a clatter. Redness suffused his face and neck. He looked so like my father at that moment with his dark looks and ruddy face, I expected a stream of Italian curses to flow from him. If I thought Rick had a hot temper, Ben had his occasional flareups, too. This one was going to be a doozy.

He pointed his finger at me. "It wasn't bad enough we had to go through all that when it happened. You want to drag it up again, bring all that pain to the surface? You can't let it rest, Trudy, can you?"

"Whoa there, big brother." Rick held his hand up like a stop sign. "Only a minute ago you were teasing me about committing a murder and this is different how? I for one am glad Trudy and Ned are looking into it. Time for some answers if any can be found."

I'd felt my own temper rise, which didn't happen often. "No, Ben, I can't let it rest, and I would think you'd want to know the truth about what happened." I softened my tone. "I'm sorry if that upsets you, but we all deserve answers."

Ben righted his chair but refused to meet my eyes. Gail tottered to her feet. "Come on home and cool off, Ben." She touched my arm as she passed me. "Good luck to you both."

At least Gail understood. Ben shot me a dark look as they left.

"Way to clear a room, Rick." Aidan looked at his husband in frustration.

"I had no idea he'd be so upset," Rick protested. "He can dish it out but can't take it when the tables are turned."

I knew I had to talk to Ben and soon. I slumped in my chair. Ned grabbed my hand.

"Better to have the air cleared," Mom said. "Ben will come around, Trudy." She busied herself putting out bowls for ice cream nobody wanted.

"I hesitate to say anything," Aidan, always the peacemaker, asked the others. "But if they can find answers, wouldn't you hope Trudy and Ned were successful?"

"I do," Rick said firmly.

"I do, too," Mom said. "As long as you keep yourselves safe."

Lying in her bed, Ned and Trudy spoke quietly in the darkened room. She had her head on his chest and he had his arm around her and inhaled her scent. The sounds in the house drifted to them. Rick and Aidan had turned on music, classic rock turned low. Ned could make out the distinctive downbeat of Paul McCartney's Wings song, "Band on the Run," and found himself mentally singing the lyrics: "If I ever get out of here . . .," an echo of Rick's frame of mind, perhaps?

"I can't believe it's Ben who's disturbed at us investigating. I'm so surprised." Trudy's voice was tight with annoyance.

Ned traced lazy circles on her back to relax her. "He'll get over it. Give him time and space to cool down."

"That's what Mom said. She thinks he's more upset that everyone else had figured out we were investigating and he hadn't a clue." Ned could feel her smile even if he couldn't see it. "He always hated being the last to know anything new."

"See? Your mom knows him best. Maybe you can talk to him tomorrow, ask him why he reacted so strongly."

Trudy sat up in bed. "I am *not* going to apologize."

"Who said anything about apologizing?" Ned motioned her back to his chest. "He's probably embarrassed by his reaction already."

"Maybe. Gail seemed to take it in her stride. She even wished us luck."

Ned hoped what he said next wouldn't set Trudy off even more. "You Genovas sure have stubborn streaks."

*DEATH in the ORCHARD*

"We get that from my dad. Mom is much more even-tempered."

"I noticed."

Trudy snuggled down to Ned. He could feel her soft breasts against his chest. His body responded against his better judgement.

Trudy yawned loudly. "What's on our agenda for tomorrow?"

Ned held in a sigh. Mood over. He rued his earlier decision to not have sex under her mother's roof. "I'll call Tony and see what he's found about Greg Dietz's past. Anything to help clear Rick will reduce the tension."

"I'll call the bank and get an appointment for us to see Mr. Graham." Trudy sighed. "I suppose I could take the baking over to Ben, save him a trip."

"A conciliatory gesture?"

She yawned again. "Maybe. Maybe not." She kissed him on his cheek. "Maybe we'll have to solve this thing so I can rub Ben's nose in it." She rolled over to her side of the bed. "Night, Ned."

"Goodnight, Trudy." Maybe being an only child wasn't so bad after all.

# CHAPTER TWENTY-ONE

*Tuesday*

It was early morning when the scent of Mom's baking reached me upstairs. I slipped out of bed without waking Ned and threw on sweats. He looked sexy with his hair flopping over his forehead and the covers pulled down to expose his muscular chest. I stifled an impulse to reach under the sheet and grab him. I'd woken in the middle of the night to find Ned's side of the bed empty, and the sound of the shower. I hope it was good and cold.

I'd heard Rick and Aidan leave before me, and once I brushed my hair and teeth, I went downstairs where Mom was cutting today's cooled apple cake into squares.

"Goodness, you're up early, Trudy. This is your vacation. Why not sleep in?"

"I'll take the tray over to Ben before he can get here. I want to ask him why he reacted like he did last night." I paused. "I am not apologizing."

*DEATH in the ORCHARD*

"No need to." Mom covered the large baking tray with plastic wrap. "I thought about his flare-up when I was baking, Trudy. I still think he's miffed because he thought he was the last to know about it."

"Says the man who didn't want anyone to know the gender of his child."

"Until he did. Maybe it's a control thing, who knows? I despair trying to totally figure any man out, Bob included."

I looked around. "Where is Bob?"

"He went home to pick up his mail and get more clothes. With work on the mural this week, it's easier if he stays here."

I surprised myself by saying, "Honestly, Mom, just move in together." I shouldered the tray. I should take my own advice when it came to Mom and Bob and let them figure it out. "Wish me luck."

"Key is in the golf cart."

I negotiated the porch stairs and carefully placed the tray on the back seat of the golf cart. Then I let the cart glide down the hill past Ben and Gail's house to the café. I parked by the kitchen door, and as I stepped out and retrieved the tray, Ben came out, his eyebrows raised at seeing me.

"Hey, I was on my way over." He took the tray from me.

"Thought I'd lend a hand before disappearing later."

No time like the present. "I wanted to see if you cooled off about Ned and me looking into Dad's death." I stood tall and hoped I didn't appear defiant. "Sorry the idea upsets you, but I need to do this, Ben." *Darn, was that sort of an apology?*

Ben looked at the tray as if apple squares held the answers he sought. "Stay right here."

He disappeared into the kitchen and returned a minute later with two coffees. The rich scent woke my stomach and I wished he'd brought an apple cake with him. "Staff have things covered for the moment." He pointed to Mom's golf cart. "Have a seat."

I did as he asked and he slid in beside me and turned to me. He opened his mouth to speak, then gulped and turned to look forward. I had no idea what he was seeing. I blew on my coffee and took a sip. He'd remembered I took it black.

A Canada goose swept over the café roof and settled in the pond in the herb garden, followed closely by its mate. The two paddled lazily around as I waited for my brother to gather his thoughts.

"Awful as this sounds, I guess Greg Dietz's death didn't upset me much. I'd barely met the guy and didn't see his body. It seemed like something out of a crime show, unreal, and I could tease Rick because it hadn't touched me the way Dad's death did." He shook his head. "That awful day changed my life, Trudy. I'd started working with Dad, learning the ropes of the business, and suddenly I was helping Mom keep the orchard going while figuring out where Dad kept things, which suppliers he used, how he hired seasonal help. It was a steep learning curve and every day I worried I'd fail—fail us all. Your sweet sixteen was ruined, Rick wanted to drop out of college, and it was all I could do to make him stay to finish."

"I remember. We were all in shock, but you swung right into action."

He turned back to me. "I had no choice."

I put my hand on his arm. "Ben, you've done a wonderful job here."

"I suppose. But I kept blinders on and couldn't allow myself to wallow in speculation. I know Mom did for a while, but I couldn't. I was angry at Dad for deserting us and leaving me holding the bag."

My dismay cut through me, wrenching my stomach. "Ben, I had no idea. You must have felt so pressured."

He grunted and took the top off his coffee and had a bracing swallow. "Last night when it came out you were dragging all that up again, well, sorry I lost it, but it brought back all kinds of negative stuff I've pushed aside for years. I don't know if I want to confront things now, Trudy, especially with our baby on the way." He looked right at me; his voice held a plea. "I'm looking to my son's future, and this feels like I'm being dragged back to the past."

I took time to form my words. "I guess as strongly as you feel about not wanting to look back, I can't look totally forward until I know what happened to Dad." I cast my mind about for a compromise. "How about I promise I won't bug you with details until there's something to tell, and if Ned and I don't uncover any answers, then I'll let it go. But I have to try, Ben."

A car pulled up and a group of women climbed out. Their chatter about their morning out and what they would order reached us.

Ben gave a nod, climbed out of the cart, and disappeared inside.

I could see Ben's viewpoint, especially considering how he stepped up, but I knew my own determination wouldn't let me stop investigating. I had to hope whatever I discovered wouldn't ruin my relationship with my brother.

Ned rolled over and found the other side of the bed empty. He could hear muffled noises floating up from the kitchen. The fragrant scent of whatever Hildy had baked, redolent with cinnamon and nutmeg, made his stomach growl. He took advantage of the empty upper floor to quickly shower. He'd squeeze in a run later or skip it today. He *was* on vacation. When he'd dressed in jeans and a sweater, he combed his damp hair and padded downstairs.

He found Hildy in the kitchen pouring herself a mug of coffee. "Yes, please," he said, and she reached for a second mug and filled it for him. On the table stood a plate of baked goods with fruit, the source of the sweet aroma.

"Help yourself." She put a plate in front of him.

He bit into delicate layers of flaky dough and cooked apples. "This is delicious."

"Second most popular item I make, next to my cinnamon rolls." Hildy cut one in half. "I can make you eggs or toast, and we always have cereal if you like."

"I'm fine with this. I'll be full after this goodie."

The front door closed. Ned heard Trudy ending a call as she came into the kitchen. She wore old sweats; her hair was pulled into a hasty ponytail and wisps escaped and curled around her face. The cool morning air had brought roses to her cheeks. Ned thought she'd never looked lovelier.

"Trying to sweeten my boyfriend?" she teased her

mother. She put an arm around Hildy's waist for a hug.

"He's sweet enough." Hildy saw the cup in Trudy's hand. "How was Ben?"

Trudy topped off her cup and sat across from Ned. "He explained his strong reaction last night. Greg Dietz's murder didn't touch him as much as us looking into Dad's death, which struck a nerve. Lots of repressed anger and stuff there he didn't want to revisit."

"Sorry, Trudy," Ned said. "How did you leave it with him?"

"I told him I appreciated his point of view, but he had to see mine was different. I said I won't mention it again until we had news, or not." She reached over and took a bite of Ned's breakfast.

"Hey, get your own."

Hildy sat down between them. "Ben had to suddenly step into Mario's shoes in the orchard. It was a stressful time for us both, trying to learn aspects of the business your father had handled while keeping things running to bring in income. At least it sounds as if you reached a working compromise, Trudy." She drained her cup and checked the clock that hung over the kitchen door. "I'll wrap a few of these to bring to Bob and Gail."

She busied herself while Ned and Trudy shared a second square. "I don't know if I like these or your cinnamon buns better, Hildy."

"Flatterer." Hildy dropped a kiss on Trudy's head. "I'll see you when I see you. Time to lend Bob a hand." She took her package and left for Gail's house.

"I called the bank on my way in. Mr. Graham has a meeting this morning but can see us after lunch at 1:30." Trudy drained her cup and put Ned's mug in the dishwasher. "I need to do my online yoga class while I call Meg, and then have a shower. Is there anything we can accomplish before we go to the bank?"

"I'll call Tony and see what he's turned up on Greg Dietz while you're upstairs."

She tossed him a smile and ran up the stairs.

At least her mood seemed brighter, even if things with Ben weren't totally resolved. Ned closeted himself in the office to check emails on his phone and then called work. From the front window, he saw Rick come out of the barn, carrying several bunches of cornstalks to restock the pumpkin patch.

Tony answered immediately. "Hi, Boss. Enjoying the rural area?"

"And Hildy's baking. She's incredible. Cinnamon rolls, apple crumble, and apple squares so far."

"You can FedEx those here, you know. Directly to me."

"Depends on what you've found for me. Anything interesting?" Ned heard his partner shuffling papers.

"Perhaps. Might take more digging. I'm making

headway on your pile of paperwork."

"Appreciate it." Ned had a pad and pen ready to take notes. "Shoot."

Tony unearthed Greg Dietz's background and rap sheet. "Stellar student, law school standout, parents paid for tuition and living until he got hooked on the stuff, and then got lifted for selling to his friends."

"Cocaine?"

"After dexies to help with studying."

"Didn't think he needed the money."

"He told the sentencing judge he used the proceeds to pay for his own drugs to keep his parents in the dark about his use. First offense, so a lighter sentence at Troy Correctional. He went through a detox program and appeared to have stayed clean after." Tony slurped his coffee. "Took an interest in helping other inmates with legal forms, gold stars all around."

Ned made notes. "Sounds like he learned his lesson."

"Maybe."

"You're not convinced?"

"I spoke to Seth Armus over in the Drugs Unit. Dietz's bunkmate was a known drug runner, Bobby Costello, who was trying to set up his own patch to Canada when he was lifted for the last time."

"Last time? That long a sentence?"

"You could say that. Died in prison not long before

Dietz was released. Any help to you?"

"Might be. Let me see what shakes out here. Thanks."

"I'll keep digging. Don't forget the sweets."

Ned sat back and tented his fingers, wondering how approachable the Troy Correctional Facility warden would be.

# CHAPTER TWENTY-TWO

I luxuriated in the shower after my yoga session, remembering many younger days when one or both of my brothers would hammer on the door to hurry me up. I'd had the temerity to enjoy baths at one point in my teens, and that closed and locked bathroom door called like a siren to Ben and Rick. Despite the second bathroom in my parents' room, they would annoy and harass me as only older brothers could do, until one of our parents called them off. I wished Ned would join me. *That* kind of annoying I could use.

I thought over the plan for today. There was no way these two cases were entwined, so I couldn't see how Ned having information on Greg Dietz could help us with my father's case. But he was the professional; I should leave it to him. I could see his point that anything that would clear Rick was a good thing.

When I entered the office Ned was sitting at Mom's desk looking at his phone. I crept up behind him and kissed

*DEATH in the ORCHARD*

the back of his neck, right where his hair started to wave over his collar. He reached back and grabbed my arm, shot his chair back, and pulled me around to sit on his lap. He kissed me all over my face and neck until I was reduced to giggling and panting, and I pulled him in for a longer, real kiss that took my breath away.

"You know there's no one else in the house right now." I let the thought simmer in the air between us.

Ned sighed and looked at his watch. "Yes, but we have places to go and people to see, so let's get a move on, my temptress."

I reluctantly agreed and grabbed my jacket as we left the house. Bob's car stood in front of the ranch house, and as we took the Benz up the drive, I wondered if Ben had given any thought to our tacit agreement. There were more cars in the parking lot now, the early lunch swarm, Mom called it. Some people came for brunch, while others would linger to shop in the storefront they had to walk through to get to the glass-walled café in the rear. The fall wreaths Gail made, along with herbs, candles and small vintage items were popular this time of year. "I need to stop in at some point and find a gift to bring back to Meg for cat-sitting. She said Wilkie is no problem, but if Tony stays over the cat tries to sleep on his head."

"I bet Tony loves that. Meg will like whatever you bring her."

He smiled and the warmth of it made me wish we had stayed home longer.

We took the hill down past the high school. The parking lot and bicycle racks were full, and the buses lined up for later in the day. I remembered the carefree days when my worry consisted of how I'd do on a biology test, or if John Maydan would kiss me at my birthday party.

Ned parked in front of the police station. When we entered, the receptionist at the front desk recognized us. A different officer sat at the other desk, talking on the phone, and I remembered Ron had said he was on late shift this week. Ned did the talking.

"Any chance of speaking with Lieutenant Hoffmann?" His smile was full-on charm.

She grinned and picked up her phone to use the intercom. A minute later one of the doors at the rear opened, and Paul Hoffmann motioned us back. He waved to two chairs in front of his desk, where a photo of three young adults and an attractive woman took pride of place. Framed certificates and diplomas hung on the wall behind him, while a large photo print on a side wall caught my attention. It showed a lake view, tall trees surrounding the shore; the blue water shimmered with dancing sparks of sunlight across its surface.

"Good morning. Have a seat."

"And to you. We're here for another look at the Genova file." Ned shifted in his chair. "Trudy was overwhelmed the other day and didn't feel she absorbed everything."

Sure, throw me under the bus. I pointed to the blown-up photo. "What a gorgeous place—is it near here?"

Paul's face lit up. "A few hours away. Lake Wallenpaupack in Pennsylvania. My family has had a home on the shore for ages. Good water skiing and even better fishing."

Ned stepped in with a few questions about what the Hoffmanns would catch (different kinds of bass, walleye too, until he'd exhausted what I hoped were fish questions and hoped they didn't move on to tackle). To my knowledge, Ned had never fished in his life, but you'd never know it.

Paul explained a town had been moved out to make the reservoir lake in the 1920s, and remnants of that old village had been found by divers.

I shook myself. "Kind of spooky to think you're pulling water skiers right over a sunken town. What an interesting story."

Paul stood. "Wait here; I'll get the file."

Once he'd left the room I turned to Ned and whispered, "When did you become Mr. Fisherman of the Year?" I turned on my phone's camera and made sure it was on silent mode.

Paul re-entered and handed me the file. "Do you want

to sit out at the table, Trudy?"

"I'll flip through it right here." I opened the Notes app on my phone. "Not sure what I'm looking for, but I want to read it over again." I put the file on the corner of the desk and flipped past the autopsy pages to look at the exhibits listing I'd ignored on Saturday, keeping my eyes on the pages in front of me but my ears wide open.

Paul sat back down behind his desk and Ned pulled out the notes he'd made. He explained he'd asked a detective on his team back in NYC to see what he could unearth about Greg Dietz. "I hoped our clearance might find information you didn't readily have access to."

Paul drew a pad from one corner of his desk in front of him. "I only have his rap sheet and the overview from Troy Correctional. You find anything else?"

The men chatted about the intel on Greg Dietz's background, arrest, and his conviction for selling, including his prison life.

"This guy, Bobby Costello, the bunkmate. You ever hear of him?" Ned asked.

"New name to me but I wouldn't necessarily know it

unless he'd been arrested around here since I've been in the area."

Ned described Costello's background and history.

"You think there might be a connection between the two men in terms of selling drugs?" Paul made a note.

"I'm having my partner look into it more, but probably the most efficient way to get good info would be to talk to the warden."

"Good idea. I can arrange that. I'll bet you'd like to ride along for that interview?"

Ned shrugged. "Once a detective . . . I wouldn't say no, that's for sure."

The two men grinned and Ned decided to chance the warm feeling in the room. He glanced at Trudy, who assiduously took notes and pretended to ignore them both. "Too early for test results on Rick's GSR?"

Paul nodded. "I'll call Rick when they come through, don't worry. Unless I have to go and arrest him." He hitched one corner of his mouth up in a crooked grin, which reassured Ned that Paul thought this was an unlikely prospect.

Trudy stirred but didn't look up.

"You can let him know I appreciated the heads-up about Gerald Dietz and his gun club. When I interviewed the parents yesterday, I inquired about Gerald's handguns. Despite the day's delay, we took GSR swabs of him and the younger brother, too. You never know. Gerald claims he doesn't own any .45s; his handguns are 9mms. Doesn't mean he couldn't have borrowed a .45 or bought one under the table. He certainly knows his way around guns."

"Something to keep in mind. He couldn't have been happy when his son went to prison."

Paul nodded. "Still waiting on the formal autopsy report for time of death, too."

No clear way to eliminate Rick yet. "I'll tell Rick tonight."

"Best let me tell him. I need to call him later about an orchard map we found in Greg Dietz's truck with marked areas. We also found a shovel in his truck. I want to know if he or Aidan saw any signs of fresh digging. You around tomorrow if I can convince the warden at Troy to see us?"

"All day. Appreciate being included."

Paul shrugged. "Let's be honest, Ned. You've worked many more murder cases than I have. Your expertise might come in handy. Officers searched Dietz's room at the hostel yesterday. Not much there, but then he hadn't lived there long."

"Still smart and necessary," Ned said. "Any of his cohorts there?"

"Ron Hanson has to go back tonight to finish interviews. Most of them were out at work. We spoke with his coworkers at the orchard, too. Nothing stood out at first glance, although one guy, Vince Russo, also a hostel resident, seemed to have taken against him in his short tenure. We're doing background checks on all of them."

"Sounds like you have things under control." Ned stood and shook Paul's hand. "You know I'm available if you have any questions or can be of help. Don't hesitate to ask."

"Appreciate it. I'll let you know the timing if the warden can see us."

Trudy took her cue and flipped the file closed. "Think I'm done now. Thanks again, Paul."

He waved her off. "No problem. Hope you make some progress." He walked them out to the front of the station and stood on the doorstep. Ned asked him to join them for lunch, but he said he had a stack of paperwork to tackle. "Especially if we can arrange a field trip tomorrow." He turned to Trudy. "One thing I wanted to ask. Those flowers you said Dietz brought to the house Sunday morning, Trudy? Can you describe them?"

While Ned would have answered "fall flowers," Trudy listed orange mums, red dahlias, sunflowers, and coral roses. "They're still on the dining room table if you want me to take a photo to send you."

Paul shook his head. "No, that description matches the

receipt we found in Dietz's truck. Not much else there, other than that map and shovel, a few snack wrappers, but the ME found a folding knife in a pocket of his cargo pants."

"To protect himself from someone he was meeting?" Trudy asked.

Paul shrugged. "Protect or threaten? Only thing certain is he didn't have a chance to use the knife, but it's likely he hadn't planned to come up against someone with a gun."

# CHAPTER TWENTY-THREE

I sat in a booth in the local café with Ned after explaining my legs dangled if we sat at the lunch counter. He bit his lip but nodded with a thoughtful expression, and managed not to tease me while we ordered lunch. "Gail and I came here after school all the time to drink egg creams and plot our debate club defenses, as well as our moves on boys. I think they're still playing the same CDs from then."

Ned sipped a chocolate egg cream. "Learn anything new from the file?"

"I learned more than I ever wanted to know about the fish in Lake Wallenpaupack."

"Hey, I'm hitching along to see the warden at Troy Correctional."

"Boys' road trip. Who knew that was a thing." I shrugged. "I guess that's progress. "

"What did you take photos of when you looked at the file?"

I unwrapped my straw and stuck it into the foam of my vanilla egg cream. "Who said I took more photos you don't want to know about?"

"I saw you turn your camera on when Paul left to get your father's file. Why do you think I talked about Bobby Costello?"

"You're getting as devious as me and changed your tune there."

"Paul said we couldn't take the file out, but he didn't specify photographs."

"It's a fine line you're crossing there, detective," I said in imitation of his father's brogue.

"You're a bad influence on me. Show me your snaps," he retorted.

"Oooh. you say the sexiest things." I took a satisfying sip. "It's only the exhibits list of the things from my father's truck. We can scrutinize it later." I frowned as a slender young woman came into the café to pick up a take-out order. She had shiny dark brown hair and hadn't changed much since she'd stolen my first love in high school. I put my head down and suddenly needed to root around in my backpack.

"If I could think of a reason, I'd say you were anxious to avoid that woman at the counter noticing you."

The rear wall had a large mirror and I realized Ned could see the takeout counter up front. "You'd think you were a detective, O'Malley." The woman left and I exhaled. "That was Jill West. When my Sweet Sixteen was canceled, she swooped in on John Maydan, my big crush, and next spring he took her to his prom." I remembered feeling totally humiliated and sad, on top of the upheaval at home. "A few years later they got married."

Ned raised his eyebrows. "Not her biggest fan, then. Sorry." He reached across to pat my hand.

"Not so much." I shrugged. "Eons ago. Old news." Then why did I want to avoid Jill West? I sipped my egg cream and thought this over. Maybe I wasn't ready to hear how ridiculously happy she and John were while she brought up phone snaps of their 2.5 kids.

While we waited for our food, I looked at the vintage photos of Schoharie that dotted the walls and pointed out the wooden covered bridge over Fox Creek. "That's near the Old Stone Fort Museum, originally a church used as a stockade during the Revolutionary War."

"Worth a look one afternoon after our business stuff is done?"

"If our business is ever done." I knew I sounded gloomy, but nothing seemed to move my father's case forward.

"Trudy, we only got here Saturday. This is Tuesday, and we had a baby shower and a death on orchard property in between. We're doing what we can."

The waitress, a young woman in the tightest tank top

I'd ever seen, snapped her gum loudly as she put our Greek salads in front of us. "And a shared plate of fries." She placed the filled platter of crispy goodness between us and plonked down a bottle of ketchup. "Getcha anything else?"

"This is fine, thanks." I dove in for a handful of warm fries and added them to my plate.

Ned poured dressing on his salad. "You sound glum."

I salted my fries, added a small pool of ketchup to the corner of my plate, and dunked a few in. "Why do greasy things taste the best?"

"I might remind you that potatoes are a veggie, no matter how they're prepared."

"Spoken like a true Irishman." I sighed. "I don't want to drop things, but it seems like there's not much left to investigate."

"Give it a few more days. What do I need to know about Wynn Graham?"

Before I answered Ned, I took another, larger handful of fries, grease be damned. I wondered what John was up to these days. He'd always be "the one who got away" when I thought of him. For all I knew, he could have turned into a real jerk. The thought cheered me, and I shook the memory of those dreamy blue eyes away and answered Ned. "Wynn Graham was one of my father's closest friends. They coached the boys' baseball teams for years. Two sons, one who died not long after my father did, and the other lives in Maine. When the Grahams divorced, Mary Graham moved to Maine, too."

"He'll be a good person to talk to about your dad's mood those last days. I'll give Larry Long a call later and check if he's unearthed anything."

I dug into my salad, trying to think of what I could ask Wynn Graham to help us move my father's case forward.

Ned watched Wynn Graham through the glass wall of a side office, which allowed the bank manager to view business while giving him a modicum of privacy. He had his head down as he read papers in front of him, while Trudy spoke to the head teller and explained they had an appointment to see him.

The First Citizens Bank retained the exterior look of one of Schoharie's historic buildings, this one of red brick with an ornate frontage on Main Street. According to Trudy, the interior had been completely renovated after the hurricane that caused extensive flooding to the town years before and almost destroyed it. Well-lit and cheery, its tile floor gleamed, and mountain landscapes by local artists on the walls alternated with plaques for the bank's sponsorship of local sports teams. With a row of tellers facing the patrons' entry, Graham's side office was opposite the huge steel safe.

The man was round-shouldered from years of poring over bank accounts, Ned assumed. Overhead lighting shone on his bald pate and glinted off his glasses.

They were shown to his office and Graham stood, his stoop pronounced, to shake hands with Ned after Trudy introduced him. A brass nameplate read: Melwynn Graham, Manager. She made small talk and asked after his son Daniel, an accountant who indeed lived with his family in Maine.

While they talked, Ned examined photos lining the two solid walls. Several showed Graham in golf clothes at tournaments, flanked by two teen boys whose resemblance made Ned decide they must be his sons. Later photos showed only one son. It was telling his ex-wife, Mary, was only in one early photo. Several were of Little League teams, and Ned wondered if an aggravated parent could have taken their ire out on Mario Genova with his kid's bat. He added it to his mental list to consider.

There were framed certificates, too. At the near end was a smaller photograph of a much younger Graham with a thatch of sandy hair, wearing fatigues, sitting amidst a group of soldiers cleaning their guns. Ned used this to enter the conversation. He pointed to the service photo. "Desert Storm? Thank you for your service."

"The guy on the end could take his gun apart and put it back together blindfolded in forty seconds." The banker's dark suit hung off his slender frame. "My time in the sandbox was long ago. Feels like another lifetime. Part of the past I don't talk about anymore."

Yet he kept a photo of himself with his squad on his wall. Interesting. Ned took one of the chairs in front of the desk at the banker's direction. "Did you play golf with Mario Genova?"

Trudy let loose with a "humph" as Graham shook his head. "Couldn't persuade Mario to even try. I love it, though. Good for thinking and great exercise with so much walking."

Ned sat in one of two leather chairs that faced the desk. Trudy remained standing, leaning against the second chair.

"Thank you for seeing us, Mr. Graham." She couldn't seem to settle and cleared her throat. "I'm up visiting for a week and wanted to ask you a few questions about my dad. I know you were great friends back then."

Ned realized Ben wasn't the only one whose past had come rushing back. This was where Trudy had learned of her father's death, and it stood to reason she must be recollecting that tragic day, with all its associated painful memories. Her throat seemed to dry up and he jumped in to help her with her explanation. "I'm an NYPD detective, Mr. Graham, and I've agreed to assist Trudy as she tries to find out what happened to her father. A cold case review, if you will."

Graham's blank face took on a puzzled look. "I thought what happened to Mario was a tragic accident, Trudy."

"That may well be the case, Mr. Graham, but it doesn't explain why my father withdrew all of my parents' savings, or what happened to their money."

"True." He pursed his lips. "But how can I help?"

"Would there be any kind of trail if my father had redeposited the money in another account?"

He shook his head. "If he'd asked for the funds in a cashier's check, we might have been able to put a tracer on it. But he requested it all in cash, and I found out afterward it almost cleaned out what we had on hand. The teller had to order more funds for the next day."

"Can you please go over the day he made the withdrawal?"

The man's face took on a look of sorrow. "I'm afraid I wasn't here when he came in, Trudy, or I might have spoken with Mario and asked him why he was closing out those accounts. It was only when you and your family came here the next day looking for answers that I pulled up the accounts and saw what had happened." Graham leaned back in his chair and looked up at the ceiling, searching his memory for the events of eleven years ago. "As I recall, the teller who helped your father was new, but Mario had the proper identification and she didn't question him once she cleared the process with the head teller. It was his money after all, and the accounts were set up to only require one signature."

Ned saw Trudy grimace as she sunk into a chair. "It was my mother's money, too, and their retirement account. It seems so out of character for Dad." She leaned over the desk, her expression earnest. "You were good friends for years before his death. He never said anything to you about needing that kind of money?"

"I'm sorry, Trudy. I saw your father a few days before when we had coffee together and he looked and acted fine."

Ned sat forward. "There was no talk of why he would have withdrawn such a large amount? No reason for an expensive purchase, say, maybe a new piece of equipment for the orchard?"

Graham shook his head. "Equipment Mario purchased for the orchard he usually did on a loan. Until harvest, they didn't have a large amount of cash. I can't recall him ever buying a large piece of equipment outright."

Trudy popped up again and moved restlessly around the office, studying the photos. "I hoped there was something we missed." She stopped in front of one of the certificates, an award of some kind. "I remember this." She turned to Ned. "Mr. Graham's son, Jake, saved a boy's life after he choked on a hot dog at a ball game. Jake did the Heimlich; the mayor gave him this award." She moved to the next certificate. "This was when he won Most Valuable Player of the team. Ben was jealous of that one."

"You must have been very proud of him," Ned said.

"I was—I keep those up there to remind me of the good times." Graham stood, indicating their interview was over. "We had some fun evenings at those games."

"You and Dad were great coaches," Trudy said.

"I suppose there was the occasional parent who became annoyed with you or Mario?" Ned threw in.

Wynn tilted his head to one side. "Rarely happened. The umpires took any blowback from what they considered a lousy call. Mario and I were there to guide the boys, teach them the rules and give them encouragement. It was a positive thing." He turned to Trudy. "I'm sorry I couldn't be of more help, Trudy." He stood and shook both their hands. "Give your mother my regards."

Out on the street, Ned walked with Trudy back to his car. "I couldn't help but notice Graham referred to those good times as in the past."

"Jake died by suicide not long after my father died, an overdose. He'd been addicted to drugs at one point but went to rehab and aced it. He'd been clean for a while, or so we thought. No one knew what sent him off the rails, but it was incredibly sad. Both Graham boys grew up with my brothers, and they all played Little League."

"That's awful."

"It was awful. We were still getting over losing my dad when Jake died." Trudy rubbed her arms.

Ned put an arm around her. "Let's go home."

# CHAPTER TWENTY-FOUR

While Ned tried to get in touch with retired detective Larry Long, I went upstairs to charge my phone and threw myself across my bed to text Meg once I'd plugged it in: **"Forgot to tell you—my bedroom is GONE! Mom put my stuff in the attic and made it a guest room. Feels weird."**

Three little bubbles appeared as Meg answered back: **"Director on warpath; late night. Wolfe was right. Talk AM."**

Meg reminded me of Wolfe's *You Can't Go Home Again*, and she was probably right. I also knew the director she had to deal with, having had my own run-ins with the guy. For the first time since we'd arrived, I was happy to be here and not there. We would talk tomorrow. She had no idea of my history with John Maydan and his wife, Jill, so I could either get over that myself, or save it for a later conversation to vent to Gail, who knew the players and the situation.

I rolled over and put my phone down. Dredging up old memories was proving more painful than I'd foolishly anticipated. Our interview with Dad's friend brought back the day my father died, and I replayed the events: the phone call that he was missing and our hurried trip to town, the fateful meeting with Mr. Graham at the bank when my mother's financial situation was revealed, Ron Hanson's sad face as he called Ben out of the office and I watched the color drain from my brother's face. How had I forgotten Ben had been the first to know Dad was dead, and then had to tell the rest of us?

The weeks after the funeral passed in a blur, encumbered by too many flowers and too much food at the house. I thought about Doug Dietz feeling the same way yesterday when Rick and I visited his house.

My eyes felt heavy as I remembered that I'd barely finished helping Mom send out notes to people who'd shown up for my father's funeral when we were attending another one. The flowers were different but the service was eerily similar, the female priest changing the readings, but reciting the same prayers for the dead. I'd felt on display in the front row only weeks before. This time I sat with my mother and brothers a few rows back, where I didn't feel my grief was on show for the gathering. Those who turned out were from the same walks of life— the Little League groups, Jake's friends we all knew, the church family. The differences were minor. Where my father's orchard employees had attended his funeral, Mr. Graham's bank colleagues attended Jake's.

Mary Graham had sobbed quietly throughout the service behind the sheer veil on her hat. Wynn Graham had stared ahead, hollow-eyed, his arm around her and his back rigid. Their younger son, Daniel, had sat huddled on the other side of his mother and stared at his brother's casket. His uncomprehending look was one I recognized.

I felt drained as my eyes closed. When I woke it was to birdsong outside my window, the lowering sun giving the outside a golden glow before sunset. I stretched and stood to look out at the neat rows of apple trees, searching for the one pear tree I knew was out there in our yard. Gail and I put a photo of it on Instagram every year around my parents' anniversary. For some reason, that tree comforted me, a solid entity amidst the sadness and unpredictability of life. I might not find the answers to my father's death, but I needed to look for them, even as I acknowledged I knew he'd loved our family and recognized that might have to be enough.

I washed my face, brushed my teeth, and wandered downstairs to find Ned standing by the kitchen island, watching my mother intently as she spatchcocked two chickens, cutting out their spines to lay them flat on a baking tray. I stood in the hallway for a moment, pleased to see how easily they interacted.

"They cook faster this way, and the skin crisps up nicely," Mom explained. "I rub olive oil and salt and pepper outside, then put herbs in a compound butter under the skin to flavor the meat."

"Giving away all your trade secrets?" I entered the kitchen and wrapped my arms around Ned's waist.

Ned squeezed me back. "Your mom is amazing. I need to import her to cook for me."

"Glad you see the Genova women for the goddesses we are." I leaned into him and when I looked up, he kissed the tip of my nose.

"Good nap?"

"Yes, but I didn't mean to doze off."

"Naps are restorative," Mom said, as she washed her hands and put the baking tray in the oven. "Ned wants to take you out to eat, Trudy, so there'll be plenty of this leftover for lunch or snacks tomorrow. Why don't you take Rick and Aidan with you? Ben and Gail are eating at her mom's tonight."

Mom saw the dismay that flicked across my face. "Nothing to do with you, Trudy. They've gone every Tuesday night for dinner during Gail's pregnancy. Her mom didn't want to miss her progress." Mom uncovered a dough bowl and sprinkled flour on the island for rolling out. "We don't always eat dinner together and when I do cook, I always make plenty so Bob and I have leftovers. All the boys know they can grab a snack here."

"You have no choice with Rick and Aidan's appetites."

Mom laughed. "They come sniffing around at least two nights a week if they're tired from work and my kitchen smells better than what they've planned."

"Who does their cooking?" Ned asked, watching as my mother cut out biscuits and placed them on a tray lined with parchment paper.

"Aidan mostly, but Rick has a few dishes he can rustle up. There's probably a fair bit of takeout, too."

I asked Ned about Larry Long. No need to hide things since Mom was clued into our investigation. "Were you able to reach him?"

"Yes, but there's no news. He's been on a buying trip with Wayne. He promised he'd browse through his notebooks when they get home and then call me. But Paul Hoffmann set up a meeting with the warden tomorrow afternoon."

I hadn't had time to answer him when the front door banged open, and Rick and Aidan rushed in. Rick had a red calico bandana tied over his hair to keep it out of his face, which meant he'd been making cider today. He carried a whiff of sweet appley scent.

"Good news. Paul Hoffmann called me. Forensics is almost finished with our house. We can go home tomorrow. Best of all, my GSR report was negative." Seeing the relief on my brother's face made me realize he'd been more upset than he'd let on.

He continued as Aidan slipped an arm over his shoulder. "The autopsy report says Dietz died between 3 and 5, and because I went home and found him around 5, I'm still not totally in the clear." He shrugged. "At least there was no gunshot residue on my hands. Tough to shoot someone without that happening, and they did the test right at the scene."

"It means a lot," Aidan said consolingly. "Let's shower before dinner."

Ned invited the boys to come out with us.

Rick brightened. "Great idea. Let's celebrate. I know just the place."

Ned followed Rick's directions, while Trudy chatted in the back seat with Aidan. He turned up a side street to their destination and parked in a lot across from The Night Owl, a pub that promised "Classics in Food, Music, and Books" under its sign, an image of a bespectacled owl reading a book.

*M.K. GRAFF*

"This used to be a laundromat," Trudy said as they ran across the street in a light drizzle, and Rick opened the door. A blast of music hit them as they entered. Mama Cass Elliott encouraged listeners to believe "Words of Love," even if soft and tender, would not be enough to win a girl's heart.

"That's an oldie," Ned said, shaking droplets off his parka.

"They play music from the 60s to the 90s," Aidan said.

Ned admired the burgundy leather chairs and booths which unified the interior. Shelves ran around all the booths and walls, holding an assortment of books. Signs posted said, "Take a book; leave a book." The far-end wall alternated racks of wine with stacks of books. A coffered ceiling added to the cozy library feel, as did shaded lights on each table, but overhead lighting kept the space from being too dark.

Trudy appeared impressed. "It's like a refined gentleman's club," she said. She had her head turned to look around when a young man with curly dark hair and startling blue eyes, wearing a navy and white pin-striped apron over jeans, arrived with a stack of menus. His crisp, white button-down was rolled to his elbows, and his wide smile and dimples gave him an air of ease and good humor.

"What a surprise—Trudy Genova." His voice was

mellow and smooth. "You look amazing."

Trudy's head whipped around. "John! Yes, a big surprise." She narrowed her eyes at her brother. "Rick didn't tell me you worked here."

John Maydan cleared his throat. "It's my place, Trudy. Opened last January." He reached out to shake her hand. "It's great to see you. Four for dinner?"

Trudy touched his arm. "Thanks."

Ned's stomach plummeted. This was the guy she'd talked about today, her first crush from high school. But Trudy hadn't seen him in ages, plus he was married. No sweat. Then why did he feel so weird?

John showed them to a comfy booth. Trudy slid in next to the bookshelf and Ned followed her, staking out his claim. Was it his imagination or did John check out Trudy's ring finger? He certainly gave her a lingering look.

The owner waited for them to settle, then handed around the menus and snowy white napkins wrapped around utensils. "We have great local brews on tap and a full bar. Your server will tell you tonight's specials." He leaned across Ned to touch Trudy's hand. "Really good to see you, Trudy."

Trudy's wide-eyed smile gave her the look of a deer in the headlights. She blinked. "And you."

In a whiff of expensive cologne, he was gone. Trudy's eyes followed him a little too long. "Why didn't you tell me John Maydan owned this place?" she hissed to Rick.

"Didn't we mention he'd been renovating the place when you were home last Christmas? I thought you'd be pleased to see an old friend."

Aidan picked up on the tension. "What am I missing here?"

Rick gave him a crooked smile. "Trudy had a crush on John you could ride a truck through in high school, until he dumped her for the gal who became his first wife."

"First wife?" Ned asked. "How many has he had?"

"Only the one, someone else from school."

"Jill West," Trudy mumbled.

Rick snapped his finger. "That's it. They were married a few years but divorced amicably I've heard. Her mom still lives in town."

"He's not married now?" Trudy clarified.

"Not to my knowledge." Rick studied his menu.

*And why do you care,* Ned thought.

It was weird seeing John Maydan after talking to Ned about him at lunch. I had to admit it freaked me out to see him after he'd been on my mind all afternoon. He was divorced! I glanced over my shoulder to get another look as John paused by a table to chat.

My cheeks felt flushed while I consulted the menu and pushed back thoughts of what might have been, even as I recalled those kisses under the bleacher. There were the typical burgers, salads, and pasta dishes, and our server told us the specials were beef tips over rice or fried flounder with fries. We settled on our meals and ordered the pale ale on tap, except for Ned, who was driving and chose a soft drink.

I probably drank my ale too fast. The music was low enough to not interrupt conversation as we ate. Rick and Aidan were excited to move back into their cabin tomorrow. Aidan told Rick he would get one of the guys to re-gravel the walk and cover any blood stains. "I still can't figure out why anyone would want to shoot that guy."

"Something in his past came back to haunt him," Rick said. "I suppose there's no movement with Dad's case or you would have told us."

I shook my head when I saw John heading our way with refills on our drinks. "Everything all right here?"

"Great," Rick assured him, as someone fiddled with a microphone on a tiny stage set in the corner with two stools.

"Tonight's karaoke night," John explained. "Trudy, I

hope we can persuade you to give us a song. You have such a lovely voice."

"Yes, you must, Trudster." Rick was insistent. "I bet Ned's never heard you sing."

I groaned inwardly and plastered a smile on my face as I drained my second beer. There was no way I was singing in public in front of Ned and John Maydan.

The bar filled quickly by eight, evidence that Schoharie was keen on weeknight karaoke. Several people had gotten up to sing with varying degrees of success. In keeping with what Aidan had said, there were no songs later than the 90s. The Beatles were favorites, as were several from Billy Joel. With each new song, Rick pushed Trudy to give them just one.

On his way back from the men's room, Ned watched Trudy drink her third beer, while John stood outside their booth, talking to her. Unusual for her to have more than one or two drinks. Then the guy leaned over and tugged Trudy's arm, urging her to sing.

Ned cursed his timing. With him out of the booth, it was easier for her to slide out. Still, he was surprised to see her capitulate to John's pleading, abetted by Rick and Aidan. He tried to decide if he needed to save her from herself, but in the end, made his way back to their booth as Trudy sat on the stool on the tiny stage and flipped through the songbook.

Ned sat back down and asked Rick, "Will she be okay with this tomorrow?"

Rick waved away his concern. "She's never sung for you?"

"No. She played her violin once but that's about it."

Rick reached out and patted Ned's arm. "You're in for a treat."

John stepped up beside Trudy. "Let's hear it for a hometown girl, Trudy Genova!"

Rick and Aidan led the gathering in whoops and whistles. Trudy caught Ned's look and rolled her eyes. Maybe this was all in good fun and he should sit back and let her get on with it, but he didn't want her to say later she wished he'd rescued her.

That idea made Ned mentally cringe at how Trudy would react if he dared share that thought with her. She'd recoil from him, angry that he'd thought he had to save her and tell him he was being overprotective, or even worse, controlling. No, he'd let her get on things. His desire to keep Trudy safe didn't mean from herself.

Trudy settled on a song and tested the microphone.

"Most people associate this song with Mama Cass Elliot, but it premiered in 1931 with the Ozzie Nelson Orchestra, and singers such as Doris Day covered it." She laughed, a nice throaty sound. "Do *not* play me at Trivial Pursuit." The audience chuckled as she stood up and hit the play button, and strains of "Dream a Little Dream of Me" started. Trudy took a deep breath and sang, her voice high and sweet. Ned had only ever heard her hum to the radio here and there, but Trudy closed her eyes and gave herself over to the music as she got into it, belting out the lyrics of night breezes whispering, "I love you."

He glanced over to the bar, where John Maydan lounged against the end near Trudy and listened to her, a giant smile on his face highlighting those damn dimples when she sang about craving her lover's kiss.

She finished to raucous applause and took a bow, while Rick whistled, and several others stood to clap. John helped her off the stage, whispering in her ear, and escorted Trudy back to their booth, one hand under her elbow. Whatever he said, she liked it and threw her head back to laugh. Ned slid all the way in so she could sit, and pointedly put his arm along the back of the booth.

"That was incredible, Trudy," John said. "I still remember your solo at the senior concert. I should offer you a job to attract people. You'd be a real draw."

Trudy's face beamed, but she shook her head. "No

*DEATH in the ORCHARD*

thanks. I'm only here for a week and this was a one-off to shut my brother up."

"Thanks for giving us a treat. Please stop in again before you leave for the Big Apple."

John left for the kitchen. Trudy sighed and drank from Ned's water glass.

"You're incredible," he told her and pulled her to him to kiss her temple. She had a look of triumph on her face and slightly glazed eyes. Was that from the third beer or John? He hoped they'd be too busy for a return visit to The Night Owl.

"I admit I didn't think you'd go for it." Rick raised his glass. "To Trudy."

"To Trudy," the others echoed in a toast.

"Let's have dessert!" Trudy said.

"Whatever you want," Ned told her, even as he thought back to the song's lyrics and wished he knew whose kiss she was craving.

An hour later, tumbled into bed, Ned and Trudy lay wrapped around each other. "I had no idea you could sing like that."

"Don't do it much these days. Who does after high school choir?" She snuggled tighter under his arm. "It was fun, but I don't know if I would have done it even to shut Rick up without that third beer."

"And John's urging," he couldn't stop himself from saying.

"Oh, my. Do I detect a hint of jealousy from the big New York detective?"

"Don't be silly. But he's obviously still infatuated with you." He bit back the words: *And made that obvious.*

"Hmm, infatuation sounds immature. I prefer to think he knows the good one got away."

"You are definitely the good one." He gave her a lingering kiss as the toilet flushed, reminding them Rick and Aidan were right next door. "Let's talk about tomorrow."

"Nice change of subject. I know you're seeing that warden with Paul later in the afternoon."

"He did say he valued my expertise."

"True." She reached over for her phone and pulled up the photos she'd taken from her father's file. "This one's a listing of the things found in Dad's truck." She flicked to the next pages. "There are several receipts, too."

Ned jabbed his finger at the receipts. "I don't have to meet Paul until afternoon. This is where we go tomorrow. Fancy a morning visit to a party store and a meat supplier?"

"Do you think anyone will recall one day from eleven years ago?"

"I've found once you've been interviewed by a detective about a death, you don't forget it. The file shows the names of the people he interviewed."

"Probably true. Okay, I'm game. We won't know unless we try."

Ned hoped he wasn't setting Trudy up for disappointment. "I wonder if these places are even still in business." He planned to keep an eye out for a company involved in Mario's past that would have benefited from an infusion of cash. Who had Mario been close enough to that he would offer such a huge loan?

Trudy gave a wide yawn that ended in a gentle burp and rolled over. "Sorry, beer got to me."

"I thought it was the standing ovation that went to your head." *And John's attention*, he thought, but didn't say out loud.

"You're hilarious."

Only a minute later Trudy was snoring gently, but Ned lay awake in the dark, wondering about ghosts of the past.

# TWENTY-FIVE

*Wednesday*

Doug Dietz closed the front door softly behind him, keeping Rusty on a leash until they reached the park near their house. His mother slept on, the pills their doctor prescribed allowing her a brief respite from her sorrow. Others she took during the day made her a zombie, but he supposed grief hit you like that, and he understood his mother's need to soften the edges of her pain. Nothing would make it go away completely, for any of them.

His father had left earlier, mumbling about needing to clear his desk at work. They hadn't been told when Greg's body would be released yet, but out-of-town relatives would arrive for that. His dad had managed to refuse offers for visits beforehand, but everyone would gather for the eventual funeral. He wasn't looking forward to that. The longer it took the better.

When he left, his father gave Doug instructions not to

disturb his mother. These past few days, his dad acted as if he and Rusty were just that—disturbances that brought visible tension to his father's face, a tightening of the jaw, words spat out through clenched teeth when he spoke to Doug at all.

He was used to being an afterthought, the son who brought home good grades, stayed away from drugs, and lived up to his father's expectations, but had always known he ran second best to his older brother. That all changed with Greg's fall from grace. Now it seemed the sight of Doug was enough to set off his father. School was in session, and while his friends had texted their condolences and a few called, they stayed away, too afraid of being in his father's presence to visit in person, although several of their parents had dropped off condolence cards with casseroles and pound cakes.

Doug had become skilled in staying invisible and keeping rein on the exuberant Rusty. The last thing he needed was for his father to say the dog was an annoyance to his mother and give it away.

These days Doug felt like Rusty was his only friend.

A pair of young mothers pushed strollers and chatted as they walked away from the park. He had the place to himself. His school had sent online work, and his teachers were sympathetic and extended deadlines for the week.

Doug walked deeper into the park. He checked to be certain no one could see him and let Rusty off leash. The Brittany spaniel leapt into a clump of bushes to flush out any doves hiding there. When he was sure he was alone, Doug sat on a bench, dug into the zippered pocket of his jacket, and brought out a small tin containing a few joints and a lighter. Before Greg died, Doug had been saving these for a special party. Screw that.

Doug had no intention of going down the road that hooked his brother. As he took a deep hit on the joint and felt the calm flow throughout his body, he realized Greg had probably told himself the same thing. A pill to keep him awake to study; another to get to sleep; then why the hell not have cocaine at a party, loosen up and feel empowered, like everyone around him was doing?

Only Greg hadn't stopped at party use. Small wonder he'd been caught selling to feed his addiction.

Doug checked for Rusty, who was having a great time snuffling in the bushes for more doves. He thought back to his visits to his brother, facilitated by the permission slip he'd had his mother sign right after Greg was incarcerated. It was tacitly understood between him and his mother that Doug would not mention these visits to his father. His father would only tolerate her calling Greg weekly. She would quiz him for details after each visit. How did Greg look? Was he eating? Were there any signs he'd taken a beating?

The prison had high barbed-wire fencing surrounding its perimeter. Armed guards scrutinized Doug at each visit as if they could see through him, right to his heart, even though he hadn't done anything wrong.

The indignity of the process had surprised him on his first visit. It still had on his last trip, as the line of visitors was herded along like sheep, except he'd gotten used to the women who had to stop in the ladies' room to remove underwire bras. Some of the women brought kids to see their fathers. It was bad enough to be there to see a sibling; he couldn't conceive of saying to a toddler, "Let's go visit Daddy today in prison," as if it were a special outing.

At Doug's early visits, Greg tried to justify his situation, rationalizing he'd gotten hooked so he could keep up his grades and not disappoint their parents. Doug supposed most people would call his father a bully. Doug had had so many years of dealing with his father, that he thought of the man as a figure to listen to and stay on the right side of to keep his own life smooth, with the attendant rewards that gave him. His mother's sweet nature made up for his father's tough side, the light and dark of parenting. She was a gardener and a reader and had taken good care of all of them. There had been family vacations they'd all enjoyed when his father would be more relaxed.

He tried to recall those now, the good times his mother revisited in her photo albums.

It hadn't been all bad, he realized, but it had all gone to shit when Greg was arrested. Now Doug wondered if they'd be able to get beyond Greg's murder.

He took another hit and pinched the end of the joint, stowing it back in the tin for future use. With a jolt of insight, Doug realized his father's recent anger was a form of heartache, too. The rage was for his older son not being stronger, and now taken from them forever, and it spilled onto Doug, the son left standing in front of him.

What had Greg gotten himself into that had led to his murder?

Doug put the tin back in his jacket pocket and pulled up the zipper. He felt the outline of what he'd hidden there. An inner pocket had a ripped lining, and he'd shoved the offending article deep inside when he'd gotten to his car after his last prison visit.

Doug sat back against the cold bench and saw Rusty's wagging tail deep in a large stand of bushes. The chill of the cool cement took him back to his last visit, and Greg's anxious face when he'd told his brother he needed Doug to do something important for him.

"Look, when I get out my bunk will be stripped, and I need to have this when I leave here. It's essential for my future. Hold onto it for a few weeks for me." He lowered his voice. "I managed to get it out of my cell, flattened inside my sock on the bottom of my sneaker."

Doug had no idea what Greg was talking about, but he knew its significance from his brother's face. He realized how serious this was, the risk he'd be taking when Greg explained he would pass Doug a small object. Greg told him to slip it into his pocket without looking at it or attracting the guards' attention, and then slide it into his own shoe in the bathroom before he left the facility. Greg had leaned down and fiddled with his sock, and then put his hand down on the table, covering the small object underneath it.

Doug still remembered he'd broken out in a cold sweat. "What's so important?"

"It's the passport to my future." Greg had looked at the guard at the head of the room. A woman started to argue with one of the guards and a second one came over to chime in.

Before Doug had time to ask more questions, Greg whispered, "Now!" and shoved the object across the table. Doug covered what felt like a tiny notebook with his own hand. "When I tell you, slip it into your pocket."

Doug's stomach turned over. The woman in the front was unpacking her copious bag to show the guards the books she'd brought to give her husband.

Doug heard the head guard explain any reading

material had to come via mail directly from a place like Amazon to the inmate. Greg whispered, "Go!" and Doug tried to casually put his hand holding the offending article into his jacket pocket, hoping no one would notice how his hand shook.

"Now go to the restroom and slide it into your sock under your foot. Keep it somewhere safe. After I'm out, I'll take it off your hands. Not the day I'm released as Mom will be there, but after that when I'm settled and come for dinner one Sunday. Thanks for doing this. I knew I could count on you."

Doug waited a few minutes, the notebook burning like hot coal in his pocket. He stretched and stood up to go to the restroom. His face felt like it was on fire; with each step, he feared the heavy hand of a guard would clamp a hand on his shoulder and yank him aside to search him. A man left the restroom and the scarred door shut behind Doug with a heavy thud. Even though he was alone in the room, he used the stall and followed Greg's instructions, tucking a notebook the size of his palm into his sock, down under his arch, and slipped his sneaker back on. As he washed his hands, Doug knew he would never forget the details of this room, from the curses scrawled on the cement block walls to the chipped mirrors and filthy sinks. He dried his hands under a blower; they still felt dirty.

*DEATH in the ORCHARD*

The rest of the visit passed in a blur of anxiety. Doug knew he had to pass the guards' penetrating stares to leave the facility and tried to keep his expression neutral. After he'd driven away without any scrutiny, Doug had breathed a huge sigh of relief.

He'd seen Greg when he picked him up from the prison but hadn't gone inside. After an emotional reunion with his mother, Greg had taken his car and driven away from the prison, and Doug rode home with his mother in the family car. Doug watched the taillights of his brother's car as he drove to his hostel to check in. He must have relished his freedom. Doug wondered if Greg had stopped along the way at a fast-food place for a burger or gone into a store to get himself ice cream or a snack, just to feel like a real person again without constraints on what he could buy or eat, where he could go.

Now he wished he'd told Greg how much he loved him and how he was proud of his brother for getting off the drugs, but all Doug had said was that he would handle things, and he'd see Greg soon. That was the last time he'd seen his brother alive.

He'd left the notebook in the lining of his jacket, stowed in his room, afraid to look at it until Sunday night when that lieutenant had come over to tell them Greg had been killed. It had been a shocking and emotional few hours after that, their family doctor calling in sedatives after a call from the policeman. He remembered Lt. Hoffmann had sent another officer to pick up the medication his mother took, but mostly things passed in a blur amidst calls to family his father made, as Doug tried to grasp he'd never see Greg alive again. He had retrieved the notebook after his parents had gone to bed, his mother with a pill on board and his father deep in his bourbon.

The little book had been wrapped in a paper towel that smelled like his brother's foot. He couldn't bring himself to throw it away. He unwrapped a small journal and slipped the paper into his desk drawer. Then he'd examined the little book before opening it, using his ruler to measure it out. 4 x 2 1/2 inches, with a blue outer cover and printed on the inside front cover, "Moleskine." He'd never seen a notebook so small.

He'd flipped the pages and saw tiny cramped handwriting unlike Greg's. At least not the Greg he knew, but then could drug use change his writing? There were lists of numbers next to dates on the first and last pages, and in the middle, several pages of what looked like a story. When Doug read it, the hair stood up on the back of his neck and he felt sick to his stomach.

He'd shoved the journal back in the lining of his jacket, not wanting to face what it all meant.

But the presence of that little book over the last three days had brought him here today, and with another glance to be certain he was still alone, Doug fished out the journal and re-read the words that had shaken him to his core.

Worst of all, he couldn't ask Greg if these were his words, his actions.

If they were Greg's, his brother had been a murderer.

Ned drove the Benz to Party Hearty, his hair still shower-damp after his early morning run, where he'd followed Aidan in a route through the woods that encircled the orchard. Trudy explained the shop was one of several event supply stores spread over the area. Mario Genova had visited it hours before he died.

"Meg was impressed when we talked this morning and I told her I sang last night," Trudy said.

"So was everyone who heard you. You surprised me."

"Stick with me, kid. I'm full of surprises."

"I think maybe you are." He ignored Trudy's sharp turn of her head in his direction and pulled into the parking lot. They entered the store, a colorful hodge-podge of aisles of plastic and paper goods, in solid colors and with different holiday themes. Halloween costumes hung in racks near the door, being picked over by a gaggle of teens, while helium balloon bouquets were weighted down and tied together in bunches behind the checkout. One wall held flat, unfilled balloons with numbers for ordering, plus banners to be personalized.

"Promise me you'll never get me an 'Over the Hill' balloon," Ned said.

"Message received." Trudy saluted. They headed straight for the front counter where the cashier handed a Spiderman costume in a plastic bag to a young boy and the receipt to his mother and turned to the man next in line, who looked suspiciously familiar to Ned.

As the man placed his carton on the counter, he noticed them when he brought out his credit card, and the man's face lit up.

"Trudy! I don't see you for years and then twice in 24 hours." John Maydan pulled her in for a long hug.

Ned stifled a groan. This guy was all over the place.

John released Trudy, who turned to Ned and shot him a look. *Be nice.*

John extended his hand as the clerk totaled his bill. "It's Ned, right?" John's handshake was firm but not overdone. "Good to see you again. You're one lucky guy."

Ned resisted the urge to put his arm around Trudy as he answered. "A fact I'm very aware of." What was wrong with him? He sounded like a stilted character from a

*DEATH in the ORCHARD*

Regency novel.

The clerk broke in. "If you'll sign this, please."

John turned back and completed the sale.

Trudy laced her fingers through Ned's hand and squeezed. When John turned back he hoisted his carton onto his shoulder and stepped away, taking in their clasped hands. "Great to see you again. The singing offer at the Night Owl stands open for you, Trudy, anytime."

"Thanks, John, I'll keep that in mind."

*What was that supposed to mean?* Ned watched John's back as he left and they stepped up to the counter. He squared his shoulders.

"Detective O'Malley to see the manager, please."

The young woman didn't flinch, as if a detective came into the store every day. She spoke into a loudspeaker. "Manager to checkout, please."

Ned and Trudy stood to one side and waited while a few more people checked out. One flustered man rushed in and ordered a bunch of pink "It's a Girl!" balloons, and they watched his sleep-deprived but radiant face as he picked out a box of pink bubble gum cigars. The cashier expertly filled one, knotted it off, added a clip to keep it closed, then tied on white and pink curling ribbons. She'd done three when a man approached them. Ned saw Trudy's face fall. This man was far too young to have worked here eleven years ago.

"Whadda ya need, Sue?"

Ned stepped forward. "Detective Ned O'Malley. I need to speak to any employee who worked here eleven years ago."

The manager frowned. "Gee, I've been here six but there's a lot of turnovers in a store like this, you know?" He thought hard for a moment, then shook his head. "Nope, can't think of anyone who's been here that long other than Mr. Chang, the owner. You're in luck; he's here today." He gestured toward the back of the store. "Come with me."

Trudy and Ned followed the manager through the store to a set of swinging doors at the back that he opened to a receiving and storage area filled with rows of tall metal shelves holding stock. A small office sat partitioned off in one corner, next to a time clock and a rack of attendance cards.

Windows into the office gave Ned a view of the slender Asian man who sat behind the desk and worked at a computer. The manager knocked on the door and was waved in. He opened the door and pointed to Ned and Trudy. "Mr. Chang, there's a detective here who needs to speak with you."

The owner stood and motioned them inside and shook hands as Ned introduced them. "Jimmy Chang. Please, have a seat. How can I help?'

Ned explained they were investigating a cold case from eleven years ago that involved Trudy's father, who had been in the store to pick up an order on the day he died. "Mr. Chang, you were interviewed at the time by a law enforcement officer." He gave him the date. "Do you recall that?"

"Let me think a moment. It was long ago but sounds familiar." He used his mouse to click open a new window. "This was my first store and now I own three," he said, his pride evident as he clicked his way to the page he wanted. "I keep excellent records. Let's look at the date." He added, "I am most sorry for your loss."

"Thank you. We appreciate your help." Ned wondered if Mario was close enough to this man to have lent him a large chunk of cash to buy his other stores. He'd wait to see how well the men had known each other before asking.

"My accountant son says I only need to keep records for seven years, but why have so much memory on this thing if I don't use it, right? I worked hard to have these stores. You never know—Ah, here it is." He turned the monitor on an angle. "Genova, a listing of supplies called in and paid for with a credit card." He looked up at them. "Do you need me to print out a copy of that order?"

"No, thanks, Mr. Chang," Trudy spoke up. "We wondered if you remember anything about my father from that day. I know it's a long time ago, but it could be important."

"I didn't know your father personally, but I do recall now when the officer at the time asked about this."

That answered one of Ned's questions.

"I was more hands-on then. The blue and green color combo was an unusual mix, and I filled the order the day before myself as we were short-staffed. This man—your father—he was anxious to get on the road and was waiting when I opened. He said he had two more stops to make. I had the cashier help him carry the boxes to a pickup truck. Does that help at all?"

Ned saw Trudy had picked up on what Mr. Chang had said. "Two stops *after* your store? You're sure he said two?"

Chang nodded vigorously. "Yes, because he said he had to take things home to his little puppy, and we laughed when I thought he was having a party for his dog. No, he said, it is a nickname for my daughter, my little princess."

I was flushed with excitement when we thanked Mr. Chang for his help and left the store.

"Two stops, Ned. My father had another stop planned

after he picked up the deli meats, one he knew he was going to when he left our house that morning. Why didn't this come up before?"

"Maybe if Mr. Chang said 'two stops,' whoever interviewed him thought he meant the party store and the meat supplier, and didn't catch the significance of what was in reality a third stop."

"I hope Mr. Jablonski will know more about it. He must be pushing seventy now. I used to ride with Dad on school holidays to get the meats and cheeses for the café. Mr. Oskar would give me a slice of bologna or cheese. Dad and I would sing in the car on the way back." I realized I found these poignant memories of my father to be comforting.

"Let's hope he has even a better memory than Mr. Chang."

"He knew Dad better. We've been going there for the meat order for years."

We drove over to the meat supplier, which had a retail delicatessen up front. The wholesale orders were picked up from a back entrance, but I told Ned to park by the main entrance. We could order lunch to eat in the car, as he had to meet Paul Hoffmann later to travel to Troy Correctional. No time for a meal out.

A sign in red over the door picked out in flowing script read: *Jablonski's Old Worlde Deli.* One side of the sign sported an American flag and on the other, the broad red and white stripes of the flag of Poland with the notation, **Oskar Jablonski, Prop**. Both signs showed their age, and I noted Ned's appraising glance.

We entered a world of savory smells that assaulted our senses and made my mouth water. There was an overlying tang of vinegar and pickling spices. Salamis, pastrami, roast beefs, hams, and other meats waited to be sliced behind glass counters, with blocks of cheeses that ranged from mild to salty. Salads included the expected coleslaw and several varieties of potato salad, but we could also order cucumbers in sour cream with dill, sweet and sour red cabbage, potato and cheese pierogi, and my favorite, crispy potato pancakes.

A hanging board listed "Sandwich Favorites" with suggestions for combinations. Opposite the main counter, a cold case held bulk selections of sausages and meats for sale. A short line of customers was served by two men behind the counter, with another cooking at a grill. I checked them all out; one looked familiar. It *had* been eleven years, I reasoned, disappointed I didn't recognize more of the servers, except the handsome young man with auburn hair who stirred my memory. He waited on us as we gave our orders: a Reuben made with kielbasa sausage for Ned, and three warmed potato pancakes with applesauce for me.

*DEATH in the ORCHARD*

As he wrote down our orders, I asked the young man if Mr. Oskar was still around, then held my breath, hoping he wouldn't tell me the owner was off that day.

Instead, he asked, "Who should I say wants him?"

"Tell him Trudy Genova is here to see him."

"I thought that was you." He barked out our orders to the grill man as my recollection clicked. This was Jan Jablonski, Oskar's son. He'd been a teenager when I last saw them. But then, so had I.

Jan opened the door to the back and shouted, "Pops, Trudy Genova's here to see you." I heard a rumble from deep on the other side before the door swung closed. "He'll be right out."

A moment later the swinging door opened again, and Mr. Oskar emerged. The tall, broad man wiped his hands on a towel hanging from his apron and hung a clipboard on a hook outside the door. His white butcher's coat was spotless and matched his mostly white hair, which still had streaks of the dark red his son had inherited. When he saw me, a smile lit his face, his pale eyes crinkling with happiness. "Trudy, how good to see you." He held out his arms and enveloped me in a bear hug. My arms didn't reach around him as I inhaled his scent of sandalwood and squeezed him back. "To what do I owe the honor?"

I introduced Ned. "Can we talk for a minute while we wait for our order?"

Mr. Oskar barked instructions in Polish to his son, who nodded. He held one side of the door open and ushered us into the back area I recognized. Large walk-in refrigerators lined one entire wall. Several butchers in bloodied white coats worked at stainless steel tables on cuts of meat or made sausages, all wearing white nets over their hair, and stopped often to wipe down their equipment. Other workers wrapped the butchered meats in clear plastic and weighed them before slapping a price label on each piece. It was a smooth, busy operation.

"In here." Mr. Oskar opened the door to his private office. His desk had neat stacks of paperwork, and clipboards hung from hooks next to it. A computer took up the center. Across the back, leather club chairs ranged by a coffee station. "Come, sit. Jan will bring your orders. I was getting ready for a coffee. Will you join me?"

"No thanks, but please, you go ahead."

I explained our mission as we sat down and he fixed his coffee, stirring in sugar and cream. As I spoke, Mr. Oskar's eyes misted over.

"Trudy, your father was my friend as well as my customer. For years we'd meet here and share a coffee before he headed back to the orchard with his order. I see your brother Ben now, but he doesn't stop for coffee, although he still brings me apple squares or cinnamon buns. How is your mother?"

"Still baking up a storm, Mr. Oskar."

The man sipped his coffee and sat down heavily. "So. You want me to tell you about the last day I saw him."

"We're trying to get a fix on his mood," Ned said. "And see if there's any new information to help us."

Mr. Oskar ran a broad hand over his face. "Trudy, I'll tell you this, he was in a hurry that day, didn't linger as he might have, no *kaffee klatch*."

"Did he mention another stop he'd make after leaving here?"

The man took the time to think back before answering, gazing over my shoulder into the past. "No, but he seemed . . . thoughtful. Almost determined, I'd say. I told the officer who interviewed me his mood was off, quieter than usual."

"Yes, I read that in your statement," Ned said.

"Mario wouldn't say what was bothering him. He wasn't here that long. I'm sorry not to be of more help."

We were interrupted by Jan, who knocked and handed me a paper bag. "On the house, Trudy."

"How kind. Thank you both." Jan went back to the front of the store, and we all stood.

"I know you live in the big city now, Trudy, but don't be a stranger when you come home."

"Thanks for your time, Mr. Oskar." I was disappointed. I'd hoped my father would have told his friend what this third stop would be.

He clasped my hand. "Your father was a good man, Trudy. I know there was speculation around the way he died, but he must have been doing something that made good sense to him at the time."

My antenna twigged. "Why do you say that?"

"When Mario left, I told him I'd see him next week and hoped he'd feel better soon. I thought maybe he was unwell." Mr. Oskar shook his head. "Mario said he wasn't sure he would feel better, but sometimes you had to do things that were unpleasant for the greater good."

# CHAPTER TWENTY-SIX

I gazed out the window as Ned drove us back to Mom's. The rolling hills and mountains wore their autumn russets and golds, while from one hill, coils of wispy smoke rose. Someone was burning leaves, and I could almost smell the acrid scent that signaled fall to me. I'd ridden this route many times before, but the familiar sights blurred together as I reviewed the new information we'd learned.

"I suppose that wasn't a wasted trip." I tried to glean positivity and not feel we'd wasted half the day.

Ned reached over and squeezed my hand. "It wasn't wasted at all. We learned from Mr. Chang your father had a third stop planned, which means it was pre-arranged before he left that morning. And Mr. Oskar told you whatever your father was doing, there was a worthy motive behind it from Mario's point of view."

"One that got him killed, though," I added. "It would be just like Dad to go tilting at windmills in some misguided idea he could make a difference."

"But that can't have been the intended outcome, Trudy. Based on what everyone has said, your dad sounds like he was an idealist."

I pondered the meaning of that word as it applied to my father. "He was a person who believed in honor. It was important to him. I remember he told us as kids over and over, 'It's not what you say but what you do that defines you.'"

"There you go. An 'actions speak louder than words' kind of guy. We must figure out what would make him feel he had to step in and try to make things right."

I shook my head. "I don't know how to make that leap, Ned."

"It's unrealistic to think we can put the pieces together in a few days. We have time, Trudy. This case hasn't been solved in eleven years. I've found a little distance from a situation sometimes lets me see things more clearly. We have new info—let's let that settle. Meanwhile, you visit Gail and I'll help Paul with the Dietz case."

I sighed. "You're right. Helping Paul wrap this up would at least be one good outcome from this week. I'm frustrated, Ned. I had this unrealistic idea you and I would stumble across something everyone else missed and solve this quickly."

"I still think we can. You knew your father better than any stranger looking into things, me included. Mr. Oskar

*DEATH in the ORCHARD*

gave us a new angle to consider."

I mulled this over. Ned was right. I needed to step back to figure out what would have made my father rush into a situation I couldn't see right now, and to do that, I'd need to take a little time to chill my brain. If I could help Ned and Paul, it would clear Rick at the same time. While Ned went in one direction, I'd go in another.

We were nearing the orchard when I told Ned to drop me at the barn. "I'll check in with Rick and Aidan, and then stop to see Gail. We've been meaning to take photos of my parents' anniversary pear tree for Instagram. See you later at the house."

"Invite the guys out to eat with us, my treat." Ned wanted to take Mom and Bob out to dinner tonight and they'd accepted.

"All right, I will." He pulled up in front of the red barn, where the number of cars said Genova Orchards was doing brisk business today. Across the way, a woman walked out of the café carrying a wreath wrapped in bittersweet vines. As I got out of the car, the side door to the  barn opened, and a man carrying two gallons of apple cider emerged.

I leaned over to give Ned a goodbye kiss. "Good luck at the prison. Not a place I'd want to be visiting."

He kissed me back. "Maybe the warden will have an idea what Greg Dietz was involved in that led to his murder."

I waved as he pulled away and I entered the barn inhaling the sweet tang of fresh crushed apples. Customers milled around, checking out the cider and cheeses for sale, while Aidan worked the till, ringing others up. Rick came out of the back, carrying a crate with more cider he placed on the end of the counter, and started to refill the glass-fronted fridge that held half and full gallons of Genova Orchards' fresh cider.

"Let me help with that." In no time at all we'd emptied the crate.

"Thanks. What brings you here?"

I noted the dark circles still under Rick's eyes. Being under suspicion in a murder investigation had taken its toll on my brother. I wanted to put my arms around him and remind him that with the negative GSR test, it was only a matter of time before he would be totally cleared, but I knew not to do that in front of customers. My resolve to help clear him intensified. "Ned and I are taking Mom and Bob out to The Bear's Steakhouse tonight. You guys want to join us?"

"Sounds tempting but I've been promised a homecooked meal and night in with Aidan. Ben and Gail going?"

"Mom said Gail has an OB visit this afternoon and they were going to eat in Albany after, a date night. I'm heading to see her now."

"Too late." Rick pointed out the front window, where

Ben drove Gail away in their SUV. "You guys go with Mom and Bob. Enjoy."

"Rick, can I borrow your truck for a while? Ned's off somewhere and I need wheels."

"Sure." He rummaged in his pocket for the keys. "Going anywhere special?"

I hesitated before replying. "Not sure yet. Need to pick up a few things."

"Leave it here if we're home when you bring it back. I'll ride with Aid in the morning."

"You mean don't stray near the cabin and disturb your night alone."

He smiled. "You read me too well."

"Hey, you working today or lounging around?" Aidan's line had gone down and he stood at the fridge, checking inventory. "We could use more goat cheese in here."

"Message received." Rick stooped to give me a quick kiss on the cheek. "Have fun, Trudster. Be careful."

I pocketed the keys. "Why would I need to be careful?"

"Because I know you, and trouble is your middle name."

Ned drove off after he dropped Trudy at the barn, thinking over their two stops this morning. The financial aspect didn't seem to apply to Mr. Chang's party stores as the man wasn't close to Mario Genova. Mr. Jablonski's shop was a different story.

The building that housed the store might need freshening outside but looked sturdy inside. Although the cost of meats and cheeses had skyrocketed in the past years, the business seemed substantial, too. He'd ask Tony to have one of their contacts unearth the financials of the meat supplier and see if there was any hint of an infusion of cash eleven years ago.

He wasn't surprised when Paul Hoffmann readily agreed to his offer to drive the Benz to Troy Correctional instead of riding in a patrol car. He'd seen the glow in the lieutenant's eyes when the officer had first spied the vintage car. They spent most of the ride talking about the car and its restoration. It turned out Paul's family had owned several classic Mercedes at one time, and he had a fondness for them.

"You can drive her home if you'd like," Ned offered once he heard that.

"I might take you up on that." Paul paused, and Ned had the feeling the man was debating what he said next. "As far as you're concerned, I've deputized you to help on this case."

Ned read between the lines. Paul needed to cover them both. "You did mention yesterday that you'd appreciate my help as I have more homicide experience. I figured that meant you'd added me to your team temporarily for the time I'm up here."

Paul nodded. "Good. Now I feel more comfortable sharing information on the case. We've been checking the backgrounds of the men at Dietz's hostel. One of them has a prior conviction over an out-of-control bar fight but nothing to do with guns. A guy hit his head on the end of the bar and sustained permanent brain damage. Another hostel guy was charged with inciting the fight, verbally setting off the two guys who got into it; he's on probation. His wife made him leave, which is why he's staying at the hostel."

"Okay. He's of interest to you because . . ."

"Because he legally owned a .45 which we confiscated last evening from the wife and sent to ballistics to compare to the shot that killed Dietz."

Ned signaled and took the exit for the prison. "Who is this guy?"

"Vince Russo. Works at Genova Orchards."

"I can talk to Rick and Aidan tonight and see what they have to say about the guy."

"Hmm. Let's wait till we get the ballistics report. We know where he is."

As he navigated the curving roads, Ned thought of what they could hope to achieve in this meeting. "You know this warden well?"

"Steve Northrup. We've talked a few times, usually a discussion over an inmate being released to our area. Met him at a law enforcement conference where he was a speaker. Seems like a reasonable guy, interested in restorative justice."

The hills they drove through undulated in pleasing bends and twists stretching up the incline to the mountains. Thrown down into the middle of this Impressionist landscape like a Brutalist installation, Troy Correctional Facility sat in stiff, boxy lines, with curling ribbons of razor wire scrolled out across the top of extensive metal fencing. It looked cold and harsh because it had to be, Ned reasoned. Nothing comfy or homey to see here.

Ned swung the Benz through to the guard post lane and stopped to show their IDs. He parked where directed and pocketed the keys as they walked to the main entrance. Two staffed towers at opposite corners of the compound looked out over a large expanse of clipped lawns; dusty recreation grounds held a group who'd shed their jackets to play hoops, while others lounged against a wall launching insults. A perimeter trail showed several groups of walkers all dressed in dark green shirts and pants with matching quilted jackets. He and Paul could hear shouts as they walked to the entry door, the heckling a mixed bag of jeers and needling from the basketball game:

"*Mierda*! Stuff it in his face!"
"You pussy! You missed by a mile!
"Who taught you to dunk, *cabron*?"

The compound had wings spread out from a central core that held the entry. CCTV had eyes on them as the door opened after Paul spoke into an intercom and they were buzzed in.

"From above this place looks like a giant letter H," Paul commented. A correctional officer behind a counter verified their appointment and took copies of their IDs, then gave them instructions to store their guns, keys, and cell phones in small lockboxes. While they stowed their gear, the guard made a call for another officer, who would take them to the warden's office.

Ned read the posters and announcements on the wall, notices about what could and could not be brought into the facility, and details on what foodstuffs could be mailed in. The odor of strong disinfectant indicated the floor had been recently mopped. He could imagine on visiting days the stringent lemony odor would quickly be overlaid with the perfume and body odors of visitors.

Rows of benches ran along the walls, decorated with carved graffiti from years of bored children waiting to see incarcerated parents.

The inner door buzzed open, and a new officer called out: "Hoffmann and O'Malley? This way."

The officer escorted them down a short hall painted the institutional shade of green that quickly became gray and sickly. He stopped in front of a robust metal door where a gold name plate read: *"Warden Steven Northrup,"* and used his card to buzz them in, then stepped aside to allow them to enter a reception area. Rows of filing cabinets and two computer stations fought for room with two desks. A young man sat at one desk and ignored them. An older woman sat at the larger desk, her frosted gray hair sprayed into a stiff helmet, but her smile warm and cheery.

"Welcome to Troy, gentlemen. The warden's finishing a call and will be with you in a moment. Can I get you a coffee in the meantime? Water?" She stood and moved to a beverage station in one corner. Ned took a bottle of cold water as the intercom on her desk dinged. "Right this way." She knocked on the interior door and opened it without waiting. The warden, a tall, stocky man, stood to greet them. She said, "Here you go," and closed the door behind them.

Steve Northrup had a bushy dark mustache streaked

with gray to match his hair. He reached out to shake their hands as introductions were made and invited them to sit.

"Thanks for seeing us, Steve," Paul said. "We know you're busy and won't take up too much time."

"After you called, I pulled the files on both Greg Dietz and his bunkmate, Bobby Costello." The warden turned to Ned. "I understand you're assisting Paul with Dietz's murder investigation. Shame, I had hopes for him."

"Paul said you're a big supporter of restorative justice, Warden. Any idea what would have made Dietz a target for someone? He hadn't been outside long."

Northrup opened Dietz's file and flipped a few pages. "None. He got clean quickly and became a model prisoner from then on. Avoided fights and stayed in the background. Helped a lot of the guys with legal forms and letters, worked in the library. Smart guy. He could have put this all behind him."

Paul asked, "You believed he would stay clean?"

Northrup's forehead wrinkled as he hesitated. "He made all the right noises, Paul, but I've seen that before and I'm not naïve. Our national average stinks. In the US almost 44% of released prisoners return their first year out. I had hopes for Greg Dietz, but there's no real way to tell on which side he'd end up."

It was Ned's turn to frown. "No fights or grievances

with someone who's also recently discharged?"

"None. Being Bobby Costello's bunkmate helped prevent that, and Dietz didn't seem naturally confrontational."

Paul spoke up. "What can you tell us about Costello?"

Steve opened a second, thicker file. "Different kettle of fish. Multi-offender for drug running, lastly the Schoharie-Cobleskill area, nicknamed the Mick for an incident years ago where he literally beat someone to death with a baseball bat. Even had the nickname airbrushed on the trunk of his car when he was arrested, right above the smiling face of Mickey Mantle." He flipped a few pages. "Never proven, of course, but that lore made him a legend among the others. Meant most of the guys gave him respect and kept out of his way. That protection extended to Dietz when Costello took him under his wing. Made his time a lot easier than the young man should have expected. He'd normally have drawn trouble from the long termers here, a nice-looking kid from a decent home."

Ned took a drink of water as Steve closed the file and leaned back in his chair, which squealed in protest. "All these guys think there's something special about them we don't know. But we do. They have their quirks and habits. We do unscheduled searches of the cells and find most things they ferret away. In here, anybody will steal

*DEATH in the ORCHARD*

anything, even from guys they consider friends. If the things they hide are harmless, we let them keep them, like books, Bibles, or magazines. Some of those things they're allowed to have, of course, but many still hide them to prevent them going walking."

"What did Bobby hide?" Ned asked.

"Any books or supplies must be sent in by an approved source directly to the inmate. Amazon's a giant here. Bobby used his stipend to order these little Moleskine journals, had them sent in regularly. Then kept stacks of them lined up under his mattress by date, filled with recollections and his daily activities here." Steve shrugged. "Maybe he was planning to write a memoir when he got out, but cancer got him first. Pancreatic; never stood a chance."

*Dead, so no chance to interview him about Greg Dietz.* Ned had to work to keep his mouth closed. "Where would those journals be now?"

"Sent back to his next of kin after he died. A cousin I recall, who probably tossed them as soon as they arrived. Bobby burned a lot of bridges, familywise." Steve tented his fingers. "Funny thing, though. When we packed up his things, the officer on his wing noted one of the journals was missing."

Ned sat up straighter. "Which one?"

"The earliest one. Covered the months leading up

to his arrest and soon after. He was caught near here, running drugs to Canada."

"What was the date of that arrest?"

Steve consulted Bobby Costello's file. "July 6th, eleven years ago."

This time Ned couldn't hide the chill that ran through him as he looked at Paul. "That's the day Trudy's father was murdered."

# CHAPTER TWENTY-SEVEN

I drove Rick's truck slowly, crawling up the orchard drive past people returning to their cars. I kept an eye on a toddler straining to break free from his mother's hand. There had been no sightings of more reporters this week, and I doubted they would show up now, days after Greg Dietz's body had been found.

It helped that the police presence had been at the rear of the orchard property. There hadn't been crime scene tape in the public areas to attract attention. Mom said she and Bob, who always watched the late local news for the next day's weather, heard the story on Monday evening and not since. It had been limited to the anchor noting that "the body of a young man from Cobleskill has been found in Schoharie, an apparent murder. Police are investigating." No mention of Rick or the orchard. No wonder we'd only had one newshound show up. It seemed possible someone living in the area might not have connected the murder with our orchard if they'd heard that news story. Had the public become so inured to multiple killings in big cities that one body in a rural setting didn't merit more airtime?

Still, it was a small mercy for my family and the business.

I paused to pair my phone to Rick's Bluetooth and headed toward Cobleskill, my plan coalescing in my mind. I wanted to learn more about Greg to figure out who would have wanted to kill him. Know the victim; know the killer, I'd learned from Ned.

I called Gail as I drove. "Bad time? Sorry I missed you at home."

"Good time. We're on our way to a routine check and Ben's choice of music is driving me nuts."

"Don't tell me he's still on that country western kick."

"Soon it will be Willie Nelson and I'll have to shut the radio off."

"Don't even think about it!" I heard Ben's voice in the background.

"What's up?" Gail asked.

"I need to vent. You can just listen."

"Turn that up," Gail told Ben. "Go ahead now. I've got this phone clamped to my ear and he can't hear."

I shared the story of the Night Owl and John Maydan, having three beers and singing, and then running into him again at the party store. "I know it was a high school crush, but at the time it seemed so important. He was happy to see me, and he's divorced now. He's still hot! But that's all in the past."

"Of course it is. Certainly."

I couldn't tell if she was being serious or poking fun at me. "I mean it. Dead end. Totally. It was good to see him, but he's not in my life anymore, divorced or not. But Ned seems jealous. I don't know how I should handle it."

"My advice? Enjoy the attention. Leave it alone. Stay mysterious. Let Ned be a bit jealous."

"I suppose you're right."

"You're not this insecure to have to worry about Ned. He seems devoted. John was lovely but he's not your present; he's your past. In the words of *Frozen*'s Elsa, let it go!"

We hung up and I took the streets to the Dietz home feeling better. Gail was always my voice of reason. I arrived and drove past the huge Colonial and parked. If Gerald Dietz were home, I had no interest in exposing myself to his wrath again and doubted I'd learn anything useful from him. Cindy Dietz might be a better bet. I scanned what I could see of the side and part of the rear garden, but she wasn't visible.

After twenty minutes I slammed the steering wheel in frustration. I couldn't sit here all day. Either I had to come up with a great excuse to ring the bell, or this had been a fool's errand. Then I looked down the street, where it ended at a small park, and a familiar orange and white spaniel ran loose.

Rusty. And where Rusty was, there would surely be Doug Dietz. Unless somehow the dog had gotten loose, and then Rusty would be my excuse to ring the Dietzes' bell.

I put the truck in gear and pulled up shy of the park. No sign of Doug, but as I walked into the park, Rusty noticed me and came bounding up, dropped a tennis ball at my feet, and burrowed his wet muzzle into my hand.

"Rusty, how are you, boy?" I picked up the slobbery ball and discreetly wiped my hand on his coat as I looked around for Doug. I tossed the ball deeper toward the trees, and Rusty tore off after it. Motion out of the corner of my eye caught my attention, and I saw Doug sitting on a swing, legs dangling in the sand beneath it, head down.

I walked over to the swings, nodding to an older man walking a Scottie dog with a tartan collar and matching leash. The man nodded back and cast a disapproving glance at Rusty running off leash as he left the park.

Doug raised his head and noticed me, but stayed on the swing and lowered his head again. I sat next to him.

"Hi, Doug. How're you doing?"

He shrugged and dug his feet into the sand to push off and take a gentle glide forward and back while dragging his feet.

I mirrored his actions. "Sorry. That was a foolish question."

"At least you didn't bring a casserole." One side of his mouth lifted in the ghost of a lopsided grin.

"One pie was enough." My heart lurched for this young man's pain. I pushed off and let my swing glide. Doug lapsed into silence. Quiet reigned until a bird chirped in a nearby tree and was answered by another, deeper into the park. A light breeze ruffled the crisp leaves fallen near us.

"No school?"

He shook his head. "They sent work online and gave me the week off."

Rusty returned the ball, panting, and hesitated between us, unsure whose feet he should drop it at. Doug won out. He tossed the ball high into the trees and the spaniel took off, barking with delight. Doug made eye contact and we shared a brief smile.

I looked for a point of connection. "Brothers are weird creatures, aren't they? I can't figure mine out and I've known them all my life."

His face drooped, tinged with sadness. "Tell me about it." He shook his head. "I thought I knew Greg, but he hid a lot from me." He stopped gliding and turned to me. "How many brothers do you have?"

"Two, both older. The one you met, Rick, and Ben."

"Rick seemed nice. I mean, he didn't deck my father when he was being an asshat to him, so he must be okay."

"You heard your father's tirade the other day?"

The young man nodded. "Running interference for my mom, keeping an eye on how he treats her. The Dietz wrath knows no bounds. Sorry he zeroed in on your brother."

"Rick's fine," I said. "But it's been tough for him being under suspicion for your brother's death—which I assure you he had nothing to do with—he'd only known Greg a few weeks. You can see why I'm trying to help clear his name."

"Sure." Doug pushed off to glide again. "I liked watching my father rage when the police checked out his guns. Then they swabbed our hands and I thought his face would turn purple."

"My boyfriend's a detective, and he says it's standard for anyone close to the, um, person in a fatal shooting." I winced inwardly. I'd almost called his brother a victim, and while it might be the truth, it sounded more like the language of a crime drama instead of the cold reality Doug was experiencing.

"Didn't bother me. I didn't shoot Greg."

Rusty returned, and this time I was the lucky recipient of the wet ball.

Doug said, "If you throw it higher into the trees, he'll

be gone longer looking for it."

"The voice of experience." I tossed the ball as high and hard as I could, into the bushy trees across the back of the park. Rusty careened into the thicket and was gone from sight. "I envy his energy."

"He's my best friend." Doug frowned. "I used to think Greg was, but now I think I didn't know him at all."

This was the second time Doug had alluded to not knowing his brother. I had the feeling he had something else to say. "Because he was killed?" I probed.

Another elaborate shrug, accompanied by a shuddering sigh.

Definitely more here than Doug had told me. "Another thing my boyfriend says he always thinks about in an investigation is the phrase *cui bono*. That's Latin for—"

"*Who benefits.* I took Latin for two years."

"Smart move. Latin is the root of many words. You interested in medicine?"

"I'm supposed to decide by graduation this June, but other than going to college, I don't know what I want to do."

"You'll figure it out. Getting back to Greg, can you think of anyone who would benefit from his death?"

Doug shook his head, then abruptly stood and whistled. Rusty came bounding back as he said, "I need to check on my mom. Thanks for coming by."

"Doug, wait." I felt he'd been right on the cusp of sharing something important with me. "Take my cell number, please."

He hesitated, then took his cell from his jeans pocket and keyed in the number I told him, then gave me his.

"Any time you want to talk, give me a call. No judgment, I promise."

Doug opened his mouth and snapped it shut again. Rusty ran up, panting, and dropped the slimy ball. Doug picked it up and snapped on the dog's leash. Teen and dog left the park without a backward glance.

The Bear's Steakhouse was a family-owned institution, and Ned was pleased Trudy had suggested it. While cuts of prime beef figured prominently on the menu, there were pork and lamb chops, plus a shrimp dish on tonight's menu, as well as a daily homemade soup.

"The old-world ambiance hasn't changed in over fifty years," Bob said, piling sour cream on his baked potato.

"I enjoy it here, but we haven't been in a while," Hildy said.

The low lighting and candle on their table gave Trudy's

face an ethereal quality, highlighting the planes of her face. Ned hoped her distracted air wasn't because she was remembering how enthusiastically John Maydan had seemed to see her again. He mentally shook himself as the others talked about the history of the place.

Ned listened with one ear, aware his English mixed grill steak-and-chop combo tasted delicious, but troubled by the knowledge Bobby Costello had been arrested near Schoharie on the same day Mario Genova had been killed. And Bobby Costello had been Greg Dietz's cellmate. These might be coincidences, but Ned's experience had shown him it didn't pay to ignore those when investigating murder and here were two.

He'd decided not to discuss the specifics with Trudy before dinner, dancing his way past her question about his interview with the warden while they changed for dinner by saying they would talk later in more detail. They needed time for a longer conversation, and by then he might have figured out a lead to follow.

He and Paul had tossed it around on their way back from Troy Correctional. The warden had given them the details about Bobby Costello's incarceration. Since his arrest hadn't been a first offense, Costello had earned a long sentence. Paul thought his car would eventually have been released to the cousin who was his next of kin.

A baseball bat had given Costello his nickname "the

Mick." Dr. Bozzelli thought Mario Genova's death had been precipitated by a crack to the head by such an implement. Third coincidence. They were mounting up.

The missing journal was intriguing, too, covering the same year as Mario's death and Costello's arrest on the same day. Fourth coincidence.

Until these coincidences could be explained, it was reasonable to arrive at the conclusion that Bobby Costello had been involved with Mario's death. He could even have been the killer. The question that bothered Ned tonight was *why?* Why would Mario Genova have been involved with Costello in the first place, and why would that lead to his murder? And since this was all speculation, would Trudy be satisfied with a dead killer, if they could even work out the rest?

While it was true a clearly established motive wasn't necessary if there was sufficient evidence to prove a crime, he still needed more of that to brand Costello a killer. A motive tended to convince a jury. In this case, there would be no jury except Trudy, who he thought wouldn't be satisfied with only knowing *who* killed her father if she didn't also know *why*. Establishing if a link existed between Bobby Costello and Mario Genova could resolve their investigation.

His phone buzzed with a text, and he pulled it from his pocket to glance at it.

It was Larry Long: **Call me**.

Hildy sat back with a satisfied smile. "That was a fine meal. Thank you for a special night out."

"You deserve it, Hildy." Ned wondered if it would be rude to call Long back now.

"You'll spoil her, Ned," Trudy said with a smile.

"Hildy deserves to be spoiled, Trudy." Bob clasped Hildy's hand.

The waitress removed their plates and listed the desserts on hand. ". . . and we have homemade strawberry cheesecake as our special tonight."

"Their portions are huge. Let's share a slice," Hildy suggested.

Ned ordered coffees all around and three forks. "Back in a minute. I need to return a call." He excused himself and walked outside to call Larry Long. The night had turned colder, and he pulled his jacket closer. Leaves crunched underfoot and swirled in a breeze around his ankles as he walked away from the noise of the building. The retired detective answered on the third ring.

"O'Malley, finally dug out those notebooks and found the one for the Genova case."

"Anything of interest?"

"At first glance, I nearly put it aside. Seemed to me almost everything I'd noted had gone into my final report."

"You said, 'almost.'"

"See, I knew you were a good detective. I had a notation circled in the margin on one page. The letter Y followed by the letter T, both in caps, with a small 's' and a question mark."

"YT's?"

"Yup. I'll take a photo and text it to you."

Ned pictured the notation. "What does it mean?"

"That's the problem. I've been wracking my brain, but after all this time I can't remember."

I slid into bed next to Ned wearing a Hamilton sweatshirt and clingy yoga pants to combat the chill. With Rick and Aidan gone, I expected Ned to return to the room they'd vacated, but he hadn't moved back into the guest room. Neither had he bridged the gap between us in terms of intimacy. It seemed his rule of chivalry meant he could share a bed but not have sex with his girlfriend under her family's roof, and now he had me doubting if I would be comfortable if we did. Part of me was impressed with his restraint and part of me thought it was absurd, considering everyone in said family assumed we were sleeping together, which we were, but sleep was all that was happening. I'd make sure to rectify that as soon as we returned to Manhattan. The lure of my own bed, my cat, my job, and a long night of privacy with Ned loomed with such attraction I could almost taste my frustration.

We were so new we had a lot to learn about each other. Ned was entitled to his feelings about the situation, and I should respect them since he'd assured me more than once it wasn't from lack of passion or wanting me.

But I wasn't going to let him off the hook when it came to ignoring what he'd learned with Paul Hoffmann today. He'd been unusually silent on the subject. And there was the call he'd taken at dinner. We were a team, which meant sharing information. I'd go first, to remind him of that.

"Great meal," I said as I snuggled up to Ned's side, pressing my breasts against his torso. Just a friendly reminder. Okay, I couldn't always let things go. I told him about my afternoon drive to Cobleskill and my conversation with Doug Dietz in the park. "He's hiding something about his brother. I thought he was ready to confide in me, but then he shut down."

"Out of fear?" Ned stroked my upper arm.

I pictured Doug's face filled with sorrow and something else. "More like disappointment? Maybe it was fear." I burrowed closer and moved my leg over his body. "Your turn."

Ned cleared his throat. "Larry Long called during dinner."

"Great. Did he find anything?"

"A definite maybe." Ned took his phone from the night table and explained the margin scribble while he showed me the photo Larry had sent.

I sat up. "YTs? Which means what?"

"That's the problem—he can't recall. He promised to sleep on it, and if he does remember, he'll call back."

"Maybe not concentrating so hard will bring the meaning flooding back." I clutched Ned's phone with both hands. YTs? Young Teenagers? Yard Time? Yellow Toes? What could those letters mean?

"Maybe."

I handed back his phone. "What about the meeting with the warden?"

Ned exhaled and plunged into the story of Greg Dietz's bunkmate, drug runner Bobby Costello.

When he told me the day Costello was arrested, my eyes grew rounder and my mouth hung open.

# CHAPTER TWENTY-EIGHT

*Thursday*

I tossed and turned, most of the night, wondering if my father had been involved with a drug runner while my thoughts ran wild. How could he have met this man? *Why* would he? And if what Ned thought was accurate, this Bobby Costello could be the man who murdered my father.

But that knowledge didn't come with the kind of relief I thought I'd find. If we proved this to be true, it raised more questions than it answered. My thoughts ran round and round, pulling up old memories of the few times my father had lost his temper and acted out.

The incident that stood out in my memory was when a Little League father had harassed his own child repeatedly from the stands for his poor performance. The boy buckled under his father's wrath and struck out.

The abuse that flew from the father's mouth was enough to send my father into the stands, where he dragged the man down and shouted at him to leave the grounds. He would bring his wife and son home after the game. A pushing match ensued until my father threw a punch that missed, but the man ducked and fell. By then other parents had circled the men, and kept the other man from hitting my father, finally escorting him from the field. He'd shouted obscenities at Dad as he left, and I remembered my mom had worried about the incident. But that had happened so many years ago when my brothers were young. I didn't even recall the family's name and it seemed too long ago to have any bearing here.

But what if there had been that kind of incident more recently, one I didn't know about, around the time of my father's death?

I woke with bags under my eyes when Ned was out on his run. I'd thought of sneaking into Ned's shower to surprise him and found I couldn't muster the effort. I couldn't summon up enthusiasm for my yoga class and skipped it. Even pulling on my favorite teal sweater didn't help my mood.

Right after breakfast, Mom and Bob left for Ben and Gail's to work on the mural. Ned suggested we have a meeting in the office after he called to check on his father. When I met him there, Ned drew up a second chair, and we sat at the desk next to each other.

"Paddy doing all right?" I liked Ned's parents.

"Mom's cracking the whip. He's doing his exercise and sticking to the heart-healthy diet. All good." He looked at me. "Let's go over what we know, maybe keep you from tossing through another night."

"Sorry I kept you awake." I plunged in. "The day Dad was murdered we know he had a third appointment no one knew about. You've told me before you don't like coincidences."

Ned dipped his head in agreement. "I don't. But let's think this through. It's likely Greg Dietz didn't know Bobby Costello before they became bunkmates. A campus dealer is in a different league from a drug runner with his own territory. Plus, there's the age difference."

"Luck of the draw for bunkies."

"Sure. But for that bunkmate to then arrive at Genova Orchards for work and be found dead shortly after?" He shook his head. "There's a connection that evolved over their time sharing a cell."

I rose and paced to the front window, trying to put my jumbled thoughts in some kind of coherent order. I could see the vehicles my family owned parked at the barn and the café, with Bob's car in Ben's drive. There were people entering the café, and a woman left carrying a white box filled with Mom's baked goodies. The side door to the café opened and Ben emerged, carrying a carton to his SUV in preparation for a delivery. I'd decided to stop worrying about us. He and I might disagree right now, but there was blood between us. We'd figure it out.

Here I was, trying to examine events of eleven years ago, looking for insights, while all that time my family had been living and working in the shadow of our father's death. They'd carried on while I'd escaped to nursing school and the city. I didn't face what they'd all had to deal with daily, but it seemed they had all moved past it in their own way.

I was trying to finally resolve the issue for my peace of mind, but at what cost if there were painful revelations? No wonder Ben was upset with me. I couldn't imagine telling any of my family that our father might have been involved with a drug dealer, or that the man who was likely responsible in some way for Dad's death was beyond justice.

My breath frosted the windowpane. "Last night when you told me about Bobby Costello's arrest the day my father died, and then his connection to Greg Dietz, I knew you were on the path to answers and this was no fluke." I turned to face him. "But for the life of me, Ned, I can't see how my father could be connected with a drug runner. I spent most of the night going back over my memories of Dad's personality, and his actions around that time."

I came back to the desk and sat one hip on the corner, counting off on my fingers. "First, there was never a hint of any kind of drug use by him. Second, he didn't know any addicts except for Jake Graham. He worked hard, went out to dinner or a movie with Mom and their friends on occasion, and coached the boys. My volleyball team was through the school, or he'd likely have coached that, too. Third, his time was well accounted for, between orchard business and our family. He was here so much, so present in our daily lives. It doesn't make sense, and if I doubt him now, it feels like a betrayal." My eyes smarted and I looked away.

Ned reached out and pulled me onto the chair next to him. "Trudy, you knew your father, as did your brothers and your mom. Everyone we've met has reinforced what a great guy your dad was, and even if you've told me his temper could flare, that means you aren't wearing blinders to his personality."

"He wasn't a saint, but he was one of the good ones, Ned." I implored him to believe me.

"Then when the facts don't line up, it means we're looking in the wrong place."

"What do you mean?" I leaned into him, hanging on to his words.

"Maybe it's not Mario we should be looking at, but someone he was close to, someone he tried to help."

"That makes a whole lot more sense to me." I was already grabbing my notebook. "Where do we start?"

Ned explained his thinking to Trudy. "We examine your father's close daily contacts and friends around the time of his death. You make a list of those people while I call Paul Hoffmann and come at this from the Costello end. We're looking for a point of convergence, right?" He paused. Would she include her mother and brothers on the list? Should she?

Trudy nodded and went to the window seat, where she flipped to a fresh page in her notebook. Ned called Paul and asked if he'd been able to find information on Bobby Costello's car beyond the make and model the warden had given them.

"Have it right here. The car was impounded and searched for drugs hidden elsewhere. It was kept until Costello was sentenced and then released, minus that spare tire that held the drugs, to his listed next-of-kin, the cousin the warden mentioned, one Sal Costello." Paul rattled off an address in the Bronx.

"I'll get my partner right on that."

"Great. Let me know what you find out. We need to explore this connection with Costello that may have led to Dietz's death."

"We're on the same page." Ned rang off and looked up to find Trudy, lips pursed, staring out the window. She stood up.

"I'm having issues remembering Dad being friends with more than a few people. I mean, he was pleasant to people he met and knew a lot of them, but the ones I can think of that he'd been truly close to are only a few."

"Who do you have so far?"

"To start, Bob Riley and Wynn Graham. He knew Mr. Jablonski well and I'd call them friends. but they didn't see each other outside work. Oh, he was good friends with Mr. Ames at the hardware store, too. Think I'll walk over to Ben and Gail's and ask Mom. I owe Gail a hug anyway. Maybe this afternoon I should try to talk to Doug Dietz again. I know he was holding out on me."

"I'll call my precinct while you check with your mom."

Trudy kissed his cheek and left the room. Ned dialed his New York partner, who answered on the first ring. "Anything for me?"

"We caught a break in that case from the summer that's been on the back burner, the snatch-and-grab ring where the bodega owner was shot," Tony said.

"I remember it."

"Shooter beat up his girlfriend one time too many. She grabbed her stuff and ran for a women's shelter. They convinced her to turn him in."

"Sweet. You find any backup evidence?"

"Sure did. This guy was laughable. He stashed the gun in the AC vent—found it in the first ten minutes of the search."

"You're racking up points with the boss, Tony."

"Yeah, the captain's happy. How's it going by you?"

"Since you have nothing to do right now—"

"Ha—spill."

"I need you to check financials on two businesses and one guy and see if they had any kind of issues eleven years ago, or major infusions of cash." Ned gave him the names and addresses of Jablonski's Meats, Ames's Hardware, and Wynn Graham. "No idea if you can work your magic for so long ago but anything would be good. Then I need you to track down Sal Costello, address in the Bronx. Off the record, an information only thing. He's not in any trouble." Ned explained the situation with Bobby Costello and gave him the address.

His partner whistled. "Think this cousin knows something?"

"Not about Mario Genova's death per se, but here's what I need you to find out."

I walked down the drive toward Gail and Ben's house and knocked on the storm door before entering. The house was quiet and felt deserted until I heard a giggle from the nursery.

"It's Trudy," I called out. "Anybody home?"

"In the nursery," Mom called out. As I walked down the hall, she stuck her head out. She had one of my father's worn shirts over her clothes; a spot of blue paint stood out on her forehead.

"I think the paint belongs on the wall." I entered a room transformed in the few days since I'd visited. The crib had been assembled and stood in one corner, draped in an old sheet, as did the glider Gail had chosen. The shower gifts had been stored in the closet, leaving the mural's bright colors to light up the room. Bob stood on a stepladder, carefully painting the wings of a bluebird perched on a high tree branch. Hence the blue paint on Mom's face.

Mom wiped the dab of paint off with a rag. "That's what I get for doing the flower border under Bob's arm."

"Total accident." Bob protested and winked at me. "But we need a break. Good thing you arrived when you did or there might be a blue stripe in your mother's hair next."

I was liking Bob more and more. I checked out the wall. "You're the dynamic duo—what amazing progress. It's a woodland fantasy come to life." I took a moment to admire the small features and shading that made the scene appear to leap off the wall. "You even put veins on the leaves."

"Little details make a big difference." Bob climbed down from the stepladder. "We hope to finish it tomorrow. Your mom has been a great helper." He wrapped an arm around my mother's waist and pulled her in for a hug. I saw her two worlds colliding: wearing my dad's shirt but being close to Bob now.

"Magic meatloaf for dinner tonight, unless you and Ned have plans or more singing in your future." She arched an eyebrow at me and for some reason, I blushed. "Rick and Aidan are coming. Waiting to hear from Ben."

"Sounds great. I love your magic meatloaf. I can help out by putting it together so it's ready for you to pop in the oven later."

"That would be great." Mom handed Bob his water bottle. "What are you up to today?"

"A few interviews." I changed the subject. "Where's Gail?"

"She's over at the shop."

"I'll get to her later then. She and I have a mission to accomplish, but right now I wanted to ask you a question about Dad."

"Excuse me, ladies." Bob discreetly ducked out and I heard the hall bathroom door close.

I chose my words carefully. There was no way I was ready to mention there might be a connection between my dad and a drug runner. "Ned and I are piecing some things together, and I'm trying to recall your close friends around the time he died. You know, people he cared a lot about, not a casual acquaintance."

Mom had the grace not to ask me why, as she sat on a step of the ladder and took a drink from her water bottle. Her forehead wrinkled as she searched eleven years ago in her memory. "Let's see. We saw Bob and his wife, and we four always got along well. Bob and your father would talk opera. There was Wynn Graham, although he was more of your father's friend. We all went out a few times as couples, all six of us, but Mario and Wynn often had lunch or meetings at the Grahams' golf club through the years. Mary lives near Daniel now and I only get a Christmas card from her."

"At the golf club? I thought Dad didn't like golf."

Mom laughed. "He hated it. But they worked on fundraisers for the rehab where Jake Graham was treated. Oh, and he enjoyed Bruce Ames at the hardware store. They could talk about John Deere equipment 'til the cows came home. We never went out as couples, though.

That's where I thought he was . . ."

Suddenly I was sixteen and sneaking a freshly baked cookie from my mom's tray in our old kitchen, trying to convince her I could run down to the hardware store to look for my father, who was late coming home with my party supplies and the meats for Ben's sandwiches. I remembered Mom's hair stuck to the back of her neck from the heat of the ovens. I only had my learner's permit, so she sent Ben instead to the hardware store to hurry my father along. Only he wasn't at the store chatting with Mr. Ames, and Dad never came home again.

"Does Mr. Ames still run the store?"

Mom screwed the cap back on her water bottle. "His daughter partners with him, but he's still there. Those are all the friends your dad spent time with. Between coaching and the orchard, Mario preferred to be with us most of the time."

Bob came back into the room. "You ready to finish those flowers, Hildy, or are we done for today?"

Mom jumped up. "We just got started. You're not getting away that easy, Mr. Riley."

# CHAPTER TWENTY-NINE

I closed the door of the ranch house, intent on hurrying back to Ned, and almost collided with someone coming up the steps. Ben.

"Whoa, Trudster. Where's the fire?"

At least we were back to nicknames. "Wanted to get back to Ned. The mural's looking great."

His face softened. "Gail is so pleased. None of our friends have anything like it. I came home to get her slippers. She insists on staying longer but her feet are aching today. She's training one of the staff on how to update the orchard's social media when she goes on maternity leave."

"I'll let you get on with it then. We want to take a photo together, but it can wait 'til she's free. Maybe I can do a load of wash for her later."

"That would be great. There's a load in the dryer I was going to fold . . ."

"I'll do it. You get her those slippers."

He stepped aside to let me down the stairs and I turned back to him before he opened the door. "See you later, Ben?"

"Wouldn't miss Mom's stuffed meatloaf." He disappeared inside the house, and I felt a stiffness in my back relax.

I walked up the drive to Mom's house and went right into the kitchen, calling out to Ned as I passed the office. I took out the packs of beef, veal, and pork my mom had defrosted overnight. One of her big stainless-steel bowls stood on the island alongside a large baking dish. I sprayed the dish with nonstick spray.

Ned appeared in the doorway. "You're cooking dinner?"

"Only helping Mom set it up. And don't look so surprised. I can cook . . . some things."

"How'd you do?"

I washed my hands, then unwrapped the meat and dumped it all in the bowl. "Do either of us seriously consider Bob Riley is mixed up in this?"

Ned took a moment to think this over. "I only met him last week, but he seems like a solid guy. And it would take a huge set of—uh, a lot of boldness if he was involved to be dating your mom now, and that doesn't fit his personality."

"I agree. I never saw a hint of anything dodgy years

ago, either." I dumped in breadcrumbs, the spices Mom liked, and cracked a few eggs on top, and a sprinkle of milk, then plunged my hands into the cold meat to mix it thoroughly. "As for drugs, it would have been difficult to teach as competently as he did if he was high all the time. And that goes for Mom and my brothers, too. I was younger but not unaware."

"I had my team run some quick background and financial checks on Oskar Jablonski, Wynn Graham, and Bruce Ames. Nothing jumps out at first glance. Solid businessmen. Jablonski's business is stable. We know Graham's a veteran. Ames is a big supporter of the Future Farmers of America."

"My dad was in that, too."

"Can I do anything to help?"

"Take the bowl of hard-boiled eggs, the pack of spinach, and the block of feta cheese out of the fridge, please."

"Your mom didn't come up with anyone else?" He did as I asked. "What are these for?"

I shook my head. "Watch and learn." I halved the meat and patted it into the pan and made a center trough, then nestled four eggs marching down the center, added a layer of spinach, and crumbled the cheese on top. Then I patted the rest of the meat on top and sealed the edges. I washed my hands thoroughly. "Nope, Mom said Dad liked Bruce Ames to talk equipment. They went out mostly with Bob and his wife, and he usually saw Wynn at his golf club after his divorce." I mixed ketchup with brown sugar and spread it over the top of the meatloaf, covered the dish with foil, and put it back in the fridge. "I told Ben I'd fold some wash for them. Gail's legs are hurting today, and I want to feel like I did some small thing to help. Maybe I'll dust and vacuum while I'm there. She shouldn't be doing that kind of stuff."

"You do that, and I'll speak to Bruce Ames at the hardware store. And maybe see if Wynn Graham can add to what he told us."

"Good thinking. You're okay going alone?"

Ned came over to me and enclosed me in a hug. "You give Gail a hand. This is what I do for a living."

I inhaled his leathery scent and reveled in the feel of his arms around me. This was my safe place. John Maydan belonged to the land of memories. Gail was right. Ned was my here and now.

We left the house together and lingered on the porch while Ned told me about his call with Tony. "He's going to visit Sal Costello about Bobby's car."

"All right. I hope it's not a waste of his time. I feel like we're so close to connecting the dots. By the way, everyone's coming for dinner. Even Ben."

Ned gave me a warm kiss as we parted. "Who could stay annoyed with you for long, Trudy?"

*DEATH in the ORCHARD*

The massive metal warehouse that served **Ames Hardware Emporium** proved easy for Ned to find. Two smaller signs underneath noted: AUTHORIZED JOHN DEERE DEALER, and on the other side, TOOLS, ANIMAL FEED, FERTILIZER & MORE! A large parking lot stretched across the property, with pickup trucks and SUVs scattered throughout. Through a chain-link fence, Ned could see new equipment in Deere green for sale, and farther back, mechanics in a garage tinkered in open-doored bays on several huge tractors. He passed a display of Adirondack chairs and entered the store to its cavernous interior, with sets of high metal shelves that stretched down both sides of a central corridor. It would take a lot of financial backing to heat and stock a place this big, but the financial check had shown this business was solvent.

People roamed the aisles, some with shopping carts holding pet food; others pulled flatbeds with pallets of livestock feed. Directly opposite the doors were the checkouts, and Ned presented himself to one of the cashiers without a customer at the moment.

"I need to speak with Bruce Ames, please."

The older woman had eyebrows penciled in high arches in the exact shade as her dyed red hair, giving her the look of an aging Lucille Ball. She looked him over appraisingly. "And you are?"

Ned had already decided he couldn't use his credentials to get the man to talk to him. "A friend of the Genova family."

The woman's face creased in a smile. "Why didn't ya say so?" She spoke into an intercom that broadcast over a loudspeaker and echoed into the rafters. "Ames needed at cashier three. Big Bruce on three."

Ned thanked her and scanned an extensive tool collection opposite the checkout. A rotund man with a rolling gait that matched his girth came out of an office set in one corner and approached Ned with a quizzical look. The cashier pointed to Ned and turned to her customer.

"Bruce Ames. How can I help?"

Ned introduced himself and put out his hand to shake. He was aware the cashier paid rapt attention. "Hildy Genova said I should speak to you about a private matter."

The man's face creased into a smile. "Sure. Call me Bruce. Come on into the office." He ushered Ned back to his domain and pointed to a chair. "Getcha anything? Water, coffee?" He pointed to a Keurig. "Things okay at the orchard? Those boys have done a great job running it."

"I'm good, thanks." Ned took the chair and Bruce settled behind the desk. "Things are fine at the orchard, humming right along."

Bruce visibly relaxed and tented his fingers.

"I'm an NYPD detective, Mr. Ames. Trudy's asked me to have a look into her father's death and Hildy's agreed. I'm getting background from anyone close to him. I take it you know the Genovas well?"

"Ever since I opened this place in 1989. Mario Genova was one of my best customers and friends, a big supporter." Bruce shook his head. "Still can't understand what happened to Mario. I don't blame Trudy for wanting more answers. Something wasn't right there."

Ned was pleased the man was willing to talk. His openness suggested he had nothing to hide. "What did you think at the time?"

"Besides being devastated I'd lost my friend?" The businessman shifted in his seat, making it creak alarmingly. "I heard the rumors he'd wiped out their finances, and Hildy admitted as much when I visited. I offered to loan her money to tide her over. For the record, she refused." He picked up a mug that said, BIG BRUCE on it, and sipped from it. "See, I knew Mario. We both worked hard to build our businesses." He shook his head.

"We spent hours together, shooting the bull over anything from equipment to politics, and there's one thing I can tell you: that man was as honest as the day was long. If you were his friend, you were a friend for life."

"Did you see him in the days before he died?" Ned wondered for a moment if the money Bruce Ames had offered to loan Hildy had been her own money.

"I did, the week before. We were tossing around the merits of upgrading an attachment to one of his tractors before winter set in."

"How did he seem? Anything bothering him?"

"Not that I recall. Mario always focused on what was in front of him. I only saw him lose his temper a few times at unfairness. He hated bullies." Bruce stroked his chin and thought back. "He had the ability to put things into perspective. Like when he was coaching, he was all about the game, not distracted by the orchard. When he worked, he gave it his all."

Ned nodded and took his time phrasing his next question. "And you'd say there was never any question of him being involved in anything . . . shady?"

"You mean illegal?" Bruce snorted and sat straight up. "Mario? He was a principled man, couldn't stand when someone was treated unfairly like I told you. That's why his actions didn't make sense. Mario would never be caught dead in anything 'shady' as you call it." He winced.

"Sorry, wrong turn of phrase."

"No, I understand. You can see why his actions don't make sense." Ned didn't want to start rumors when none were founded. "We're trying to figure out if he might have been trying to help a friend."

"Son, let me tell you something. He'd do anything for me, but he loved his family more than heaven on earth. He wouldn't do anything that would hurt them unless they were under threat and he had no choice."

Ned realized this was an angle he and Trudy hadn't considered. Could Mario have been trying to protect his family? Was one of his boys in trouble, and Mario had kept that knowledge from Trudy and Hildy?

They hadn't considered that the threat might have been close to home.

# CHAPTER THIRTY

Ned called ahead. Wynn Graham had a customer in his office but could see him in forty-five minutes if he didn't need too much of the man's time. He pulled in at the police station and found Paul Hoffmann talking to Ron Hanson up front; the receptionist was out. Both men smiled when Ned entered.

"Just the men I wanted to see," Ned said, hoping his question would come out the right way.

"Any news on Costello's cousin?" Paul asked.

"I asked my partner to track him down and get back to me. I'll call or text if I learn anything."

Paul nodded. "Good. What can we do for you in the meantime?"

Ned was glad the two men were alone. "This is a weird question; please don't take offense. I know you both know the Genova brothers, but I don't, so humor me. Were Ben or Rick ever known to use drugs?"

Ned watched the two men carefully. Paul shook his

head immediately, but Ron's fair face reddened.

"Never heard of anything about either of them. Certainly, no arrests since I've been here and I didn't see any on Rick's record when I called him in," Paul said. "Ron, you went to school with them. Anything there?"

Ron cleared his throat. Ned held his breath. "There was a group of guys who would meet behind the school at dances when we were seniors. Someone would bring a flask to pass, you know, and sometimes a joint would go with it. We all took a hit. Ben, too. Rick never did, said it tasted skanky."

Ned almost chuckled. "That's it? An occasional puff of a shared spliff?"

Ron held up his hands. "Promise. Not all of us, and not all the time." His sheepish look made Paul and Ned laugh. "One of the kids stole it from his older brother and for a time we thought we were high and mighty teens, you know? We weren't potheads by any stretch of the imagination."

"A little dancing around at the edge of the line." Ned cracked a smile.

"Don't recall seeing that on your application form." Paul put on an exaggerated frown.

Ron looked between the two men and rolled his eyes. "Give it up, guys. Seriously, Ned, neither of the Genova brothers were involved with drugs of any kind, buying or selling."

All great to hear, Ned thought. But then what was Mario's motive for being involved with Bobby Costello?

Ned moved the Benz to the bank parking lot. He took a swig from his water bottle and realized he'd missed lunch when his stomach growled. He locked up and walked the half block to the café where he and Trudy had eaten the other day and ordered two hot dogs to eat at the counter. He'd needed this break from work. He couldn't recall the last time he'd taken an entire week off—his weeks of accrued vacation time spoke for itself. Despite still being involved in an investigation, he felt more relaxed. Now if only he could pin down something useful to help Trudy.

Trudy. He realized he was falling in love with her, harder and more deeply than anyone in his life before. They'd been here since last Saturday, days without the intimacy that was new and exciting, yet those hours sleeping beside her, listening to her breath, feeling her warmth, filled him with comfort and satisfaction. It took all his self-control to keep her at arm's length. He shook his head.

He admired the determined way Trudy forged ahead, dealing with anything in her path. She was convinced he and she together, working as a team, would solve the mystery of her father's death. He hoped he wouldn't let her down.

He'd taken the last bite of his second hot dogs when his phone rang.

"News here, boss," Tony said. "I off-loaded your deep financial stuff to that new civilian geek who knows computers. Nothing showed up on the financials of any of those businesses you asked me to check out. All solvent with high marks from the Better Business Bureau, bills and taxes paid on time, too."

"All right, tell him I appreciate the effort. What's your real news then?"

"I tracked Sal Costello down at home. Nice house in Pelham Bay. He's a web designer, works out of a home office with tons of computer stuff I've never seen. Sounds like he was a world away from his cousin Bobby. They grew up close, but when Sal went to college, Bobby decided selling drugs would net him more money faster and they drifted apart quickly."

"A different road taken."

"For sure. Sal said he was surprised when he was contacted as Bobby's next of kin to take possession of the car."

Ned put money and a tip on top of the bill, waved to the waitress, and left the café to walk back to the bank as he listened to his partner recap his interview with Bobby Costello's cousin.

"Car was a classic '79 Chevy Nova that Bobby had restored and painted a bright purple. Sal said it looked like a giant grape. He sold it to a collector within a month, put the money in his son's college fund. Figured it had been bought with drug money, but this way it could go to something good."

"Smart guy."

"Ned, he had a photo of it, and on the trunk, there was an airbrushed head and shoulders of Mickey Mantle with a big grin. It said 'The Mick' over his head. Weird."

Ned described the sordid meaning behind the airbrushed nickname he'd learned from the warden at Troy Correctional.

"Holy crap, that's creepy."

"I'll say. What about the contents, anything there?"

"There wasn't much but an old blanket and a baseball bat."

Ned's pulse rose as he paused outside the bank. Through the large main window, he could see Wynn Graham on the phone. "Please tell me it was wood, not aluminum."

"A Louisville Slugger, all wood. Sal kept it for his son to

*DEATH in the ORCHARD*

use but the kid never liked it, and they got him a lighter aluminum one."

"Now tell me he still has that bat." What were the chances?

"Had, as in past tense. We poked around the garage and found it sitting in a bin with hockey and lacrosse sticks."

"Yes! Where is it now?"

"He signed it over to me for chain of evidence and will sign a statement as to where it came from. It's next to me on the front seat, wrapped in an evidence bag, soon to be on its way by State Trooper up to you. The Albany lab should have it in a few hours."

"Fantastic. I'll call Paul Hoffmann and give him a heads up. If that bat has traces of Mario Genova's blood, we'll have a big break in our case. I owe you one, buddy."

State Trooper Wes Brady loved these kinds of assignments. Close to retirement, he had first pick of the choice and unusual assignments. When the call from NYPD came in for an evidence transfer to the Albany forensics lab, he immediately volunteered.

*M.K. GRAFF*

What could be better than a drive during nice fall weather down to the city and back. He picked up a huge Italian sub, threw in a large bag of chips, and added two diet sodas. Lots of napkins, and he was set for a long ride. This trip would take up the rest of his shift, and he could leave the thruway losers to the others.

As he drove south to meet a detective from the 2-0 precinct, he pondered the details he'd written down with the case number. Genova didn't sound familiar. But taken from and belonging to a Costello. Now that name definitely rang a big bell in his memory.

Brady hit a knot of traffic near Westchester and used his lights to clear his way. The siren would be unfair and unnecessary. He was almost to the city line when he flashed on a memory of the day he and a new rookie had arrested a Costello after drugs were found in the spare tire of his trunk. Could this be related?

He was picking up a baseball bat to be delivered to the lab for testing. He cast his mind back to Serving Since Breakfast, the rookie he'd mentored, now an eleven-year veteran, who had turned into a good trooper and worked the Buffalo area. Then other specifics about that arrest came to mind, like that horrid purple car with the painting of Mickey Mantle across the trunk.

There had been a baseball bat in that trunk. This must be the evidence he was collecting.

He remembered the weasel who had thrown himself back against the squad car seat in disgust when Brady had shown the rookie the cache of drugs secreted in the spare tire. If this bat had inflicted damage to a person, Brady would help make sure Costello didn't get away with it.

He wrapped the remaining half of his sub for the return trip, cleaned his hands, and used a wet wipe to get the rest of the oil off his fingers. He tossed the used napkins and wipes into the bag with the chips.

Time to get serious. He added the siren to his lights and made his way into the Big Apple.

# CHAPTER THIRTY-ONE

Rick only raised an eyebrow when I asked to borrow his truck again. Up to his elbows making cider, he threw the keys to me and said he'd see me at dinner. After a stop at the pet store, I was off to Cobleskill, eating the banana I'd grabbed on my way out the door.

The twenty-minute drive gave me time to gather my thoughts. I wondered if Ned had made any headway this afternoon. I turned onto the Dietzes' road and kept going right to the end. The park had more people in it this afternoon, mostly young mothers with toddlers, but I knew when school was out later it would be a different story.

I parked in a spot near the entrance and pulled up Doug Dietz's number. It rang and rang and went to voicemail. "Doug, this is Trudy Genova. I have something for you. Could you meet me at the park, please? I won't take up a lot of your time, I promise."

I sipped my water and decided I would wait twenty

minutes. Doug had said he had the week off from school, but there was a chance he couldn't handle the atmosphere at home and had gone back early. More likely, he was deciding if he was coming to see me or not. A light breeze made the tops of the surrounding trees sway. There was a dark cloud in the distance, and I wouldn't be surprised if it rained later.

A knock on my window startled me. Doug had decided to come. I pointed to the passenger seat, and he climbed in beside me as I muted my phone. This could be an important conversation and I didn't want to be disturbed. "No Rusty today?"

"He was sleeping in my room, so I left him home."

I reached behind me and handed him the bag from the pet store. "I thought you both would enjoy this." He pulled out a blue plastic device that lets you chuck the enclosed balls, flinging them farther away than an arm could throw.

"I've seen ads for this. Thanks a lot." His voice trailed off and he looked out the side window.

"How are things at home?"

"They've stopped talking to each other."

And to you, I read between the lines. Poor kid.

"Mom keeps looking at our old photo albums and Dad disappears into his office. We don't eat together; we microwave plates when we're hungry. It's like Greg is this unspoken presence between us all."

"Even in death Greg still gets most of the attention?"

He shrugged. "It's not the attention, it's that his murder sucks all the oxygen out of the room, you know. Even though I loved my brother." He turned to face me. "I was the one who supported him, the one who stood by him. Now I'm wondering if that was a smart idea. I'm not sure I knew the real Greg."

"Why do you feel that way? Because of the drugs?"

Doug kept silent, watching the small children on the swings. What I said next would make a big difference. I looked out the windshield, too, and kept my voice low and steady.

"My father died eleven years ago, Doug. I was sixteen at the time. We never found out who killed him, and all these years I've wondered about the person who did it. Did he ever think about our family, about how devastated we would be? Did he understand that not knowing why he died would haunt us for years?"

The car was silent except for the shouts of the children playing. One little boy scraped his knee, and his mother comforted him.

I kept talking. "My family coped in different ways. My mother spent many lonely years wondering what she'd missed that led to my father's death, and if she should love him or hate him. My brothers threw themselves into the business so we wouldn't lose it, yet my older brother still can't talk about that day. I went to nursing school and the first chance I had, I moved to Manhattan to get away from the pity and the grief and the memories."

Doug cleared his throat.

I kept looking forward and spoke again. "I do know, firsthand, how death changes everything in its path. I'm sorry it's happened to you, too. Your life will go on, but it will be forever transformed. But you can't let Greg's death define your future."

I finally looked over at Doug, who had tears running down his face. He hadn't moved or made a sound. Those tears made my heart twist with sadness for this young man on the cusp of adulthood who had his whole life before him.

In a choked voice, Doug said, "I know all about your father. I think Greg did it."

I frowned. "Did what?"

He rummaged in the pocket of his denim jacket but then withdrew his hand. "I think my brother killed your father." He bolted from the car and took off into the woods.

Ned called Trudy's phone, but it went to voicemail. She was either on a call or in a location with spotty coverage. "Call me when you get this, Trudy. Tony came up trumps."

He entered the bank and told the head teller he was there for a meeting with Wynn Graham. She looked familiar.

"I met you the other day at Gail's shower," the young woman said. "I was in Ben's class." She tapped a few computer keys. "You just missed him. Mr. Graham was called away suddenly and asked if you could reschedule for tomorrow. He can see you at 10:30 if that would work."

Ned glanced through the glass at Graham's neat office and the framed photos on the wall. He saw a back door that led directly to the parking lot. "I suppose so." He made a show of checking his phone calendar. "I wanted to talk to him about one of the photos on his wall. One of the men from his Army outfit might be someone who served with my uncle." Then, as if the thought had just occurred to him: "Say, is there any chance you could let me have a look?"

She hesitated and he leaned in to add: "Since you know the Genovas, I'll tell you in confidence that Trudy and I hope to bring resolution to the family on our trip here."

"It's about time someone figured out what happened to that lovely man. Once he bought five cartons of my niece's Girl Scout cookies so she'd win a badge." She shook her head and put a "closed" sign on her window and moved away, calling to the teller next to her. "I'm taking my break." She came out from behind the counter. "I suppose if I were to come with you that would be all right."

"Thank you." Ned backed away to allow her to lead the way into Graham's office. She unlocked the door and stood inside it, watching him as he moved slowly down the row of photos.

"I'll never forget that day. It's burned on my memory. I was relatively new, but I knew the family through school. Mrs. Genova's eyes were as big as saucers when I brought them in to see Mr. Graham. Then the police came, and we heard Mr. Genova was found dead." She shook her head. "It felt awful, seeing the family's heartache on display right in the middle of the bank."

"It must have been hard," Ned agreed. "If you were here then, were you around the day before when Mario came in to make those withdrawals?"

Her cheeks flamed. "I followed all proper procedures," she said.

Ned realized this was the teller who had given Mario his funds. "I'm sure you did," he assured her. "It had to be a tough time for you. Mr. Graham was at work before the Genovas showed up, I expect?"

She tilted her head to one side as she remembered.

"Hmm, he arrived a little before they did. I remember he changed into a shirt and tie out of his golf shirt. He'd had a meeting at the golf club about the fundraiser they were planning. It was to help the rehab clinic where Wynn's son had gone. Jake was still alive then and we all thought he'd beaten the drugs thing."

Ned nodded. "Was Mario at that meeting, too?"

She shrugged. "Maybe. He was on the committee with Mr. Graham. I don't know."

"Trudy went over the things recovered from her father's truck, and there was a bag with gold golf tees engraved with 'MG,' but I'd heard Mario hated golf."

Now the woman smiled. "We all knew Mr. Genova teased Mr. Graham about wasting time batting a tiny ball around. It was Mr. Graham's birthday that week. I bet they were a gift for him: his first name is Melwynn." She frowned. "But that doesn't make sense. If they were at the golf club meeting earlier, why didn't Mr. Genova give them to Mr. Graham then?"

That was an excellent question and it dawned on Ned that Larry Long's "YTs" notation likely referred to these golf tees. Long must have learned Mario hated golf. He'd have to tell Trudy. One tiny mystery solved.

Ned stopped at the photo of Wynn Graham with his Army unit and used his phone to take a photo. "I'll send this to my uncle. It would be some coincidence if his pal was in the same unit." The image had resonated with him, especially with the way Wynn Graham had spoken about that time. If you didn't like to talk about your war experience, why keep a photo from that time on the wall of your office?

The teller nodded. He couldn't tell if she bought his story or not. Ned moved down the wall to a golf tournament photo of Graham flanked by his two sons and studied it for a moment, before turning to follow her out of the office.

"Must have been another tough time when Jake died," he said as she locked the office behind him.

"Especially since we thought Jake had knocked his habit. His death came out of the blue. Mr. Graham was never the same after that. But I suppose drugs are like that once they get a hold of you."

"Could I ask you if you've seen this man at the bank?" Ned brought up a photo of Greg Dietz from his phone. He turned the phone to her.

She nodded in recognition. "That's the young man who showed up near the end of last week, maybe Friday. Mr. Graham said he'd made the appointment personally and forgotten to log it in his diary."

Ned hid his surprise. "I suppose you wouldn't have any idea what their meeting was about . . ."

"I couldn't say. They spoke privately in Mr. Graham's

office." She frowned. "It did become heated before the man left. Mr. Graham seemed angry, body language, you know, red in the face, and their voices became loud. After the man left, Mr. Graham said he had a headache and went home early."

A customer stepped up to ask a question, and Ned thanked her and left the bank.

Once back in his car, he texted Trudy, then sent the Army photo to Tony with a text: **"Great work on bat. Pls ck archives BBC Intern'tl + NY Times unusual stories on MELWYNN GRAHAM and/ or this unit."**

I decided against trying to follow Doug into the woods. I'd only spook him and what would I do if I caught up to him? I cursed and hit the steering wheel. Why did Doug think his brother could have killed my dad? He wasn't thinking clearly.

I left the Dietzes' road and pulled over in a nearby Dunkin' Donuts parking lot to read Ned's text, which asked me to check with Mom about my father having a meeting at the golf club on the day he died. I couldn't imagine that hadn't come out previously if he had, but I did as Ned asked before I called him back. My heart raced. Could this be the third appointment my dad had that day?

Mom answered on the second ring. "Hello, dear. You should see the mural! We should finish tonight."

"Wonderful, Mom. Hey, I need to ask you a painful question. Think back to the day Dad died. Do you know if he was supposed to have a meeting with Wynn Graham at the golf club?"

"Goodness, no, Trudy. It was summer and we were busy. Those meetings were always after work on the first Tuesday evening of the month. They'd already had July's and I would have known if he'd another scheduled. All he had that day was the party store and Oskar's deli."

"Thanks, Mom, that's helpful."

"You're getting somewhere, aren't you?"

"Maybe. I promise when I have something more concrete, I'll tell you."

"Please be careful, Trudy. Ned, too."

I promised her and called Ned back to tell him my mom had no knowledge of any plans Dad might have had for a golf club meeting the morning he died. It was unlikely that it was his third appointment.

"Trudy, I have news. Tony went to see Sal Costello. He still had a bat found in Bobby's car when he was arrested."

I had a sudden mental image of a bat hitting my father on the back of his head. I shuddered. "Where is it now?" I fought down a wave of nausea and reached for my water bottle.

"On its way to the Albany forensics lab with a State Trooper." His tone changed. "Trudy, I know what this means for your dad's death. I'm so sorry."

I gulped a swallow of the cool liquid. If I were to help my dad, I needed to step back from my emotions and concentrate on the case as if it were any other we'd worked together. "Thanks, Ned, but this means we're on the right track. And it makes sense with his injuries." I took a deep breath and put on my nursing cap. "If my father was hit from behind with the bat, that's the first fracture and matches what the medical examiner told you. He'd have fallen off the platform and hit his head on the trailer hitch on his way down, fracture number two. It fits the autopsy findings." I inhaled to steady myself. "But Ned, what are the chances if this bat *was* used to hit my father there would still be blood on it after all these years?"

"Tony said it looked wiped to the naked eye but don't forget Costello's arrest happened the same day your father died, only hours later. He wouldn't have had time to do any type of deep cleaning. Wood is porous. There are new tests they do now. We'll get there."

*DEATH in the ORCHARD*

I realized my hands were shaking. "This might be evidence to prove Bobby Costello killed my dad, but we still don't know *why*." My thoughts whirled. I desperately needed to know why my father would have set up a meeting with a known drug dealer.

Ned recounted that the teller told him Greg Dietz had visited Wynn Graham last week, and that Wynn said he'd had a golf club meeting the morning my father died. He also mentioned the mystery of YTs likely referring to the golf tees found in Mario's truck.

"Of course, MG was Melwynn Graham. We knew about those tees in the truck; why didn't I see that sooner?"

"Because you've had other things on your mind. And get this, Graham was supposed to meet me this afternoon and canceled at the last minute. I'd seen him through the bank's front window minutes before, yet when I came inside, he'd left and rescheduled me for tomorrow. And somehow Desert Storm comes into play."

"Desert Storm? I don't get that."

"Call it my detective's intuition. I'll explain tonight if it bears fruit."

"Ned, I feel like we're coming so close to the truth. But I still can't see how a drug dealer like Bobby Costello and Wynn Graham are connected, nor why Greg Dietz would be involved with Wynn, or how that leads to my dad."

Ned's tone was grim. "I can—Graham's son, Jake."

# CHAPTER THIRTY-TWO

For the second time that day, Ned drove his car back to the police station. This time when he reached the doorway, he met Paul Hoffmann coming down the street toward him, holding a large brown paper bag and two cans of soda. The officer called out to him.

"I was on my way to call you." He waited to get closer to finish his thought. "I have the ballistics back on the gun we confiscated from Vince Russo. Not a match by a long shot. Your face says you have news, too. Come on in." He put the bag on the receptionist's desk and told Ned to take a seat as Ron ambled over. "Ron and I have been clearing up monthly reports while our receptionist's off for a few days."

Ron reached into the bag and pulled out a sub. "This one mine?"

"They're the same." Paul spread a layer of paper napkins on the desk.

Ron sat back at his desk and unwrapped his sub and

popped the tab on his soda can.

"Want half of mine, O'Malley?" Paul offered up half his meatball sub.

"No, thanks. Saving myself for Hildy's stuffed meatloaf. I have news."

"Legendary meatloaf," Ron said between bites.

"So I hear. You two go ahead while I catch you up." Ned told them about the visit Greg Dietz paid to Wynn Graham last week, and about the trooper on his way to the Albany forensics lab with Bobby Costello's bat. "I had the case number from your file, so we're good."

Paul's eyes opened wide. "Amazing. Now let's hope the lab can find Mario's blood on it. You may have helped close a cold case. But why would Costello kill Mario or Dietz visit Wynn?"

"When I think about the Dietz connection I think about drugs and Jake Graham. I'm hopeful heat from the trunk would have set any blood stains deeper in the wood. There's a lot riding on this." Ned told them Wynn Graham had told his staff he had a meeting at his golf club the day Mario died and would be in late, a meeting which had been disputed by Hildy and Trudy, with good reasons. "Plus, before I even knew any of this, I'd set up to see Wynn today, and when I arrived for it, he ducked out the back door, 'called away' suddenly."

Paul frowned. "I don't see any good reason why Wynn

would have lied to his staff about his whereabouts any day, or why Greg Dietz would visit him privately."

"Or why he'd avoid me now unless he's worried I'm getting close to figuring out what happened that day, which indicates he's involved."

"You believe Wynn Graham is implicated?" Paul sipped his soda and looked in the distance as he mulled this idea over.

"It's the only logical thing when you consider all these pieces." Ned laid out the information they'd gathered. "We know Bobby Costello was a drug dealer whose area was Schoharie and Cobleskill. We also know Jake Graham had a history of drug abuse and had been in rehab with relapses. It's not a stretch to think Bobby's crew were Jake's dealers and Jake owed him big time. Then we have Mario Genova, who withdrew his family's savings, and with no reason for that concerning his own family that's ever come to light—but I've learned that he would do anything to help a friend, and he and Wynn were close."

Ron nodded. "That's all true."

"Someone said to me today that once drugs get their hooks into you, it's hard to get away, and we know debts to dealers pile up quickly. Isn't it possible Wynn Graham asked Mario to help him pay off Jake's liability to keep the boy out of trouble with his dealers, and Wynn would pay Mario back over time? If it had worked out, Hildy wouldn't even have known the accounts were temporarily raided, and it would be easier and safer than if Wynn, the bank president, tried to embezzle bank funds from someone else's account."

"It makes a weird kind of sense," Paul admitted. "But no money was found on Bobby when he was arrested."

Ned felt like he was on a roll, his years of investigative experience putting the pieces together. "Because if Mario didn't bring the money to the railroad meet that day, Bobby never received it—and if Bobby killed Mario because of that, he'd known he had to get away from this area quickly. He likely planned to come back at a later time for the money if he knew where it was, but instead his arrest meant he went to prison for years. Didn't the warden tell us Bobby was close to getting his sentence reduced when he died of cancer?"

"That's right." Paul whistled. "Once Costello knew he was dying, he told his roommate Greg Dietz, who'd befriended him, where he could get the money."

"Which is why a law student would want to work in an orchard, but not any orchard. It had to be Genova Orchards to give him access to look for the money Bobby knew was hidden there." Ned paused as Paul spoke up.

"And when Dietz became frustrated, that explains why he might visit the only other person who would know where the money was, Wynn Graham." Paul paced the office. "It fits. If Mario didn't pay off Costello, where else would he hide it but his orchard, amongst all those acres? I think you're right, Ned, but I also think Dietz quickly realized the enormity of his search and tried to blackmail Wynn with that knowledge when he couldn't find the money himself."

Ron had been listening intently. He balled up his paper, wiped his mouth, and threw the garbage in the can. "Gotta say that all holds together, especially if that bat has Mario Genova's blood on it. Mario dies helping Wynn, Wynn keeps silent all these years, and then some kid comes along to spill the beans? There's your motive for the Dietz killing. The question then is: does Wynn Graham own a gun?"

Ned took out his phone and started scrolling through his photos. "I took this photo of Wynn in Desert Storm with his squad. The men are all holding guns. If I'm not mistaken, they're all Colt .45s."

I turned around and drove back past the Dietz house to the park. I'd only been gone ten minutes and I hoped I hadn't missed Doug.

*DEATH in the ORCHARD*

No, there he was, on the swings. I parked up before the swings and waited. I saw him notice Rick's truck. A few kids walked into the park as I deliberated getting out, but before I could move, Doug left the swings, walked right to me and opened the passenger door.

"You came back." He handed me a small notebook as he got in. "Read it."

I stared at Doug and then at the small notebook in my hands. "Look, let's settle one thing first. My father died eleven years ago. Your brother would have been, what fourteen or so? Last year of middle school, right?"

"I guess."

"Our families didn't know each other, to my knowledge. Was Greg involved with drugs then?"

Doug shook his head. "Only an occasional joint. He started using years later, pills and cocaine in law school." He frowned as he thought this through and saw the sense of what I was explaining.

"By then my father was long dead. Greg didn't kill him, Doug." I opened the little journal. "What made you think that? Where did you get this?"

Doug haltingly told me how his brother had urged him to smuggle the journal out of the prison, while I flicked through the pages. There were lists of dates with dollar signs and amounts, initials, and here and there, place names with check marks. It seemed to be an accounting going back a long time.

I heard the tension in Doug's voice as he recounted hiding the notebook in his sock. "That must have been scary. I'm sorry he involved you."

"I figured it was Greg keeping track of his deals, but why would he have that in prison, especially if he was going straight?" Doug shook his head. "He was insistent he would need it when he came out, said it was for his future." He picked at a hangnail. "Then I saw the part about the killing, and I freaked out."

No wonder the kid was muddled. "I can see you'd be confused." I kept flipping the pages. "I'll bet this goes back months if not years." At the back I saw the listing that had upset Douglas. It was the last notation, and it was for the date my father died. I took a quick photo of it. The entry in pen read:

7/6 $120K p/off MG 4JG; Schoh tr st 10A

And added under it in pencil: *The bat kills again.*

Bobby Costello. A death on the date my father was murdered. Did "MG 4JG" stand for "Mario Genova for Jake Graham?" My heart sped up, knocking against my ribs. "Doug, does this entry look like your brother's handwriting?"

Hope sprang into his eyes. "Hard to tell with all those numbers, but it doesn't look like his. I haven't been able to get into his room to compare it to old notebooks. My mom keeps it like a shrine and yells at me to stay away if I go near it."

"Mm. I'll tell you another reason why I don't think your brother had anything to do with my father's death." I showed him the last notation that had upset him. "This is the day my father died, when we've already established your brother was in middle school." I made eye contact with the teen. "Doug, this journal belonged to someone who gave it to your brother. And I have a feeling I know who."

Paul and Ron scrutinized the photo Ned showed them. "Forward it to me and I'll print it out," Paul said.

The three men watched the printer as the page slowly descended from it. Paul wrapped up what was left of his sub. Ned knew how he felt; his appetite had deserted him.

Once the copy was in the tray, Paul waited a moment for the ink to dry, then picked it up and tacked it to a bulletin board hanging on one wall.

The three men huddled around it, examining the photo. "Wait, there's a magnifier in the desk." Paul retrieved it and they ran it over the picture of the cluster of men, five in the squad, all in desert camouflage fatigues with grimy faces. A cigarette dangled from the corner of one man's mouth. Their grins were tepid, if you could call their expressions smiles. Each man held a gun in some stage of cleaning. Wynn Graham was in the center of the group, pulling a wad through his barrel.

"Ned, you're right." Paul pointed to the photo. "Those are all 1911 Colt .45s. But wouldn't Wynn have had to return his to the Army when he left the desert?"

"I wouldn't know." Ned indicated the man Wynn had pointed out. "Graham told me this guy holding his gun up in triumph could take his gun apart and put it back together in under forty seconds blindfolded. Then he told me he didn't like to talk about his time 'in the sandbox.' Yet he kept this photo on his wall."

"Ron, check with licensing and see if there are any firearms registered to Wynn Graham. I'll check on the policy of Army personnel returning to the States and their guns."

Ned's phone rang. "It's Trudy; I'd better take this." He answered and heard the frantic note in her voice.

"I know what links Bobby Costello to my father. Where are you?"

"At the station with Paul and Ron. You manage to get Doug to open up to you?"

*DEATH in the ORCHARD*

"He's grieving and confused, but he finally gave me a journal Greg had him smuggle out of the prison."

"Poor kid."

"Listen to this last notation." Trudy read it to him. "I bet this is Bobby Costello's missing journal, the one the warden told you about."

"Bobby must have given it to Greg. I'll ask Paul to obtain a sample of Costello's writing."

"See you shortly."

"Don't get a ticket speeding here." Ned told Paul and Ron about the journal Trudy was bringing, and what the entry spelled out. "Can we get Steve Northrup to fax us a handwriting sample from Bobby Costello's file? It might still be in his office."

"On it." Paul rang the warden's office and explained what they needed. "Preferably a sample with numbers if it's available . . . thanks." He recited their fax number and hung up. "Steve said he'll get a sample to us shortly."

Ned's phone rang again. Tony. "Anything?" The shorthand let his partner know Ned was up to his eyeballs.

"Maybe. A BBC journalist wrote about an incident in that squad's province when Graham was there, where an innocent child was killed. He insinuated a hushed investigation into the incident was a coverup, but it's all classified. That's all I could find."

"All right. Thanks for digging, Tony."

*M.K. GRAFF*

Ned told the men what Tony had unearthed while he paced the tiny office. "Not sure if that adds anything to our case here. Still, things seem to be coming together swiftly. We know Mario Genova withdrew funds and Bobby Costello likely killed him. We know Jake Graham had a drug debt, according to this entry if it matches Bobby's handwriting. Wynn lying about a meeting that day is suspicious. But where is the money and why Mario was involved are still questions that need answering."

"We need more evidence concerning Wynn Graham." Paul consulted his computer screen. "Looks like the Army's policy is for vets to turn in their arms before returning stateside. Unless Wynn figured out a way to smuggle his home, the gun in that photo can't be the one used to kill Greg Dietz."

Ned sighed. "I was afraid of that."

Paul's inbox dinged with a new email. "Hold on. Incoming from the medical examiner's office." He scanned the email. "They've had time to examine Greg Dietz's stomach contents and correlate it with statements from the hostel of what he ate at lunch and when. Based on that, he's narrowed the time of death to between three and four pm. That totally clears Rick."

"Trudy will be thrilled to hear that. I wish we had better news on Graham's gun."

"The Lord giveth and He taketh away," Rick intoned,

paging through his own computer.

"Today you're a comic?" Paul continued to read the full revised autopsy report.

"Hey, a little levity never hurt." Ron stopped scrolling and Ned saw his eyes widen. "And He just giveth again."

Paul looked up from his own screen. "What have you found?"

"Wynn Graham's ex-wife, Mary, has a 1911 Colt .45 registered in her name." Ron looked up. "She's living in Maine now. We need to call and ask if she took her gun with her."

"I'll do that if I can find her number." Paul opened his laptop. "You get a warrant application started for Wynn's office and home."

The fax machine burst into life while Paul tried to locate Mary Graham's number in Maine from a database. Ned spoke to the two men.

"Trudy will be here any second. I don't think we should tell her about the warrant at this point. She'll want to come along on any search, and I don't want to put her in jeopardy."

Paul nodded. "Makes sense."

Trudy ran into the office at that moment, brandishing a tiny journal held aloft as if it were the Holy Grail. "Here it is!"

Paul grabbed the faxed pages from the warden's office.

Ned explained to Trudy what they were, and they all crowded around the worktable in the back of the office. Trudy flipped to the last page as they compared the handwriting.

Steve Northrup had included a page with Bobby Costello's dated signature, and Ned noted several similarities, including the way he formed his numbers. "See the way he put that little hook on the number '1'"?

Ron said, "Catholic school."

Ned pointed to the last page of the journal. "It matches numbers throughout all the pages of this journal. The slant of the writing is the same, too, as is the way he makes an 'o' more like a little oval. I'm not a handwriting expert, but to the naked eye, these look the same."

"I agree," Paul said.

"Where do we go from here?" Trudy's eyes were shining, the end of a long eleven years close at hand.

Paul looked at the wall clock. At Ned's nod, Paul turned to Trudy. "Trudy, I know what this means to you, and the effort you've invested. We've had confirmation that the official time of death for Greg totally clears Rick. Could you go home and let Rick know he's no longer under suspicion? I promise we'll keep in touch if anything develops."

Ned watched Trudy's face fall, but she put her chin up immediately. "Of course."

*DEATH in the ORCHARD*

"All right. I have a call I need to make." He went into his private office and Ron went back to typing up the warrant application.

Ned put his arm around Trudy and kissed her, then left his arm around her and whispered, "We're almost there."

# CHAPTER THIRTY-THREE

Harry Holland swore in frustration, threw his pen on the scratch pad he was using, and rubbed his temples to ease his pounding headache. The slip of paper he was working on fluttered to the ground at his feet.

For days he'd tried to make heads or tails of the string of numbers on the paper fragment he'd found in Greg Dietz's room. He'd been dismayed it wasn't a written message but then figured if Dietz had something important to hide, he wouldn't be so obvious about documenting it. He'd worked on it during his sick leave this week between naps, trying to keep what he was doing from the other idiots at the hostel. Each evening the quiet got to him, and he'd gone to the common room to catch up on the day's news and left the paper behind.

Today the hostel was quiet in the late afternoon, so he sat in the common room alone. This had started out as an intriguing puzzle; now it irritated him that he couldn't figure out what those numbers meant. Were they dates?

*DEATH in the ORCHARD*

Latitude and longitude lines? He'd used his phone to look up any destination using those same numbers and they all led to dead ends.

He knew they were important. Otherwise, why bother to hide the paper in the first place? Harry closed eyes, massaging his forehead, when he heard Vince Russo say, "What the fuck's this?"

Screw it. He hadn't heard Vince come in and now the crackhead was holding up Dietz's paper slip, looking at the line of numbers. Harry couldn't let Vince know this was important to him, or the guy would eat the paper just to annoy him.

Harry shrugged and yawned. "A puzzle my niece sent me. I tell you, that kid's smart. I can't figure out what this means." Harry didn't have a niece, but Vince wouldn't know that.

Vince pulled a chair over and sat down next to Harry, the whiff of strong oniony perspiration coming off him after his shift at the orchard where he worked. "I like puzzles. What's it supposed to be?"

Christ, now the jerk was going to try to solve it for him. "That's the whole point. It's some kind of message I guess."

Vince took the pad and flipped past Harry's scratched notes to a clean page. "Maybe it's in code, you know, to hide the message."

Harry sat up straighter. He'd not thought of that. "That's the kind of thing this kid would do. So how do I figure it out?"

Vince was writing the numbers one to twenty-six on the page. "The simplest code is to use a number for each letter. That's like the key, you know, 1 is for A, 2 is for B."

"Hey, I think I saw that in a spy movie once." Harry watched Vince go back and add a letter under each number. "Yeah, this could work, right? Thanks, I'll take it from here in case it's private."

Vince gave him a withering look. "What? From a kid? Probably wants you to send her candy." On a fresh line, Vince wrote out the string of numbers: 6 21 3 11 15 6 6 8 1 18 18 25. "Now we figure out what the kid's trying to say."

Harry watched Vince write the letters under the line of numbers as the message slowly took shape. Both men sat back in surprise, then Vince handed him his pen. "Not a request for candy then. Think your niece needs her mouth washed out with soap."

Harry had been played by Greg Dietz.

The message read: FUCKOFFHARRY.

*DEATH in the ORCHARD*

Paul got through to Mary Graham in Maine and told her she was on speakerphone.

"Mary, we have a situation here with Wynn. I need to ask you about the gun registered to you, a Colt. Do you have it with you in Maine?"

Mary Graham's sigh came down the line. "No. I bought it for Wynn when he came home from Desert Storm. As a spouse on base, it was easy to get a gun permit. The boys were so proud of their dad, and I had the misguided idea he'd want a memento." Her breath shuddered and it was clear she held back tears. "I put it in a lovely display case, but he hated it and put it in a closet, said what he needed was to forget his time there."

"Where's the gun, Mary?"

"What aren't you telling me, Paul?"

"We're concerned the gun might have been used in the commission of a crime. It needs to be checked to see if it's been recently fired. Where is it, Mary?"

"In his study, on the closet shelf." Mary's voice caught as she started to cry. "Wynn hasn't been himself since Jake died, Paul, you know that. But the change started with Desert Storm. He was never the same but hid it well from most people."

"War can do that, Mary."

"There was this shadow around him. When Jake had his drug problem it became worse. We thought our poor boy kicked the drug habit in rehab. But then Jake overdosed. We never knew if it was deliberate or not."

"I'm so sorry, Mary. We heard—"

"—it was suicide. I know. In a way it was, because he'd been clean for months, but whether he meant to die then or not we'll never know. Mario died, and then Jake a few weeks later. Wynn never recovered." She cried openly now. "What has he done, Paul?"

"I promise once we know the details, I'll call you back, Mary. For now, can you tell me if there's a place Wynn likes to go when he's upset?"

Mary sniffed and blew her nose. "Um, maybe the golf club. The back fairway has a bench that looks out over the course. We put it there in memory of Jake. Wynn sits there sometimes, says it helps him think." Her voice broke again. "Please, make sure he's safe, Paul."

"That's up to Wynn. We'll do our best, I promise."

I snapped my seat belt on and revved Rick's engine, my temper simmering. Just as things were coming to a close, I was being sent home like a kindergartner. A phone call to Rick would have been fine, so why was I being shunted aside?

I pulled the truck around the corner and started up the hill toward home. By Schoharie High School, buses were lined up for the end of the school day, stretching along the curb in a bright yellow line. Memories of my days there came flooding back, and I pulled over to the side of the road to calm down.

I remembered Gail and I sharing secrets and makeup tips and giggling in the halls; volleyball games and the smack of the ball sailing over the net with the thrill of scoring; debates where we'd argued our side with coherent points. I thought of hoping John would ask me to Homecoming and his prom, and how my father's death had changed the trajectory of our lives. It was tempting to think that if my birthday party had gone ahead, John and I might have become a long-term couple and married like Ben had married Gail. My future would have turned out very differently.

But then I remembered John was divorced, so maybe life with him wouldn't have been golden. Instead, I had a good career, and I'd moved away and eventually met Ned, who I loved and respected. It hit me then that I *did* love Ned, even when he frustrated me, like now. He must love me, too, or he wouldn't have taken on this task to help me track my father's killer.

I took a slug of warm water from the bottle sitting in

the cup holder. I should have been excited at being able to drive home and tell my family that Rick was definitively cleared for Greg Dietz's death. Soon I hoped I'd be able to tell them Ned and I were certain we'd unearthed my father's killer, Bobby Costello, after forensic testing for confirmation came through.

We'd done what we came to do. Ned and I had found out who had murdered my dad. After all these years of my knowing deep down his death hadn't been an accident, I'd been proved right, but it felt like an empty victory. I thought of my father, and how happy he'd be I'd persevered to find out what had happened to him.

I should have been thrilled at knowing the identity of his killer, but I still had too many unanswered questions.

There could be no elation yet. I didn't know *why* my father had to die, or why my parents' bank accounts had been raided. Instead, I was disheartened I only knew half the story. I knew Ned would say I was stubborn, but I was bringing my family half-answers. I had to know the whole story. The *why* mattered to me so much; it would matter to my mother and my brothers, too.

Ned said Wynn Graham knew more than he had said, and Jake Graham had to have been involved somehow. Costello's journal pointed to that.

I decided I had to do two things before I could go home.

First, I called Rick at the orchard, and he answered his cell on the third ring.

"Trudster! You run away with my truck?"

"Only need it for another hour. I have great news. You're totally cleared." I explained about the timing and how he was no longer a person of interest. I left out the bit about knowing who'd killed Dad. Some things had to be done in person.

I could hear the relief in Rick's voice. He told me dinner would be delayed tonight so Mom and Bob could finish the mural. "That fits in with our plans. Ned and I will see you then and we'll celebrate your close escape." I hoped that wasn't all we would celebrate.

Ned retrieved three cold bottles of water from the station's fridge as Paul reassured Mary Graham and finished his call. He knew Trudy was unhappy at being dismissed, but his first goal was to protect her, and he didn't know how volatile Wynn Graham could be. He could apologize later.

He handed a bottle to Ron, who was faxing the warrant application to the judge's chambers and thanked him for pulling it together.

"Judge gave us a verbal go-ahead. He'll sign off."

"All set. Ready to go?" Paul took a hard copy of the warrant application with him. "Just in case there's a question or we need to show something. I can get away with you coming with us, but you're better off driving your own car."

The two cars set off down the road, Ron driving the squad car. They'd agreed to check at the bank first since it was only a few blocks away. If Graham had returned to the bank, he could be brought in for questioning right away without a warrant.

When they pulled up outside the bank, Paul went inside but returned only moments later. Ned rolled down his window as Paul shared with them what the head teller had told him. "Wynn never returned today. Said he might get in a game of golf while the weather held. Let's head there first to the bench Mary mentioned. The club's not far away in Cobleskill. Follow me."

Ned knew Paul was concerned Wynn Graham could be suicidal or dangerous. Paul went back to his car and Ron pulled out with Ned following. They snaked up onto River Road and raced to the golf course. Paul used his siren to clear the road in front of him and Ned followed in his wake.

It was a tense drive to the golf course as Ned followed

the sheriff's car, his pulse pounding at what they would find. When the manicured lawns of the club came into view, the siren shut off. Ned followed them to the car park.

Paul led the men up a rise at a run, past golfers getting ready to tee off on this pleasant autumn afternoon, unaware of the drama unfolding yards from them.

Once he hit the top of the hill, Paul slowed to a walk and pointed to a stand of trees ahead of them. "Jake's bench is on the other side of those trees. I'll go ahead, and if I see Wynn, I'll come back for you two. In the meantime, find the clubhouse manager, Ron. Explain no one can come up this way temporarily and have him post someone to block the hill."

Behind them at the base of the hill, curious golfers made their way back to the clubhouse, sweaty and comparing scorecards. Ron ran down the hill to the clubhouse and reappeared with a man who took up a post at the base of the rise. Paul rejoined them as Ron chugged up. "There's someone there but I can't tell if it's Wynn without giving myself away." He pointed to the golfers returning to the clubhouse. "They're all away from the action."

Ron said, "Manager's clued in. All set."

"He won't recognize me as easily," Ned said. "I'll get his attention first while you move in." Ned pointed to each side and behind. Paul and Ron nodded; the men walked quickly but cautiously to the trees along the rise.

Ned took his position hidden by a thick oak near the bench. He saw Paul move into place opposite him on the other side of the bench. Ron brought up the rear. On the bench ahead of him to his left, a man surveyed the landscape in front of him. He wore a baseball cap that hid his hair and the shape of his head. There was a magnificent view from here with the fairway down beneath them, clumps of golfers like colorful ants moving and swinging their clubs as they played through. In the distance, Ned could see the blue ribbon of the Schoharie River shining, and further still, the undulating peaks of the Catskill Mountains.

At Paul's wave, Ned sauntered out from behind the tree, his heart beating fast, one hand protectively down near his gun in case Wynn had come here armed. He approached the bench and called out, "Wynn?"

The man turned and looked at Ned in surprise.

It wasn't Wynn Graham.

# CHAPTER THIRTY-FOUR

I made a U-turn to complete the second thing I had to accomplish before I went home and headed toward Wynn Graham's house. Ned said Wynn had missed a meeting with him earlier today, and that Jake had to be at the root of this, somehow. If Wynn was at home, I would ask him what he knew about the day my father had died. I needed answers.

Wynn Graham's house was a large brick Colonial on River Street in Middleburgh, set back from the road. I drove up the lane that ran next to the right side of the house and led to two other houses hidden in the woods, then turned left onto the Grahams' driveway at the back of the property, where it led to a large garage past a modern glassed-in addition with a flagstone patio. There had been barbecues here with both our families. I remembered playing and laughing with my brothers, and Jake and Daniel, wolfing down hot dogs before drugs and murder had infected and changed us all.

I parked on the drive behind the sedan Wynn drove and decided this conversation didn't need interruptions. After I turned my cell on silent, I stuck it in the pocket of my barn jacket and walked up to the glassed-in room. To the left of its sliding doors, there was a seating area, with a large duffel bag gaping open on a coffee table. Two closed suitcases stood in front of a counter that fronted the kitchen. A half-full glass and an open bottle of Jack Daniels stood next to the duffel. A side window next to the patio doors by the seating was cranked open; the strains of a familiar song reached me: Bob Dylan's "Knocking on Heaven's Door."

The first feelings of doubt about my actions hit me. What if we'd gotten it wrong, and not just knowing more than he'd admitted, Wynn was the one who had killed my father? I felt incredibly exposed and foolish in equal measure.

A shadow fell over me and I realized Wynn Graham stood on the other side of the glass, looking out at me with a smile that didn't reach his eyes as he slid the door open and reached out for me. Crap. Too late to run now. I returned a weak smile and raised my hand in greeting.

Ned left the country club and followed Paul and Ron as they rode toward Wynn Graham's house. He'd tried to call Trudy to update her, but her phone went straight to voicemail. It was time to come clean about the gun and warrants with her safely at home.

A thread of unease ran through him when she didn't answer after several attempts. He called Rick's cell phone, and when Trudy's brother answered, asked if Trudy was with him.

"With me? She said you two had a few things to tie up and we'd see you at dinner later. What's going on?"

Ned feigned nonchalance. "Must have gotten our wires crossed. See you later, Rick." He hung up quickly before Rick could ask more questions. He had a feeling he knew where Trudy had driven to, and his urgency rose.

Ned thought about what must be going through Wynn Graham's mind. He deduced Wynn had asked Mario for financial help to pay off Jake's drug debt, which somehow resulted in his best friend's death by Bobby Costello. Why that happened he didn't yet know, but he was hopeful that the bat on its way to Albany would yield definitive evidence that pointed to Costello as Mario's killer. The criminal might be beyond justice, but Trudy's family would know the truth.

Then Jake had either relapsed or, ridden with guilt over Mario's death, taken a deliberate overdose. Wynn had carried the weight of both deaths around for eleven years, eating away at him. When Greg Dietz arrived, he was primed by Bobby Costello to recover the missing Genova money.

It had to be somewhere at the orchard because Dietz had gone out of his way to get a job there. Knowing Dietz had visited Wynn at the bank and left in anger had presumably led to a confrontation near Rick's house. At least, that's how he had it figured out.

He needed that gun and the ballistics to match to prove his theory. He hoped Trudy hadn't put herself in jeopardy to find out the end to this story.

Ned called Paul's cell. "I'm afraid Trudy might have beaten us to Wynn Graham's house."

Wynn grabbed my arm, pulling me inside. With a sinking feeling, I stepped over the threshold, and averted my eyes from the suitcases and duffel bag, determined not to aggravate him as I remembered no one knew I was here.

"Sit down, Trudy." He pointed to a loveseat at a right angle to the open window and I sat down. "I shouldn't be surprised to see you. I knew the minute you and your hotshot boyfriend were reopening your father's case this would all come out, especially after he clocked my squad photo." Wynn sat in a club chair opposite me and picked up the glass that was next to the whiskey bottle.

I shrugged nonchalantly as if I had all the time in the world. What was Wynn planning?

We hadn't been as discreet investigating as we thought, but then at first neither of us thought Wynn Graham had been anything but my father's good friend. I tried to grab a look inside the open duffel, but I was too low where I sat. "We've figured out some of it, I think." I remembered what Ned had told me. "Did it start for you back in Desert Storm?" I didn't have the connection Ned seemed to have made but it was worth asking in order to stall things. I broke out in a cold sweat as my shoulders tightened. I was glad I was sitting because my legs felt weak.

I'd never felt so alone.

Wynn took a greedy gulp of whiskey. He nodded, his face a contorted mask of pain. "We were ambushed on a patrol by a man who dashed out of a hut, shooting an AK-47. It was shoot or be shot. One of my buddies was wounded but we sprayed the man with so many bullets his body slammed against the wall." His voice quaked. "A woman ran out, screaming at us, carrying the body of a child. Some of the bullets had gone through the wall and killed her little boy. There was blood all over the small body of her son, on her face and clothes, on the wall behind her, on the dead father." He shuddered.

I didn't have to fake my horror. "My God, how awful."

"I couldn't sleep for months. When I closed my eyes, I'd see that child being held in his mother's arms. Some nights I still do. When we came home and Mary gave me a gun as a present, I almost vomited."

Wynn had access to a gun. Oh, boy. I felt my terror ratchet up. Where was that gun now? I had to keep Wynn talking. What was he planning? "Then why do you keep that photo of your squad on your wall?"

"So that I never forget what we did. Then my penance became a son for a son when Jake died." He drained his glass and poured another measure, hesitated, and kept pouring, almost filling the glass. "My VA therapist told me over and over I'm not responsible for what happened in wartime." He gave a mirthless laugh. "Try telling that to the woman who lost her entire family in the space of a minute."

I struggled to keep my voice level and not quaver. "War is . . . inhumane." I wanted to run but knew I wouldn't get far. Things seemed to be moving too fast for me to process. My heart stuttered in my chest.

"Why do you think Daniel lives in Maine and Mary left me? I came back haunted. I hid it well until Jake died. Then they had to get away from me." Wynn took another deep swallow. "Jake had beat the drugs, Trudy, he really did. When he came out of rehab, this dealer said his nut had quadrupled. By the time Jake confessed to me, he owed this creep over a hundred thousand."

The pieces fell into place in my mind with a resounding clunk. I tried to keep an accusatory tone out of my voice, but it was tough. I was hurt and angry that this man had presumed too much from his friendship with my father. "Which is why my dad depleted his savings—to pay the dealer for you."

"Only temporarily," he protested. "I'd started the process for a second mortgage on our house, but Jake was harassed and physically threatened. We called it a bridge loan. Once my loan came through, I would put the money back in your parents' account. Two weeks after your father died, the loan fell through."

Despite my fear and trembling, I asked, "Why?"

"The home office said I had too many open accounts, and despite or maybe because of being a bank manager, they had to make an example of me and denied the second mortgage. That wasn't supposed to happen!"

This time I couldn't keep the anger from my tone. "What *was* supposed to happen that day, Mr. Graham? I deserve to know." Tension gripped my temples; a headache flared.

I knew I'd have to face Ned and Paul once this was over

if I was alive to tell them, but I had waited eleven long years to hear this. I was aware of a bird chirping outside. Down the block someone used a leaf blower, the distant buzz reaching me inside the room. Sounds of normalcy.

Wynn rubbed the coolness of his glass against his forehead. I hoped he had a whopper of a headache of his own. My father had been the best friend this man had ever had, and Wynn felt sorry for himself? Eleven years had passed where he could have made an effort to say what had happened that day to a man who had paid with his life for their friendship.

My fury surged.

"Yes, you do deserve to know." Wynn must have read my thoughts. "Over the years I thought of how to pay your family back, at least for the money I owed them. I helped here and there, but your mother would have noticed a sudden deposit in her accounts."

I placated him to get to the truth of that horrendous day, clenching my fists on either side of my thighs. "I suppose that's true."

"I funded the scholarships you and Rick 'won' to college. I thought not worrying about tuition would at least help Hildy."

I felt stunned and shifted in my seat. Dread ate away at me. My stomach was rock hard with tension, and my pounding headache started to blur my vision. We had always thought our scholarships were needs-based, not down to one person, and we'd both had good grades.

But I wasn't offering any gratitude if that's what Wynn thought he deserved.

Paul parked on the shoulder of the road and spoke briefly to Ned at his window. "Go up the lane and don't stop at the Grahams' drive. The trees get thick there. Park up by the next house and creep back, let me know if you see the truck Trudy was driving or Graham's sedan."

Ned closed his window. Paul was right not to spook Wynn. Trudy couldn't have been here much longer than a few minutes ahead of them. He had to hope she was all right and hadn't been hurt. His heart thumping, he did as Paul instructed and passed Graham's drive, saw the two cars there, then parked behind a thick copse of trees at the next house. No cars were in this drive, and he hoped no nosy neighbors were home. He texted Paul: **2 Cars—Trudy + Graham**.

Paul texted back: **We have front/side doors. U get low--glass patio doors-- cover back.**

Ned texted a thumbs up and left his car. Remembering

Paul's instruction, he stuck to the far side of the lane as he walked inside the tree line back down to the Graham house and continued past it, then crossed the lane where he couldn't be seen from the house. He stepped quietly past a row of hydrangea bushes with papery brown heads. Once he cleared the edge of the house, he could hear voices from inside the addition. He dropped low and sidled, duck-walking, until he was under the open window and could clearly hear voices. His heart caught in his throat: it was Trudy, talking to Wynn Graham. At least she sounded unhurt; that was a relief.

He sent Paul a text: **2 by window. Hear but no eyes--give posit away.**

Paul texted back: **Hold posit 4 now. Bk-up soon.**

Ned pulled his gun out in case things changed suddenly, and settled on his haunches, wondering how long his runner's legs could stay in this position without cramping. He closed his eyes, leaned against the house, and listened to the conversation happening inside.

My stomach roiled and my hands were sweaty and clammy from panic mixed with rage.

*DEATH in the ORCHARD*

"I still don't understand what went wrong," I said to prompt Wynn. "Dad was supposed to meet Bobby Costello at the old Schoharie train station to hand over the payment, right?"

Wynn's eyes opened wide. "You really have put the pieces together. I'm impressed." He looked off into the distance. "We both met him there. Bobby brought a bat and your father brought a note."

"A note?" I squeaked. This was not what I'd been prepared to hear.

"Mario demanded Bobby sign a note saying Jake's debt was fully paid, and that Costello and his crew would disappear from his life. Your father would keep the note in his safety deposit box for security."

"I'm guessing Costello refused to play along?" *Dad, oh Dad. You didn't know who you were playing with.*

"Mario told Costello he'd buried the money at the orchard, and he wouldn't get it until he signed the paper. Costello exploded, demanded to know where the money was and your father said, 'After you sign this, I'll take you there myself. A new ending for Tosca.' I had no idea what he meant by that."

I picked my head up at that, but Wynn kept spooling out his story.

"Costello became enraged and swung the bat at your father. It missed and Mario launched himself at the man and tried to fight him off, but Costello still had the bat. He struck your father in the head and Mario fell off the platform and hit the hitch on his way down, and . . . well, you know the rest."

I realized I was screaming. "You didn't try to help Dad? You left him there to die? This man who had wiped out his family's savings to help you and your son?"

Wynn shrank back from my rage. "I panicked. Bobby and I saw the blood on Mario's head and knew he was dead. Costello took off and so did I. I never saw him again." He looked down at his hands. "I burned the note on my way back to the bank."

My voice seemed to come from far away, my wrath making my voice hard and quiet, more malicious than if I'd yelled. "If you'd called an ambulance, there was a chance my father's life could have been saved." I felt light-headed from my emotions; my fingers tingled.

Wynn's eyes opened wide. He shook his head and sat back in his chair. He looked like the whiskey was getting to him. He struggled to keep his eyes open and his head up, as if it weighed too much. Finally, he propped his head with his hands on his knees when I asked, "Where does Greg Dietz fall into all of this?"

"He saw me at the bank, said he had Costello's journal with my name in it and wanted to meet Sunday afternoon. He was impatient—he couldn't find the money and wanted my inside information. He said I owed him that."

"*You* owed *him*? Why would he think that?"

"Costello told him your father hadn't shown up with his money. They were going into business together after they dug it up. Before Bobby died, he gave Greg his journal to make me tell him where the money was hidden. It had a reference to me and Jake."

He fell silent. A pair of doves hooted in a nearby tree. Ned had always told me silence could be effective, so I waited while I tried to process what I was learning. Greg had been murdered at the orchard, the place my father had spent his life building. It was all connected to Dad's death eleven years ago. The violence was unending.

Wynn looked at me with sad eyes. "I wanted that journal, so I went to meet Dietz. I'd been as surprised as Costello when Mario showed up without the money. I knew he'd withdrawn it." His hands started to shake. "Dietz didn't believe me when I told him I had no idea where the money was buried. He screamed at me and reached into the pocket of his pants. Suddenly I was back in the desert with a man screaming outside his hut and pointing a gun at me. The next thing I knew Dietz had fallen by my feet."

I'd had enough. I stood up, shaking with so many mixed emotions that I was glad I didn't have a gun in my own hand at that moment.

Then I saw Graham's gun inside the duffel bag. I tried not to react and thought quickly about what was at hand. "And once again you ran away from a tough situation. I need a drink." I reached for Wynn's glass and helped myself to a sip, then cradled the glass as Wynn stood up across from me. I felt an urge to reach for that gun and take Wynn Graham's life in the same cavalier fashion he'd allowed Bobby Costello to take my father's.

I watched him while actions ran through my mind in a wild tumult as I pretended to take another sip. The little bit of whiskey that had touched my lips burned while I tried to focus my thoughts. The gun lay between us, and all Wynn had to do was reach inside and fire. At this close range, I was dead, unless I could get to it first.

I thought of my father and how he had had his future taken from him.

I thought of my mom and my brothers and how their lives had been impacted.

I thought of Ned and the future I was starting to see in front of us.

Then I looked at Wynn, whose reaction through all these years had been to flee. He wanted to get away. I saw in the glaze of his eyes that he had nothing left. He was registering his options, too.

Time slowed . . .

until Wynn reached for the gun.

*DEATH in the ORCHARD*

I threw the whiskey in his face. He yelped and clutched at his eyes.

I grabbed the gun and held it on him with shaking hands, my chest heaving. "You don't get to run away again!"

# CHAPTER THIRTY-FIVE

After Wynn Graham was handcuffed by Paul, Ned rushed in to hold me while I howled, crying in relief and in frustration at how my father's life had been taken.

Hours later, I told the entire saga to my family as we sat around the large dining room table eating Mom's magic meatloaf. Mom and Gail cried openly, my brothers and Bob teared up, and even Aidan, who hadn't known my dad, was moved when he learned how my father had died trying to be a good friend.

I didn't expound on my great relief when Paul rushed in and took the gun from my shaking hands. I might have skipped over the extent of the danger I'd been in, too, preferring to let the diatribe I'd received from Paul while Ned held me to his chest suffice. Ron led a sobbing Wynn Graham away; I was never so happy to see the back of someone.

I would go to the station tomorrow with Ned to give a formal statement, but for this evening Paul had told us to go home and get some rest. He had the difficult job of calling Mary and Daniel Graham in Maine and explaining the situation to them.

But before we left, Paul told us that the bat had shown clear evidence of my father's blood on it, tying it to Bobby Costello and Wynn Graham's story of that awful day.

"Thanks for clearing me, too, guys," Rick said.

"We didn't do that; the evidence did, and Wynn's confession confirmed it. Paul, Ron, and I heard it all," Ned said.

"Time for a drink." Ben followed me into the kitchen and grabbed a bottle of sparkling apple juice for Gail and a chilled bottle of cabernet while I gathered wine glasses.

He stopped me at the kitchen door. "I realize now you were helping to find answers I didn't want to know. I guess a small part of me was afraid the truth would show Dad had done something wrong. Thanks for ignoring me, Trudy." He kissed my forehead, and we rejoined the family and filled the glasses.

Ben raised a toast. "To Mario."

"Best friend but stubborn lug head," Mom added, and we all laughed.

"To Mario," we chorused.

"Any idea what you'll do when you find the money, Hildy?" Ned asked.

Mom sipped her wine. "Lots to think about. There are

grandbabies in my future to start college funds for, but I think our town will soon have a Mario Genova Little League Field."

After dinner, we sat around talking over coffee about how the day had turned out. I was finally relaxing, my adrenaline surge calmed down. Suddenly, I remembered what Wynn said my father told Costello about the money; I told the others he'd said it was his "new ending for Tosca."

Gail and I locked eyes. She said, "We never did get our Insta photo by the pear tree."

I stood up. "We could rectify that right now before your baby comes."

Mom protested. "It's getting chilly, ladies, and the sun is almost down. Tomorrow might be better."

Gail struggled to her feet, in command. "Hildy, I'm overruling you. Rick, get the backhoe. Ben, you and Aidan grab a few shovels. We meet in the driveway in five minutes before the light is gone."

"Never argue with a pregnant lady," Bob said. He and Ned went with the men to gather tools.

*DEATH in the ORCHARD*

"At least put jackets on," Mom said. "And I'm coming with you."

We met up at the side of the house, where Rick steered a small backhoe up the driveway. The other men walked beside him, holding an assortment of shovels and a pickaxe.

Mom disappeared behind the house, and the others followed. I waited for Gail to catch up and we locked arms. Soon we gathered around one tall Tosca pear tree, reaching to the sun, anchoring a corner of the yard, away from surrounding shrubs and plantings in the garden.

Mom craned her neck and pointed out scars in the wood which had grown up high as the tree grew over the years. "That's where Mario carved our initials. I was upset it would kill the tree, but he insisted it would heal over." Years later, the crooked outline of a heart was barely discernible, and the squiggles that represented their initials were difficult to read.

"Where to dig, though?" Bob asked.

Ben and Aidan walked around the tree, searching the ground. It had been too many years since Dad had dug his hole for there to remain any obvious signs of disturbance to follow.

Mom scrutinized the tree. "Your father always had a reason for what he did. He'd want to be able to find it quickly himself. Three was his lucky number, for you kids." She backed into the tree under the initials and paced off three large steps. "Dig here, Rick, and watch for roots."

Everyone stood back while Rick went to work. The noise of the motor cut through the peace of the evening air. I shivered, not from the cold, and Ned wrapped an arm around my shoulder.

Rick carefully dug layers of dirt on either side of the roots he encountered and placed the clumps aside. When we heard a *clunk* over the motor, he backed the machine away and turned it off.

I felt my heart pounding as I thought of the day Dad had buried this box thinking he was helping his old friend. He'd had no idea it would all go so horribly wrong.

But our family had survived without him. I missed him more than ever at this moment and hoped he knew we were about to finally end what he'd started eleven years ago.

Aidan and Ben took the shovels and dug out a metal box, sealed with duct tape, and wrapped in several layers of burlap bags stamped with **GENOVA ORCHARDS: Sweetest Apples in the Catskills** inside a wreath of rosy apples.

Ben bent down, unwrapped the box from the burlap, and handed it to Mom. "You do the honors."

We were all teary by then. Ned tightened his hold

on my shoulders. Bob helped her peel off the duct tape. Mom opened the lid and found bundles of large musty bills stacked in currency straps.

A hundred and twenty thousand to be precise.

*NEW YORK CITY*
*Sunday*

I leaned my computer bag against the wall and clamped a stack of accumulated mail under my arm to unlock my apartment door. I held it open for Ned as he rolled my suitcase off the elevator and carried my backpack on one shoulder into the kitchen.

"I know it's only been eight days, but it feels longer."

I was filled with a huge sense of relief at being home in familiar surroundings. While I poured cool water into ice-filled glasses, I thought back over our last days in Schoharie. We had given detailed statements to Paul Hoffmann. Then there were calls to the people Ned and I had involved in reopening my father's case, explaining the resolution. I'd talked endlessly with Mom and my brothers, too. Even Ben admitted that finding out what happened to Dad had been more than worth any anxiety and dredged-up grief. There had even been a call to Veronica's Vintage to ask for the measurements of the table Ned admired. We could pick it up on our trip back to Schoharie to see my new nephew after he was born.

Yesterday, after the orchard closed and the sun was getting low in the sky, we drove in two cars to the cemetery to lay a wreath on Dad's grave. I brought an apple to place inside the circle of grape vines intertwined with leaves and acorns that I'd helped Gail fashion— all materials gathered from Genova land. Fallen leaves crunched under our feet, and the chill in the air was persistent, autumn in full as signs of summer receded. We told Dad we loved him, knew why things had happened as they did, and would always miss him.

Now I handed Ned a glass and sipped mine as I pulled out my basket of takeout menus and handed it to him. I felt relieved to return to my normal world and leave murder behind. There was a sense of satisfaction, too, that we'd completed the mystery of my father's death when we headed to my hometown. I needed to thank Ned for taking this journey with me. Or better yet, I could show him.

"Feel like Italian?" Ned asked.

"Sure. Let's order from Broadway Pizza." I kicked off my shoes and started to unbutton my shirt. Ned still had his head in the menus, and I felt a swell of desire, waiting for him to notice.

"Why not Giovanni's? It's closer, and Broadway's will take an awfully lot longer to get here." He lifted his head, then raised his eyebrow when he saw me take off my shirt and throw it over my shoulder.

"Precisely." I walked down the hall toward my bedroom and may have swayed my hips more than usual. Ned trailed behind me. I paused by the door to unzip my jeans and gave him what I hoped was a sexy look when I saw he'd unbuttoned his own shirt. My anticipation built.

"It's good to be home," he murmured. He wrapped his arms around me and bent to nuzzle my neck, his warm breath giving me chills.

Our lips met, and when I came up for air, I breathed out, "I love you, Detective O'Malley," just as Ned whispered, "Love you, Trudy."

We smiled and headed into the bedroom with our arms wrapped around each other.

THE END

*M.K. GRAFF*

# ACKNOWLEDGEMENTS

Schoharie, New York is a real place about three hours north of Manhattan, and I've been mostly faithful to its layout, with changes made to its Main Street to suit my needs. The site of the orchard was loosely inspired by Wellington's Herbs and Spices, which was run by the delightful Carolyn and Frederick Wellington, a place I visited often when in the area.

Other liberties include creating The Night Owl, and changing how the Schoharie Police Department is structured and placed. In reality, they are a part-time department called to incidents in the village, with the County Sheriff's office called on to assist. Thanks to Lt. Jason Temple for the clarification. Also, there is no Troy Correctional Prison.

I received enormous help in the policing, prison, and gun aspects of this story from Sean C. Burk, who helped me construct many of those scenes with brainstorming sessions and brought realism to them with his input. I am grateful for your expertise and love.

Any errors are entirely my own, while some may even have been deliberate choices to suit the plotline.

So many people helped to bring Trudy's story of going home to life. Kimberly Zimmer, who grew up in nearby Berne and lives in Schoharie, is the director of

The Community Library in Cobleskill and was a great help refreshing my memory of the town and bringing me up to speed on changes since I last visited. Kim's father, George, was not a coroner but an engineer, as well as a multi-decorated Viet Nam War veteran. George earned three Purple Hearts among his many awards and medals, and I remember him for his sense of humor and dedication to his community and family. Frank Bozzelli was a favorite uncle of mine, as far from a medical examiner as you could get, a man who loved antiques and his girls, my cousins, Cindy and Dana.

Paul Hoffmann and I grew up across the street from each other on Mayfair Avenue in Floral Park, NY, and are still good friends. Although he is not a police lieutenant, he and his family have had a cottage on Lake Wallenpaupack for decades.

Copyeditor Jennifer Brecht brought her eagle eye to the manuscript and made it far better with her keen observations and modern eye. She was a delight to work with and it won't be our last collaboration. Beth Cole worked her magic, creating the stunning cover and interior design, helping to bring another Trudy Genova story to readers. Beth has helped me with Nora Tierney books, too, and is always patient and creative. It was a delight to work with both of these talented women.

Beta readers Anne Jacobs, Barbara Jancovic, Joyce

McLennan, and Kim Zimmer all read later drafts and answered my questions. I truly appreciate your time and efforts. Thanks to Peter F. Bruno for the Italian lessons. And loving thanks to special author friends Mandy Morton, for the blurb, and Nicola Upson for both standing behind this project. Love you all. It wouldn't be a book without your intervention.

Melissa Westemeier, Lauren Small, and I have been workshopping our novels together for twenty years. I would be lost without their wisdom to help define my vision for every book. I count on these clever women to help me shape each novel from its early days.

The writing community is unique, from local writers to far-away colleagues. We support each other's work and glory in each other's successes. There's nothing else like it that I've experienced, and I'm proud to be a member of it. Thanks to my fellow Miss Demeanors, and to the many authors I count as friends. To my readers, thank you for your validation by reading this book, and thanks, too, to those who are always asking when the next one will be out. It spurs me to work harder, and I love hearing from you and meeting you at events. You're the reason for all of this hard work. Thanks to Kimberly Werntz for the lovely new website design that will allow you to find me easier.

My husband Arthur's support sustains me. I'd be lost

without him. Thanks for corralling the pups when I'm working, and for being my biggest advocate and fan. He's the reason I'm able to write full-time, a gift I don't take lightly.

This book is dedicated to exceptional friends from my home on Long Island who stayed in my corner when we moved to North Carolina. Anne Jacobs remains a constant in my life. Her encouragement and love are the true definition of unconditional friendship. Likewise for the women listed as The Sisters of No Mercy, which refers to the Hallowe'en costumes we four wore one year as we made our rounds at the Port Jefferson hospital where we worked together. Those were special times with many laughs along the way.

Each one of these strong women holds a tender place in my heart, along with memories of tough times endured and joyful ones shared. This one's for you.


April 2024
Montgomery Point, NC

## ABOUT THE AUTHOR

Marni Graff is the award-winning author of *The Nora Tierney English Mysteries* and *The Trudy Genova Manhattan Mysteries*. Her short stories are in several anthologies, including the Anthony Award-winning Malice Domestic's *Murder Most Edible*. She is Managing Editor of Bridle Path Press, a crime book reviewer, and blogs for Miss Demeanors, a popular blog written by crime writers.

Marni is a member of Sisters in Crime, Mavens of Mayhem SinC, Triangle SinC, Mystery People UK, and the International Association of Crime Writers. She lives in eastern NC with her husband and two Aussiedoodles, Seamus and Fiona. Marni enjoys hearing from readers, so feel free to reach out to her at: bluevirgin.graff@gmail.com; on Twitter @GraffMarni; or her website: https://www.MarniGraff.com.